John Morey

THE SIGN of the]

G000081298

A novel by John Mor

First published in Great Britain 2021
Copyright © 2021 by John Morey
Second Impression April 2021
Third Impression September 2021
All rights reserved
The moral right of the author has been asserted.

Acknowledgements:
Copy editing: Jane Morey; Cover design: Gomangocreative
Dedicated to my wife, Jane Morey, for her continual support

The 'Love should never be this hard' series
The Sign of the Rose (Bk 1)
The Black Rose of Blaby (Bk 2)
Rose: The Missing Years (Bk 3)
Finding Rose (Bk 4)

PREFACE

Our story begins in Southern Ireland after the Potato Famine of the mid-19th Century. The history books chronicle the realities of that terrible time much better than I can. They read like a work of fiction.

Unfortunately they were so real. The telling of the simple facts – handed down by document and word of mouth over the centuries – requires no embellishment. They record one of the darkest periods of Anglo-Irish history, and shame the English.

But *The Sign of the Rose* is pure fiction. It's aim is to take you on a journey taken by the Irish ancestors of two young people, Rosalee and Sean, descendants of those who became the main characters from *Finding Rose* and *Rose: The Missing Years* decades later.

This introduction explains the context and circumstances within which our story begins. I hope you enjoy the chronicle, but let me emphasise one thing: as light and entertaining as *The Sign of the Rose* is, or is meant to be, in no way does it ignore the darkness surrounding what took place between two nations over 150 years ago.

But let's get into the story now, embracing all the fortunes and misfortunes – and, above all, joy – that beset two young people as they moved from youth to maturity.

The background to our opening scenes draw from the real tragedy of simple, impoverished families evicted from their cottages and livelihoods by cruel landlords.

Like so many distressing episodes that beset humankind, there is usually hope and optimism for a better future through opportunity, notwithstanding the countless challenges along the way.

Their story is no different...

Chapter One

An all too familiar scene in a small Irish village, late 1800's...

"Run, Sean!," his father whispered. "Slip out the back door so they don't see you. Take this duffel bag with you, and the bedroll and tarp for shelter."

"Where should I run to, father?"

"Go out the back, over the sheep pen, and climb the hillside behind the back pasture. You remember where I showed you the circle of stones?"

"Halfway up the hill, overlooking the valley, on the other side of the Fergus River?"

"That's right, boy," continued Frankie, his father. The soldiers won't follow you there. Look for the over-hanging rocks just above the stones. You can camp there. Lay low for two nights, use the tarp for shelter, but don't light a fire. Not until the second night, anyway."

"What shall I do then?" Sean sensed danger in the way his father was behaving but he was a big lad for his sixteen years. He could hold his own in a fight with the other lads in the village, but the fear in his father's voice was totally new to him. He knew something was very wrong.

"Look out for a girl about the same age as you. She'll be coming from across the valley." His father, Frankie's, voice was shaking as he knew the soldiers – and the local constabulary – were only minutes away.

"This girl. Who is she?"

"She's your...cousin I suppose. Well, she's not really. She's my brother's wife's girl. You remember I told you about Billy marrying a gypsy woman who lost her husband?"

"*Uncle* Billy? Who we see sometimes at the monthly market?" His Dad had shown him the spot where his brother had the farm they could see in the distance, on the other side of the Fergus. "He has a daughter?" asked Sean.

"Step-daughter," corrected Frankie. "Anyway, there's no time to talk about it now. I promised him *on my life* that you would look after her. Now promise *me* you will protect her with *your* life. But do as I say. Run!"

"But what about Mam, and Declan, Bridie and Seamus?" Sean's younger brother was only twelve, and his sister and youngest brother only a year apart, at six and seven.

"Don't worry about us. Your Mam and me will look after them. Look after *yourself*, boy. And take Lurch with you, and this." He handed Sean a silver necklace on a chain. It was in the shape of a rose. "Your mother says you must wear this at all times and it will keep you safe. It was her grandmother's and carries a Romani blessing."

Sean slipped the chain over his neck, thinking little of it. He was more concerned about Lurch, their lurcher. *Sean's* lurcher. He had trained him from a pup, having bought him at the market two years ago. He had paid the princely sum of a flagon of poitin (pron. 'potcheen'). Since potatoes, the main ingredient, were still recovering from the blight of some years previously, this forty percent (plus!) spirit fetched a premium price.

But Lurch was worth it. Half whippet and half terrier, the little sight-hound weighed little more than the couple of sugar beet – the vegetables that might go into a poitin mash - but he was worth his weight in... I guess, poitin.

Lurch had become another bread-winner for the whole family. He was a master at catching the plentiful rabbits that populated the county ever since they were introduced by the Viking Norsemen, centuries earlier. He also provided a more varied addition to their diet.

Rabbits were exceptionally nourishing in times when good food was scarce. It also meant that, on a good day when he might catch a surplus of rabbits, Sean was able to trade them for other essentials such as clothing, medicines, other foods – including bread and cheese. Theirs was one of several small-holder's cottages in this area of Southern Ireland. It was a tight community where everyone looked after each other – at least when they could.

To look at Lurch you would think he was deprived and wanting in nourishment and love. Not a bit of it. His rag-taggle look – with his rough grey coat that caught every burr and thistle he brushed against – gave him the appearance of an orphan. But despite that he was fitter than most other unwashed curs in the area and, as for love and kindness, he was given and returned more affection in a week than most other dogs, and people, could expect in a lifetime.

If you want to understand the behaviour of a pet animal, look at the master they often say. Lurch was a prime example.

The one thing Lurch lacked, of course, was a full *human* vocabulary. But he could sense what was happening was serious. He cleaved even closer to Sean now, with frequent glances to his master, searching his face for signs of anxiety, fear, danger – even hope. It was an unwritten, unspoken, secret language they shared. Sean and Lurch worked together without words. Instead they used instinct.

The occasional growl was the first clue that Lurch had spotted, or thought he had spotted, something that wasn't right. He didn't bark. He couldn't. It wasn't part of his breed characteristic. A high pitched yelp was all you were going to get if danger presented itself. *Read the signs* Sean's father would say.

On this occasion it was Lurch's 'Yelp' that startled Sean, forewarning him that the soldiers had entered the village, looting, burning, killing. Then he heard the unmistakable sound of a gunshot. It felt as if it had passed right through him, it seemed so close.

Then there was a second.

He waited for the third.... Nothing.

Then a fourth..... Nothing.

A fifth?.... Still nothing.

He stopped, turned, looking to where he'd heard the gunshots. It was in his family's cottage. He pulled Lurch close. Closer. He feared the worst, knowing right away that his beloved Mammy – 'the beautiful Colleen' his father called her, because that was her maiden name, Annie Colleen McGowan when he first met her - was no more. Shot, just like his father, Francis John Baker Sercombe - Frankie.

Although English by birth they were classed as Irish and therefore 'non persons' in the eyes of the 19th century legal system. The English could kill - no, murder them - legally. Legally? What a joke. But what of his sister and brothers?

He was too far away to hear what he imagined would be the the cries of disbelief followed by the sobbing of first the sister, then the boys, learning that the military had dispensed of their parents. Why? The answer was simple. They *were* dispensable. Of no value. Irish.

And why was that? Because Trevelyan, Assistant Secretary to Her Majesty's Treasury, said so. To keep them alive let alone let them prosper, was not in his budget.

Sean pondered on what might happen to his brothers and sister. At twelve years old Declan might be considered 'useful' and probably sold off to become a cabin boy on one of the many 'coffin ships'. Loaded with unfortunates seeking a better life, these ships were leaving so frequently now from the Irish ports, including Kilrush, bound for Canada and America. But few survived the passage, dying either from disease or hunger.

After all, what was the point of feeding them well? the ship owners would say. Many of the evicted men, women, and children were already malnourished, suffering from cholera, dysentry, consumption – and typhus. *Why waste too much food on so many when only 60% -* the lucky ones *– would survive the perilous journey to New York or Newfoundland?*

The future was no more promising for his siblings. The English politician, Peel, had funded the building of new workhouses for the poor, which is where Bridie and Seamus would probably end up. If they were lucky.

It was the sudden flash as bright flames engulfed the roof of their cottage that struck dread into his heart. The mix of cane and peat turf used to keep out the rain caught light easily, fuelled by tar torches brandished by the constabulary. They were now so skilled at burning out their own kind. They made sure of that – for the money and spoils was good.

"So this really *is* the end," said Sean, out loud, even though his canine companion could not understand his words. But Lurch understood the meaning and signs of sorrow. They were the smell of acrid smoke from a burning home. His *home.* Sean's and his, Lurch. His faithful friend nuzzled closer as if he was more in need of comfort than his master. Sean wiped the solitary tear from the lurcher's eye.

So dogs, and all animals, can feel grief and pain, he thought. That one tear told Sean that all the kindness his father and mother had also lavished on Lurch was felt, appreciated, and would remain with him long after their passing.

It was Lurch who first broke away from Sean's hold as if to say, *No turning back, now.* They set out ahead making their way down to the Fergus, looking for the section of low water, still but just deep enough, where they had a currach moored. Lurch led way. He had taken over. By the time Sean caught up Lurch was in the front of the small river craft, having already undone the loose knot of the tethered mooring rope!

Come on, now, Sean, he seemed to be saying – before going back to stare straight ahead, his body rigid as he stood with his nose pointed across the river to the opposite bank. It was where he, Sean and his father, had crossed on so many previous occasions – *but much happier times*, he reflected.

Obediently, Sean pulled the craft to the water's edge and boarded before taking the oar to push away from the bank to row across the gentle current of the River Fergus. There was not a sound. Nothing stirred. The noise and chaos of soldiers ransacking his village was now a memory, but still raw.

Landing on the opposite bank he recognised the familiar and well-used dry slope leading up a gentle gradient to the standing stones – the stone circle. Sean tied the currach securely and away from the water's edge, just in case floods threatened. But he knew he was unlikely to return or need it again. Lurch started up the hill path ahead of Sean, looking round only now and again to check that he had chosen the route his master had intended.

Sean rarely looked too far ahead, merely keeping his head down and focussing on the rocky ascent to the place on the hillside where the standing stones had been undisturbed for centuries. Waiting. After another half an hour of steady climbing Sean reached their destination. Lurch was already there, patiently waiting. As soon as he saw his master come into sight he relaxed, lying down with his paws outstretched, resting his head on his legs. He yawned.

Sean ignored Lurch's bored expression, walking past him – deliberately right in front of Lurch – so close than he had to move his paws. He was heading for the overhanging rocks, and shelter. It was exactly as his father had described, with a clear view downhill and across the valley, just in case they might be followed. Sean was learning to be vigilant and learning fast. He also remembered to keep an eye out for the girl.

It was only then he realised how heavy the tarp and duffel bag that his Dad had handed him – already prepared for him before the soldiers came – had become. He dropped it at his feet like a lead weight, immediately feeling the relief to his right shoulder. Lurch ignored Sean's protests. He dozed.

Don't light a fire, his father had said, *at least not on the first night.* Sean could see why.

He could see everything for miles; but everything and everyone could also see *him*. He unrolled the tarp first, then found a branch – it had to be fairly straight and some eight foot long. He started to assemble his shelter. *Their* shelter. Already he was thinking about the girl and his pledge to his father that he would look after her, at all costs.

I hope she's not going to be a bother, he thought. But then a stark reminder of how alone he was struck him, even with Lurch for comfort. He needed someone, anyone – human contact, as long as it was friendly. *What* would *she be like?*

Dismissing those thoughts for a while, he set about more practical, and pressing, tasks – a camp. The principle for building a shelter was simple. You took an elevation or a wall, or an over-hanging rock, leaned the branch against it, and anchored it to the ground in front at the far end. Then he recalled how his father had taught him all this during their nights out with the flock during lambing season.

He had said, *You then drape the tarp over the branch, pinning it down on either side about four feet apart. The slope of the tarp, with the ridge pole sloping downwards, deflects any wind, rain, snow – the weather – over you.* Sean could hear him now, as he followed his instructions. As soon as the shelter was finished Lurch joined him, settling back again to doze.

It was now time to see what was in the duffel bag – the rough canvas bag such as sailors would carry for *all* their belongings, secured by a drawstring at one end. He had not even noticed his Dad preparing this escape package, let alone realised he would soon be on such an escapade in the first place. But he *had* noticed *one* thing.

The cottage that he could just about see in the far distance but had never visited – the one belonging to Uncle Billy – was now gone. Its white walls were no longer visible, replaced by a plume of black smoke spiralling heavenwards in the still night air. He wondered if there *was* a heaven after all.

His attention turned back to the duffel. He laid its contents on the short-cropped turf grazed nearly bare by hillside sheep and goats. *Ah, there was the flint stone for the fire,* he muttered. Next he found a lodestone. It was his navigation if the sun and stars decided not to shine – another relic from the Viking age. Then there was something soft - food!

Neatly wrapped in paper was bacon. It would have been all the bacon they possessed. He found a few crusts of bread   then the all-familiar, cut up, pieces of rabbit, skinned and boned. Cooked. One potato. (Also their last.) The eggs were hard-boiled, two of them, with a small bag of salt.

Apart from a cooking pot the heaviest of the items were also the most surprising. Again, he fought to hold back the tears. His father's boots. His best pair. Another sign that, *I won't be needing these any more* (he could hear his father say). Guilt racked Sean as he realised he hadn't noticed his father wearing his old boots when they had said their last goodbyes. *How could he be so insensitive?*

Lurch sensed Sean's remorse, creeping forward on his belly as if he were a collie sheepdog, before resting his head on his master's knee. Finally he looked up to catch some sign of acknowledgement.

Sean reached down to stroke Lurch's head, playing gently with the hound's ears until he, and Lurch, both drifted into a near slumber. It was now dusk but the alarm call of a nearby blackbird brought them both back to wakefulness, and an awareness of where they were. Back to the *shock* of where they were, and what they had gone through just a few short hours beforehand when life was oh, so different. It was not perfect, now, but it was better. Safe.

It was soon dark. Looking across the river Sean could still make out the smouldering remains of their family home. Just. It lit up the sky every now and then when the dry roofing thatch ignited fragile timbers below, helped by the animal fat-impregnated material used to keep the weather from blowing through the crude openings used for windows.

To the right of that now, and way into the distance on the same side of the river as he sat silently, he could just make out a similar scene marking the same fate that had struck his uncle's cottage. And, he presumed, the girl's family - the girl he was about to meet – and very soon.

The military-backed constabulary from the troubled town of Ennis would spare no-one. Recent food riots by local townsfolk had led to the introduction of even more British forces, involving more brutality. With recent riots quelled – at least for now – the cynical government authorities used Trevelyan's Law as an excuse.

It led to bands of Anglo-Irish task forces being deployed, to cause even more misery and resentment for all local cottage dwelling farmers, in scattered settlements along the banks of the Fergus and the Shannon, on towards Kilrush.

Sean turned his head away from the tragic scene to attend to immediate matters. With the temporary shelter assembled he topped up his water bottle from the nearby spring. Then he would try to get some sleep, hopefully until dawn. He was exhausted but the distress of the day kept his mind racing, searching for reasons and solutions.

Where would he go, and what would he do next? And who was this girl? How would she find him, and when? He took out the one, small cooking pot and filled that, too, with water.

A small blanket – child's size, the one once used in his younger

13

brother, Seamus's, cot not so many years before – lined the bottom of his duffel bag.

It provided little warmth to take him through the night, but at least there was Lurch to keep his feet warm, and his spirits from sinking even lower.

Chapter Two
Sean awakes to an unexpected intrusion...

His faithful hound served him well for warmth that night, as he always had. Skinny, sinewy and with a tatty covering of coarse grey hair, Lurch gave up as much body heat as he could to his master, hoping, of course, for more in return. Neither were disappointed. Thankfully, although rain threatened it remained dry with just a gentle spring breeze that night.

They both woke up early but refreshed, courtesy of the dawn alarm from a stray cockerel across the valley. It had been spared the brutality of a soldier's bayonet. Lurch instinctively sniffed the air. Something wasn't right. It was the scent of another human. Someone was nearby. He gave a low growl, the hairs on his neck bristling. Sean tensed.

Lurch's instincts were returned by a low growl, followed by a sharp bark. Then silence again.

What the...? Sean thought. Then something stirred. Just the outline of a dark figure, a willowy female shape by the standing stones.

Were the stories true? Was the stone circle magical like the villagers said? Haunted? Would he soon witness the twelve maidens dancing in and out of the stones, laying down a curse on anyone and everyone unlucky enough to see their secret ritual? To turn them *to stone, too?* Then he remembered, and relaxed. Instinctively, Lurch wagged his tail.

Emerging from behind the tall granite stone nearest to him – but still some twenty feet from where he and Lurch had spent the night – *she* appeared. It *was* a young maiden, but without the other eleven, if they *did* exist that was. Like the myths and legends of the stones, she was *so* beautiful. He remained still, speechless, almost as if he *had* been turned to stone, just like the legend said. It took his breath away as her face, lit up by the morning sun and casting its light over his shoulder, appeared in full view before him.

Sean recovered from his state of inertia. His innate shyness still left him feeling awkward. He replaced his initial mistaken fears for *what* she was, with a realisation for *who* she truly was. That's if his father was right. He still didn't know her name, his father had not said. That part was soon remedied.

"Good morning," she said, sleepily. The growling exchange of their two canine protectors – their sole companions – had startled *her* as much as it had Sean. "You must be... I mean, I hope you are... Sean Sercombe? I'm sorry..."

But why should *she* apologise?

"Yes," Sean replied. "And this is... my dog." He very nearly said 'Lurch' but stopped just in time, wondering *who on earth introduces their dog*?

She laughed before hastening to hide her rudeness, and her mouth, behind a very delicate hand. He noticed how long and slender her fingers were for someone little over five feet tall. Perhaps five foot five.

"My Dad – my step-father – said that I should head south keeping the banks of the Fergus on my left all the way until I came to the stone circle, partway up the hill. I would know where to start climbing when I saw a currach moored."

It answered his first question, *How did you find us? In the dark?* Sean remembered that it was pitch black when he and Lurch finally dropped off to sleep the night before, and she still had not arrived.

"After my Mam and Dad told me to run, I took off straight away. That was at mid-day. Yesterday. Before they came. The soldiers, I mean. Then I saw your cottage burning in the distance and knew you would be coming here too. Just like my Dad said. He's your brother's Dad?"

"How come you were so sure I'd *be* here?"

"My Dad – your uncle – said they had worked out a plan together if the English soldiers ever came calling. That was a few weeks ago when they met up at Ennis market.

"He told me to run just before the troops came, then follow the river and look for the stones. There – or so he promised - I would find you. His brother's son."

"But it was pitch black. Weren't you afraid of getting lost?"

"I know. I was. I slept for a while when it first got dark, then woke up with the moon shining down on me. It was almost like daylight. It seemed to *want* to wake me, to guide me here. I was *so* worried in case you couldn't wait so I carried on walking. I was desperate. I had nowhere else to go. No-*one* else..." Her voice was faltering as she fought back the tears.

"Don't worry. You're here now. You're safe with me. With us." Sean fought the need to walk over to comfort her, to put his arms around her. Instead, he turned to look down at Lurch who was already peering up at his master, wagging his rope-like tail. Sean assumed Lurch meant he was in agreement. He was wrong. Lurch was looking right past Sean, having just spotted the black and white collie-cross at her feet.

"I'm Rosalee," she added. "Rosalee Ryan. It's my *real* Dad's name but he died before I was born. I've known your uncle as the only father to me. He's a Sercombe, too."

"Are you hungry?" Sean needed a distraction so he could think straight, to think about their next step. He needn't have bothered, she was ahead of him.

"We must carry on down river. My Dad said to find our way to Kilrush on the Shannon. But yes. I'm starving." Rosalee had answered both questions going through his head. Telepathy?

"Is rabbit OK?"

"Do I have a choice?"

"It's cold, though." Sean felt she deserved an explanation. "We can't risk a fire until we're sure the English are way out of sight. They were headed down river too. They may have camped just ahead of us overnight. It's hard to say. It's likely they were exhausted after... after... ," Sean couldn't finish the sentence.

He found it impossible to describe the indescribable, even though he hadn't actually *seen* the atrocities. The memory of the two shots followed by screams was still too raw.

"I know," interrupted Rosalee. "I know what they did. They killed my Mam and Dad too. I heard the shots. I just kept on running like Dad told me." Lurch walked slowly over to where Rosalee and her collie had now sat, next to the stones.

He wanted his ears fondled again but by this new person. Sean guessed Lurch also wanted to provide her with some comfort, as well as getting to know the collie.

"It's alright, Peggy," said Rosalee, reassuring the collie that this skinny hound was a friend. A new friend. Sean smiled to himself then prepared two helpings of breakfast – strips of cooked rabbit, two small chunks of bread, a couple of apples, and water.

Sean and Rosalee finished breakfast in silence, sharing any remaining scraps with their two canine companions. It was Sean who spoke next.

"So. What did your Dad say we should do, once you *had* found me?"

Rosalee didn't answer immediately, instead packing up her makeshift bed from the night before, rolled up her tarp. Only then did she explain the plan further.

"You're right about not starting a fire. At least not yet. And we should only light one once it gets dark, in a hollow so it can't be noticed, and at night in case any smoke could be seen during the day. It also makes sense to stay close to the river."

"That's about right," agreed Sean. The two brothers had given the same instructions. "How much food did you bring?"

"Some bacon. A couple of small potatoes. Some stale bread, and dripping. There's some cooked chicken – our last. Some wild hazel nuts – last years. And a bottle of poitin."

"Do *you* drink that stuff?"

Rosalee laughed. They both did, out of relief more than anything. "No," she said, still giggling. "Dad said I may need it to barter for food, or..."

"A passage to England?"

She looked up at him in surprise. "Why do you say that, of all things? Those bastards are our sworn enemies. Have you forgotten what they've just done – to us both, to our families?"

"No. But it's something I remember my Dad saying before all of this happened."

"What?"

"You Dad's – your Step-Dad's – name is Sercombe. Right?"

"Yes. 'Baker Sercombe' to be exact." Rosalee had become rather irritated by Sean's attitude. Now she needed answers – good answers – before calming down. She fell silent again, giving Sean the chance to carry on with his story.

"We have relatives over there. In Devon or Cornwall, on the border I think. So does your Step-Dad. He was named after *his* father – *William* Baker Sercombe. He would be your grandfather by marriage."

Sean had to explain it all fully so that he himself would understand, as well as for Rosalee's benefit. He explained *all* that his Dad had told him. Rosalee drew closer.

"My Dad said that one day, if things here got much worse, we should go back."

"To England? Have you ever been?"

"No," said Sean. "But he said we had to get down to Kilrush and buy a passage to Bristol, on one of the food ships taken provisions across to England."

"But that's why we're all starving," said Rosalee, becoming irritated again. "The English are stealing our food."

"I know," agreed Sean. "But it may be our only chance."

"You mean we have to stow away?"

"Not necessarily. I have this." He handed her a coin.

"What is it?"

"A silver dollar. It's not our Irish money, but the silver in it is valuable." He took the coin back.

"Will that be *enough*? For both of us?" She was interested now, mulling the plan over in her mind, starting to realise it might make good sense after all.

"This, and your bottle of poitin, should be enough - if not to buy a ticket then to bribe one of the crew. Maybe we get him to drink the poitin first then he may let us on free." He laughed at his own joke. "Or we could *work* our passage."

Either way, he had now reassured himself that the plan was sound, as long as they made it to Kilrush.

"We'd better get going if we mean to get there." she said.

It would be their first real test of facing the outside world on their own. In the few years prior, his father had tested him to make sure he could hold his own, proving his worth on their occasion trips together to Ennis market. *But would it be too much for Rosalee to cope with?*

"Ready when you are." She had collected her belongings as a signal that she was up for the plan. Sean followed suit then scanned the the valley towards the river, and downstream for signs of the English militia or the constabulary.

There was only one way to find out...

Chapter Three
Sean and Rosalee make progress – in more ways than one.

"It looks all clear," he said. "But we had better be careful. I know most of the troops are on foot, but some will be on horseback. If they *do* spot us we won't have a chance. We won't be able to outrun them."

"Yes, *sir!*" replied Rosalee, offering a fake salute. But she knew what he meant and kept close, stopping every now and then to check they weren't being followed. They headed downhill closer to the river.

It was still early but Sean knew that the soldiers – even the sloppy English – were sufficiently disciplined to rise at dawn, have breakfast, and be on their way within the hour. He guessed – he hoped – they were well ahead of them, but he felt it might be safer if they could actually *see* the enemy.

As soon as they reached the river Sean stopped, relieving his shoulders of the weight of his bedding, shelter, and provisions.

"Shouldn't we keep going?" asked Rosalee.

"We need food. More food at least. It's best if we forage for it now, rather than wait until late in the day – just in case."

She said nothing but it made total sense. "I'll go and look for mushrooms," she said. I know it's not the season, but it *has* been wet and *some* fungi should be around. Morels. Mammy told me the best places to look. What will you be doing?"

"Have you ever tickled trout?"

"What else is there to do with them?"

"I'll take that as a 'yes', then. Care to join me? There's the perfect spot just here. I'll walk downstream and find another spot for myself. We'll meet back here." He was already walking before she could answer.

A few yards downstream he saw another perfect spot. In theory.

It was a bank *low enough* to the water so he could lie face down and place *both* hands gently into the river, about two feet apart. His approaching footsteps may have startled them but that didn't matter. Hopefully one, or more, would have sought refuge *under* the lip of the bank. He lay face down, spread himself out, and got into position.

He doubted he would fare as well as Rosalee. If her mother had taught her foraging then she had almost certainly taught her how to tickle trout. But his first exploration of the still waters under the bank was promising. He connected.

It was slimy, barely moving, allowing him to caress the underside of its body. He gradually worked his fingers close to the head. *So far, so good*, he thought, then he closed his hands around his prey, then up, and out. Perfect. The fish must have been near a couple of pounds.

Using a stout stick he quickly struck the fish a quick blow, killing it instantly rather than allowing it to slowly suffocate and die. Tying it with a piece of string to his belt he walked a few yards back up stream for another spot. It was not as good as the first, but it would have to do. He needn't have bothered. Several more minutes – several tedious minutes – lapsed and, nothing. Finally, the squeal of delight made up his mind.

Somebody else had just got lucky. *Now who might that be?* He made his way back to where he had left Rosalee. As soon as she saw him she held up her prize – triumphant. It was easily two pounds. But her joy was short-lived as she saw that he, too, was sporting a beautiful trout of his own, albeit not quite as large. Thankfully.

"Well, that's supper taken care of." It was both of them this time, matching each other word for word. They laughed. Lurch and Peggy wagged their tails in agreement.

It was a great start to the day. One fish should suffice for them both, with the head and tale enough to keep the dogs happy. It could be cooked on a spit – Sean had a metal spike in his bag – over a low fire. Hopefully they could find some wood sorrel. There were plenty of dandelion leaves, and perhaps some early hawthorn leaves and nettles for lightly wilted – not over-boiled – greens. They would cook nicely in the pot over the same fire, but they would still have to wait until dark.

Inwardly pleased with themselves they set out once again, but this time climbing *up* the gentle gradient overlooking the river. Once there they could keep an eye on the horizon and the way ahead. It lightened their moods and allowed them, for now at least, to forget the recent horrors of the previous day.

They reached a flatter pathway half-way up the slope, enough for them to walk side by side, chatting. Ahead, Lurch and Peggy did similar, apart from the occasional foray into the gorse and new growth of bracken. And without chatting!

The sun had long since risen to its height and was now dropping down towards the opposite horizon, casting longer shadows from the trees and rocks along the way. The countryside was fresh with the oncoming spring, the hillside adorned with the ever-present yellow flowers of gorse, interspersed with heather. Soaring skylarks, emerging from the thick undergrowth at the side of the animal track, also brightened their moods. It was now past mid-day and they had made good progress without seeing another living soul.

"There's still plenty of daylight left but we had best not go too far in case we catch up with the soldiers," said Sean. "At least we can be fairly certain there won't be another platoon following on behind. Above all, we must make sure we don't overtake them without knowing."

Rosalee was becoming increasingly reassured. She sensed already that Sean was smart, practical and vigilant. It made her feel safe once again.

"What about those rocks over there?" she asked. She was

pointing down the hillside to granite stones. They would create a wind-break from prevailing westerlies with a dip in the centre, perfect for a fire unseen from any direction.

"Just the job," he agreed. Soon they were exploring their new 'camp', setting down their belongings, putting up a shelter, and sorting out provisions for supper.

They both worked on automatic, in silence and seeming to know instinctively what had to be done next. Neither assumed the role of leader, and each respected the other's skills. They were settling down into a natural routine.

"I'll take Peggy and look for some dry wood," said Rosalee. He didn't reply, taking Lurch off into the opposite direction to look for 'greens'. "Don't go too far," she added. It was her nervousness of being alone once more suddenly taking over.

Soon they reunited back at base camp with their finds. "How many days old are the chicken pieces?" he asked.

"A couple of days now. Perhaps we'd better cook and eat them first before your rabbit – or the fish."

"Yes, to be on the safe side," he said. "I still have a couple of eggs we can save for breakfast – already hard-boiled."

"Mam made sure I had a packet of salt in my supplies," she said. "Perhaps we cook *both* fish tomorrow night, even though one will do both of us. I can then rub salt into the second one – *yours* – to preserve it for the next day."

She laughed at her own joke. *'Yours,'* she said, as if it were inferior. He hid his smile. *I won't give her the satisfaction of finding her funny*, he thought.

As soon as the light faded they lit the fire, really looking forward to a cooked meal, not to mention the warmth that the fire would afford. They placed small granite stones around the fire. They had sited it as close as was sensible to where they intended to sleep that night. Later they could use the hot stones to warm the earth under their beds before they retired for the night That would help them get to sleep.

Whilst Rosalee was out collecting kindling she came across a small spring. Luckily she had her water bottle tied to her belt. She also came across a handful of edible fungi. Morels. She filled the inside pockets of her overcoat with enough to keep them going a few days. It was more protein and perfect for adding extra flavour to their basic diet.

Their conversations became sparse and intermittent at times. The fate of their parents during the previous day invaded their quieter moments. But 'misery likes company' as they say, and it eventually opened them up enough to occasionally share their inner thoughts in an attempt to heal each other's wounds.

Both their sets of parents were lost. Killed. Murdered. They were certain of that. The native born Irish were considered 'non-persons' and of little worth to the English. Sean's siblings would be spared. They were useful or, at least, in the new workhouses they would cost little in keep until they were old enough for useful, productive work. A source of income.

For Rosalee it was slightly different. She loved *both* parents, even though Sean's uncle was not her *real* father. He had been good to her, loving her as her own. During the time her mother, Maureen, had been with Billy, however, she had been unable to bear more children. They could not afford to consult doctors for a reason but the local gypsy seer – who was also the mid-wife – said that the birth of Rosalee was *so* traumatic she was not surprised. In hindsight, it was a blessing.

Sharing this, the recent happenings and the background to each of their families, helped them both understand each other. Sean's father had hardly mentioned his brother Billy, apart from occasional references when he had met him by chance at Ennis market, the nearest town. But when it came down to it they were family and their first instinct was to look out for each other.

Rosalee knew much, much more than Sean about the relationship between the two brothers and their past life. Her step-Dad, Billy, was older and more confident than Sean's Dad - his brother Frankie. She explained how they came to Ireland from England – or, to be more exact, from Cornwall. Their father, William Senior, had lost his first wife after several years' struggle with consumption. If that wasn't bad enough, he immediately took up with a local barmaid from the village tavern in Callington. Their own mother was hardly cold in her grave before, within the year, William married the barmaid.

Billy (William Jnr) and Frankie were suspicious and distraught about the new – sudden - romance. Had he been 'carrying on' whilst their mother was on her death bed? They confronted their father whose answer was simple. *If you don't like it, you can clear off! Both of you. Here's £100 each. Don't come back until you learn some manners.*

They set sail for Ireland three days later, leaving behind their two sisters who were not much more than toddlers.

Sean was amazed at this story but it explained why his father, Frankie, rarely mentioned his *own* father or his brother, Billy. But now he understood. It also put into context why he made Sean aware that he *did* have family in Devon and Cornwall – in particular his aunties Florence and Mary Alice – also 'Baker Sercombes', his full family name.

The £100 they each received instead of an inheritance was enough for the brothers to buy farms in Ireland, encouraged by notices posted by the English government of rich promises.

"How come they – we – lived so far apart?" Sean wanted to know. "Dad hardly spoke of his brother, let alone go and see him. I didn't even know you existed. 'Till yesterday."

Rosalee had the answers – as usual. "Apparently they had to take whatever tenancy farms were on offer for the money they had. They were lucky to be as close as they were, in terms of distance. You know what long hours your Dad worked. Mine was the same. They hardly had *any* time for socialising. But the landlords were the same wherever you were, ready to evict us both as soon as it was convenient."

Thanks to the greens and the seasoning, the blandness of the cold chicken became palatable. Careful to exclude the bones (for it was mainly strips anyway) there was a little left over for the dogs. Even so, Sean raided their own reserves of rabbit – meant for the next day – for Lurch and Peggy. In any case they had an abundance of trout. With supper finished and cleared away, it was time to get some well-earned sleep. But should that be under the *one* 'roof', or should they make two *separate* shelters? They agreed to be practical and share.

Now they had two tarps it allowed them to improvise a little on the design of the shelter, and sleeping arrangements. They combined the two and so covered a greater area (but still only six foot square). It was just as well when the west wind decided to blow in a series of quite heavy showers.

The first squall doused the fire slightly, but they were able to salvage most of the hot stones for comfort and warmth, heating the ground upon which they were about to lay. In parts, their tarps were double skinned. It helped keep them dry when the rain was at its heaviest.

Sean suggested their dogs be placed on either side of himself and Rosalee – on the outer edges - but that met with resistance. She was adamant that the lurcher and collie should sleep *between* them, on the basis that they would provide more warmth.

Plus, of course, it would keep her and Sean at a respectable distance. *Her mother had brought her up well*, he thought.

Again, when Sean was selecting a site for their night's shelter, he had chosen the flat upright surface of one of the rocks against which to rest their 'ridge' branches. As before, the tarps were draped over them, but this time there were two eight foot struts, spaced three feet apart. It was enough to accommodate all four of them. Whilst supper was cooking, Sean had cut two lengths of hazel especially for the purpose.

"What on earth have you got there?" she asked, marvelling at Sean's knife. It did its job in minutes once he had located a suitable source of hazel.

"It's called a Bowie knife. My Dad gave it to me. He bought it from a crew member of one of the timber-carrying ships from Canada that docked in Limerick. It's named after the American backwoodsman who invented it. Apparently he used it for knife fights."

"It looks more like a sword," she concluded, grasping one end of the recently cut poles to take them back to camp. Some lighter lengths of hazel were laid against the main poles at right angles so that side 'walls' could be created.

From the top, where the main ridge branches rested against the upright rocks sloping down to the ground where they anchored at the bottom, any rainfall was again able to run downwards and to the side, and away. Rosalee was amazed at how cosy they were. With their provisions, plus Sean's duffel bag placed on the perimeter, they had everything secure, ready to catch some well-earned sleep.

Even so, Rosalee waited for Sean's gentle snoring, before closing her own eyes, hoping for another good day tomorrow.

Chapter Four
Their last days in Ireland – a new world awaits...

Next morning it was Rosalee who woke first – or rather before Sean, but third. Lurch and Peggy had already risen together to go out to make themselves comfortable, without disturbing her or Sean. He was still sleeping soundly, dreaming perhaps of goodness knows what, but perhaps happier times, going by the peaceful look on his face.

She remained still for several moments before rising, secretly studying his face, noting how the corners of his mouth turned up in a smile. With his fine features, dark hair, strong nose and healthy complexion, she found him quite handsome. She had noticed how much taller he was than her, perhaps six foot or more, and broad.

She was at the age 'when she was noticing boys' as her mother had said. It was followed by her warning to be careful and not to let fanciful thoughts get the better of her. But she felt so safe with Sean, confident in his ability to look after her, and so... attracted to him.

Suddenly realising what she had been thinking she blushed, dismissing such thoughts as wicked, and just in time. Sean stirred, opened his eyes, yawned, and turned to face her. "Who...? Where...?" He couldn't remember. Then he came to his full senses and sat up. "Good morning," he said.

"Did you sleep well?" she began.

The cool morning breeze sent a chill through him. Rosalee remained snug under her coarse woollen blanket.

"Fine, apart from this damned hard..." he felt under where his shoulder had lain "... rock." It had cooled hours ago. He threw it out then got to his feet.

Despite the chill air they were bathed in bright warm light from the early sunrise. They had purposely placed their shelter with the westerlies behind them which, in turn, gave them the benefit of an early warmth from the east.

"What's for breakfast?" she asked, still refusing to move.

"Eggs," he replied.

"Cold?"

"Yes."

"Ugh!" she was looking for a reason to get up. All she found was an excuse to stay put in her makeshift – but warm – bed.

"So, warm brown trout wrapped in dock leaves, sorrel and nettles doesn't really excite you?"

"How on ....?" *That* made her sit up. Her face lit in disbelief.

"Oh, just something I rustled together, whilst you... had disappeared for a while. *(He was careful to spare her blushes by referring to the real purpose for her sneaking off behind the bushes.)* I had picked the leaves just after I caught the fish then, before the rain put the fire out totally, I wrapped the trout in them after dampening them down. That way the embers wouldn't scorch the fish too much."

He got up, reaching over to dig out the trout buried in the embers from the night before, using his Bowie knife.

"It looks pretty good. Edible at least. And the juices from the leaves should have seeped deep into the flesh of the fish." She was impressed.

She held out her hands for her breakfast, impatient as she watched him behead the fish, strip out the backbone then pass over her portion, laid across a bed of dock leaves. They tucked into nature's bounty as if it were their last meal.

"This is really good," she said, pausing to take a breath. "Where did you learn to do this?"

"There's lots you don't know about me," he replied, hoping she wanted to know more in the first place. He looked down at her to measure her approval, but she was too engrossed. It didn't stop him carrying on with his story.

"My Irish Romani mother, Annie Colleen McGowan (before she

married) taught me. I do a similar dish with hedgehogs and squirrels." He laughed then looked across to see if she thought it funny.

She didn't, or she wasn't really listening, which I suppose was a compliment if she was *so* absorbed with the trout breakfast he had prepared. They both took extra time over their breakfast, partly because of the bones, but also to relish its taste and make it last.

Rosalee finished first. "That was *so* good, Sean," she said. He liked the way she called him by name.

Having kept a respectful distance while they ate, Lurch and Peggy finally joined them, sniffing round to find out what the meal was that they were in danger of missing. Sean split the fish head and tail in half. Rosalee donated her cold boiled egg to them, not wishing to mask the taste of such a delicious starter. Seeing this, Sean did the same.

In the short time they had been together, Sean and Rosalee had already worked out a system to quickly pack up and prepare for the next leg of their journey. There was no real need for urgency at the moment. Rather the reverse, they wanted the English troops to make as much distance from them as possible. Even so, it was instinctive within them to be ready and responsive to any event, to any potential danger.

"How far is Kilrush?" she asked.

"If we follow the river – first the Fergus, then the Shannon as it opens up into the estuary – it's about fifty miles." He said no more, fascinated to see her mind working, calculating how long it might take them.

Finally, her next question came. "Is four hours a day enough walking?"

"Sounds about right," he answered.

"Is ten miles a day about right?"

"In this terrain. Yes. We should only use proper roads, and only then if we think it's safe." He automatically weighed up the dangers.

"Five days, then," she said. "At the most."

"And if the weather holds," he replied. "Talking of which, we'd better get going in case those dark clouds head our way."

She needed no more encouragement. For two sixteen year olds thrust into the most tragic of situations, they were coping in a way that was *way* beyond their years. As it turned out they found drovers' roads on their route, still keeping sight of the river. They were able to make good time, finding the going much easier than trudging through bracken and rough animal tracks.

During the day their main focus was to make good progress addressing the fifty mile journey. They stopped only occasionally, snacking on meagre cold rations. Their main meals were breakfast and a hearty supper.

With only four to five hours devoted to walking it gave them time, and enough daylight, to choose the best place to camp overnight. They needed good, warm shelter – a fire for cooking and with water close by. That would ensure they kept fit and healthy, and in good shape to face up to 'who knows what kind of future' they might expect in England. Limiting their walking time also ensured they could pick, gather, and hunt for enough food.

Enter Lurch with his special skills.

They followed the rivers as a sure method to avoid getting lost. It also acted as a defence against the possible dangers that the main highways presented, as well as providing another food source – fresh fish. However, the more they travelled *down*stream the wider the river became, leaving the delicate skill of trout tickling less of an opportunity.

But the sight of the Shannon, as it widened to provide them with a view across the broad expanse of water to the county of Limerick, was spellbinding. It was hard to imagine a country so beautiful could turn out to be so cruel and force people to leave, rather than stay in their motherland.

"Is that the ocean?" asked Rosalee, never having seen anything wider than the River Fergus just outside of Ennis.

"No, not quite. But we're not far." Your trout tickling days are over for a while, I'm afraid," he said. "Time for Lurch to earn his keep now."

Rabbits were still in plentiful supply – ever since the first Viking invasion introduced them centuries earlier. Lurch not only relished the chance to please his master, who rewarded him with praise and hugs with every catch, he also quite liked rabbit in his own diet, so it had a double benefit. Whilst there were some natural and redundant warrens to be found along the way, it was sometimes a bit hit and miss. Usually it was all down to patience.

In the circumstances they decided on a fixed routine. First make camp, prepare the shelter and food for supper, then take Lurch out hunting. They could spot the best areas to start by the abundant rabbit droppings. Burrows were then quickly identified and it was simply sit and wait. Sean hoped that a couple of sessions would provide a brace of rabbits – enough to supplement their rations and sufficient for them to 'survive' until they reached Kilrush.

Rosalee proved excellent at tickling trout but her opportunities would run out after a couple of days as the wider river proved unsuitable for such a fine skill. That said, she spent most of one afternoon while still on the narrow parts of the Fergus to yield another four trout – nearly ten pounds of fish. If she could preserve – and keep back - two of them until they reached port, they could be used to buy or barter other provisions.

As the roads became straighter and easier underfoot they were getting close to their destination.

The evening of day five saw them camped just a few miles outside of the bustling port of Kilrush. The only other town of any size Sean had experienced was Ennis, on market days. *What could be so different?* he asked himself.

The truth was that it represented a major sea port for the area, where a third of its inhabitants were 'just passing through'. They might be seafarers travelling the world on merchant ships or tea clippers, or merchants themselves, hoping to find buyers for their goods and services – or a passage to England, Scotland, or the New Worlds of America and Canada.

What little law and order existed was not enough to curb the criminal activities, and lack of morals, of most of the transient population. Even the locals, hardened to the worldly mores of matelots and sharp-dealing merchants had grown wary. They were capable of looking after themselves in a different way from the simpler villagers among whom Sean and Rosalee had been raised. Sean would have to adapt quickly and use all his wits to survive.

But that was for tomorrow. If they set out soon after dawn they would be there before noon the following day. If they found a ship, they might even make the evening tide and be spared the uncertainties that lurked in the depths of the colourful community that was Kilrush.

They could soon be on a vessel bound for Bristol.

Chapter Five

Fleeing the English in Ireland – for the English in Devon

Neither of them slept well that night. It was a mixture of excitement and anticipation – but mostly fear. Fear of the unknown. It was all new to them. Their parents being wiped out so suddenly and so recently left a gaping hole in their lives.

Billy and Frankie had expected the day would come – might come – when the creeping threat of the British-led eviction squads would be knocking at their door. It was no surprise when it did. They knew whole families were being murdered, which is why they both vowed to save their eldest.

On their own their older children just might have a chance of a better future, but Rosalee was a mere girl. How could she stand up to the savagery that surrounded them? In their last meeting, at the marketplace in Ennis only a few weeks earlier, Frankie and Billy made an agreement. Their last testament, you might say. Sean and Rosalee would have a better life in England, if only they could find their own father again.

Each would prepare an escape package – one for Sean, the other for Rosalee: materials for shelter, food, provisions to survive. But they would say nothing to either of them until the very last moment. They – the heads of the family – could bear that burden; there was no reason to put the fear of god in either of their eldest until it was time.

Their plan – to tell them to go down river to the nearest port with ships to England – was the only option. No matter what the threat, family always looked out for family. It was true, both brothers had left England under a cloud, but that was a long time ago now and the dispute was with their father, not with their sisters. Their mother had died shortly before they left their birthplace in Cornwall for Ireland.

"We will send them back," said Frankie, meaning Sean and Rosalee. He was always the one who yearned to return to England himself, or at least see his sisters again. Billy, perhaps because he was a little older, had fewer emotional attachments to his siblings, given that they were so much younger than he was. But he agreed.

"But what about us, Frankie? And our wives? Have you considered that? And the younger children?" He and Frankie were treating themselves to a few glasses of porter in one of the many taverns, and the drink was making him feel sentimental, and worried.

This time Frankie took the lead, the part of the more practical of the two. "We cannot run. We'll be too slow when the time comes. And the money it would take to pay for ship packages for *all* of us - well, we just don't have it. If we *do* get caught I just hope they'll spare the boys and their sister – they should take them in at the nearest workhouse, at least."

Sean and Rosalee knew little of this beforehand - that they were both part of a plan, one that they had nothing to do with creating, but one that would shape their futures together. Their destinies.

On the last morning before they were due to arrive in Kilrush they awoke and, making an exception on the final day, they revived the embers from the previous night to cook the last of the bacon. On the previous day they had passed an abandoned farm cottage – left vacant by the evicted tenants – to discover a clutch of fresh eggs in the hen house.

They were still warm, with the mother hen clucking at them while they raided her bounty. They had wrapped them individually and carefully in moss, determined that they survive the journey unbroken until they could treat themselves the following morning, with the bacon. It was their first proper cooked breakfast but they still made sure kindling was dry, making no unnecessary smoke to attract unwelcome attention.

"What's the plan when we get there?" Rosalee wanted to know. Sean took out his Bowie knife, advancing towards her. "Hang on," she blurted, nervously. "What are you going to do with that thing now?"

She only relaxed once she saw him laughing and dropping the hand holding his knife to his side. Then he explained. "You need a haircut," he said, walking towards her once more.

"I certainly do *not*," she replied, quite adamant and backing up as he came closer. "Peggy! Save me!"

"You can't be a girl any more," he said. "It's not safe."

"So you're going to make me a boy?" she said, with an air of disbelief again, "a boy wearing a dress?"

He reached down into his duffel bag. "Here. Put these on." He threw her a pair of his own trousers. "You'll have to tuck the bottoms into your boots." He turned round, signalling her to change her clothes behind a nearby hawthorn bush.

"Keep your eyes straight ahead," she warned. "This bush hasn't got its summer leaves on yet."

"Tell me when you're ready."

"You can turn round now," she said after a few moments. "How do I look?"

"Wonderful," he said. "But you'll be all the more convincing with a haircut." She gave in and walked up to him, turning her back so that he could get to work with his Bowie knife.

It was sad to see such luxuriant, black hair fall in tresses from the back of her neck, resting in a pile at her feet. He could see her face, her beautiful face, even more clearly now. It was the closest intimacy they had shared. He had to force himself to prevent his hands from trembling as he sliced through the last of her hair. It revealed her neck, an inviting neck that he longed to kiss.

"You're still too pretty," he declared, before scooping up a handful of peaty soil to smear over her freshly washed cheeks and chin. "There. You look much better with a beard." Her faced dropped.

Was she about to cry? He hoped not and immediately regretted his spontaneous, yet well-intentioned, foolishness. "Look. I'm sorry," he whispered, but then his heart leapt as she pressed her head into his chest, grasping him to her.

"It's OK," she whispered back, his chin resting on the top of her newly-shorn head. But wait. Now her shoulders were shaking. *Oh my god, what have I done now?* he was thinking.

"Please don't cry. I'm truly, *truly* sorry," he repeated. He stroked her remaining hair in an attempt to comfort her. But she her shoulders continued to shake even more. Suddenly he realised, at the point when she was rubbing her face back and forth across his chest against his shirt – his '*newly washed in the stream the night before and dried by the fire*' shirt – that she was shaking with uncontrollable laughter.

She looked up at his face. "Nice shirt," she smirked. "Nice *clean* shirt." He looked down, first at her still smudged face before noticing the streaks of peaty soil, smeared across the front of his shirt. Before he could think of a way to retaliate she let go of him and ran to take cover behind Peggy. Lurch joined his new companion, and Rosalee. And growled.

"Traitor!" yelled Sean at his beloved lurcher. "Who's side are you on?" But he beamed at the scene in front of him, glad to see at least some joy and laughter was left in the world. "OK. You're forgiven. All of you. I deserved that – I'll let you off just this once."

Seeing it was now safe, Lurch ran up to him, jumped up to earn some serious ear tweaking – and leaving even more mud on his shirt.

Soon they were on their way, the episode of tom foolery lightening their moods, deceptively hiding their sense of apprehension for the challenges they knew lay ahead. Both dogs bounced on before them, keeping to the well-worn path into the port, only briefly making an excursion into the bushes by the side of the road. The hedgerows formed a welcome shield from the elements, and other travellers. Sean decided to discuss, rather than dictate, his thoughts with Rosalee. After all, the whole venture was new to him, too. Beginning to trust her judgement, he was glad of a second opinion.

"Have you been here before?" she asked.

"I've only heard what Dad used to talk about when he told me of the towns and places he used to go to. That was before we settled on the farm near Ennis."

"What do you think it'll be like?"

Sean didn't want to frighten her. "Like anywhere else, I guess, apart from being a port with lots of merchants, sailors and people passing through from other parts, other countries even. He stressed that we just have to be careful, and trust no-one in all places like this."

That included when they arrived in England. She knew she just had to stick to Sean, and follow his lead.

"Will they guess I'm a girl?"

"Not if you pull your hat well down over your face, turn the collar of your coat up – and don't talk. Do you think you can manage all that?"

She didn't like his tone much, but knew he was probably only trying to get his own back for his dirty shirt.

"How will we get a passage to Bristol?"

"We could sign on as crew," he replied, "but I expect most of the ships preparing for tonight's evening tide are all sorted. We'll head for the docks straight away to see if there is a ship, and see how busy they are. If they look as if they are behind in their loading, we may get lucky."

"My Dad told me about ships leaving every day over-loaded with food and provisions, even though we're starving. Why is that?" she wanted to know.

"I don't really understand any of it. None of it makes sense. But it seems they just want us out, out of our cottages, off our land and, well, off the face of the earth."

They were approaching town now, the roads were busier with more houses and buildings, and people. Sean drew the dogs in closer, tying string to each of their collars together and keeping them to heal.

"We have to look as though we're going some place with a purpose," said Sean. "If we look lost, hungry, or homeless, we'll get caught by the constabulary and taken to a workhouse. That's one thing my Dad told me."

They followed the main flow of traffic – most were on foot, some on horseback, some in carriages or on carts. They paid particular notice of the carts loaded with provisions – wheat, vegetables, whisky, bacon, fresh meat. Some were even loaded with live sheep, cattle and pigs – all bound for England. The streets were narrow, muddy in parts but those with crushed stone made it easier for the carts. Poorer areas were dirty with refuse, visibly infested with rats from an open sewer.

Soon the welcome sight of masts and rigging rising above the warehouses and offices signalled their arrival at the docks.

"Here we are," said Sean (they had talked very little since arriving, taking in all the unfamiliar sites and surroundings). "What's that vessel over there?"

They made their way to the only ship being loaded – a two-masted merchant ship with foresails off it's bowsprit, and a small mast and sail aft. The sign on her bow said 'ELLEN', she was clearly being prepared for a sailing that very evening. It would need good winds and a strong tide to ease their departure from the Shannon estuary and, if it were bound for Bristol, a nicely turning tide to take them swiftly up the Bristol Channel, via the North Devon coast. The quartermaster was supervising the loading.

"Excuse me. Sir?" Sean could see immediately that the man was agitated, probably behind schedule in getting all the produce on board. "Are you by any chance bound for Bristol."

"Yes. What of it?" he replied. (He later found out the man's name was Andrews.) "Who's asking?"

"Are you still looking for crew?"

"Let's have a look at you," replied Andrews. "You look OK. Strong enough. But what about the scrawny one?"

"He's my brother, Lee." That was a surprise to Rosalee but she kept quiet, letting Sean come up with all the answers. "He's tougher than he looks, and he doesn't eat much."

"Oh, I'm not so sure. We've no room for passengers if you know what I mean." Andrews thought he had just made a joke. Sean laughed, just in case.

"Plus," Sean jumped in before Andrews could walk off, "he comes with an excellent rat catcher at no extra charge." He was referring to Lurch.

"Well, we usually have Jack Russells for that, but OK," said Andrews. "What are your names. I need it for the Log."

"Sean and Lee Sercombe, age sixteen and fourteen."

"That's an English name. You're not from round here then?"

"No," said Sean. "But we're going back home to Devon. Tavistock, to be precise. We're going back to family."

"That's settled then. OK. I've got to get this loaded before we miss the tide. See that lazy bunch over there?" Andrews pointed to six or seven men unloading sacks from a line of carts, carrying them up a rear gang plank. "Tell a bloke called Steve Dawe who you are and that I've signed you on, then take your orders from him. Give him these."

With that he left to check in a new delivery of whiskey from the Limerick distillery, but first he gave Sean two pieces of paper with numbers on them and the ship's stamp 'Ellen'. He was told to keep them safe.

"Are you Steve?" asked Sean, going up to the one who seemed

most in control.

"Yes. Have you just signed on?"

"Yes. Me and my brother. I'm Sean, and this is..."

"... Lee," broke in Rosalee, just to remind Sean of her new name.

"Can I see your Muster numbers? For the List?"

Sean showed him their papers, then returned 'Lee's' to Rosalee. "Keep this safe at all times," he told her.

"Just follow those blokes there," he said. "Do what they do. Whatever they load, you join in and help. And no wandering off or you'll start the voyage in the brig with no rations."

They worked in pairs – the same as the other crew – loading sacks of grain until all the carts were empty. The cart drivers would at last be glad to spend their wages in the local Kilrush taverns. Sean and 'Lee', as well as Lurch and Peggy, followed the crew when all the carts were loaded up. The dogs had been left to guard their belongings while their masters pitched in loading the good ship 'Ellen'.

They followed behind the crew up the gangplank, tired, but thankful that the hard work – for now – seemed to be over. Judging by the comments from the rest of the crew they were about to be fed. One of the youngest of the work gang – a clean looking fair-haired lad about the same age as Sean - turned, his hand outstretched, inviting a hand-shake.

"I'm Davey. Is this your first sign-up?" he asked.

"Yes. I'm Sean. And this is..."

"... his brother, Lee," said Rosalee, looking vacant and bored.

"He's only fourteen," explained Sean. "His voice hasn't even broken yet. And he's got an attitude. Ignore him."

"This is only my second ticket," said Davey. "I worked my way across from Bristol the other month to join my uncle on his farm. The fever had just taken his eldest so he needed an extra hand. I got there – at a place near Ennis – and found it had been burnt down. They'd all been evicted, or worse. I couldn't find them so I made my way back here, to go home."

"I'm sorry about that," said Sean. "We were burnt out too. We're off to find what family we have left. In Devon. Or Cornwall. I'm not exactly sure."

"What's your family name?" asked Davey.

"Sercombe."

Davey pondered a while over the name before answering. "It's not too common a name, that's for sure. It should be easy to track them down though. And easier the further down from Bristol you go. There's not too many farmers - with land - once you get past Taunton. I take it they are farmers?"

"More like labourers or builders as far as we know," answered 'Lee', not wanting to be totally left out of the conversation. "Or tenant farmers."

"Your best bet is to ask at the railway station when we get to Bristol. If they're farmers of any size they'll be sending vegetables or cattle up to the markets in London, through Bristol. They may have an address for you." With that, Davey caught up with the rest of the crew with Sean and Rosalee close behind.

Most of all they were looking forward to a hearty supper – and sleep.

Chapter Six
The young couple's resilience is tested on the high seas...

Davey had warned them not have too many expectations about their meals and rations. His main advice was to eat well early on in the voyage. Because the food used would not be that fresh even when they cast off, by the time they were about to dock in Bristol, it would barely be edible.

They took his advice though they expected to be no more than three days or so at sea, given the prevailing westerlies. They were really starting to blow as soon as they left the shelter of the Shannon estuary. The Ellen was in for a stormy first night. So were they.

Because they were not seasoned deck-hands, Sean, 'Lee' – and Davey – were given less demanding roles in terms of working on the rigging and sails. Theirs were the more monotonous jobs of keeping the decks clean, checking and readjusting the food supplies in the hold so that none would spoil (with 'Lee' and Peggy deployed to reduce the rat infestation level to a minimum), and helping Cook before and after meal-times.

It wasn't hard work but they were long hours and sleep came easy with a hammock - a real luxury compared with those hands unfortunate to have the most uncomfortable bunks imaginable. Their main worry was losing their belongings – theft of all they had in the world. But Cook was a benign soul who took a liking to Sean and 'Lee', so he promised to keep them safe.

Despite this, Sean was careful to keep his silver dollar secure on his person – their lifeline in case of emergencies – and his Bowie knife, on his belt, was a visible deterrent to anyone even thinking of messing with them. The seasoned crew were mostly thin, wiry, and looked malnourished compared with the strapping Sean and the likes of Davey, but they included some devious chancers, for whom

Davey warned you had to be on the look-out. But it wasn't until the start of day three that the first real danger occurred.

Dawn was usually sounded by the bell or bellow from the watch-keeper, who also assigned them their jobs for the day. This morning's sound was different - an almighty crack as one of the two main masts gave way under the weight of the rain-sodden sail, and gale force winds. It also tore through the second mainsail, literally, rendering both sails useless.

The next cry sent alarm through the whole crew, even Lurch and Peggy stood up erect, ears pinned forward.

"Rocks! Hard to port! To port!" came the cry from the bowman. He had seen the rocks first. There was nobody on look-out on the landing on the masts due to the storm, so the rocks were only spotted until it was too late. Or was it?

The helmsman responded immediately but he only had the foresails and the sail aft – now both fully reefed – for power. The main power was the savage force of the westerly, aided by the brown-water currents as they neared the Bristol Channel.

If that wasn't enough, there was another deafening splitting sound as one of the rock overhangs, luckily not one of the submerged jagged edges, sliced into the bow. Fortunately, it was just above the normal waterline.

"Curses," called the helmsman. They're not ordinary rocks. It's Lundy." He turned towards the second mate on the bridge. "What shall we do now?"

He was right. It *was* Lundy off the North Devon coast – indistinguishable at sea level to anyone on board as they were approaching it through the mist and spray thrown up by the head-on waves, and the torrential rain. Caught in a vortex, they were heading straight for the cliffs.

"Hard to port! Hard to port!" yelled the second mate. "Keep 'er steady called the bosun. Take her away from the island."

The second mate offered more help, making a three-man team and using all their knowledge and experience to save the ship from disaster. From sinking!

"He's right. Head away from the rocks if you can then, as soon as you feel we are in the lea of the island and sheltered from the westerlies, bring 'er round. We'll sit it out until she blows out – as long as we don't take on too much sea in the meantime"

It was a tough job for the helmsman to turn the vessel onto a beam reach and switching from a following wind, but he had to do it. The bosun joined him at the wheel so they could hold a steady course, at least long enough to sail past the headland.

"Now!" screamed the second mate as he could see the slightly calmer waters over to starboard.

The helmsman shifted position, temporarily causing the bosun to lose balance. "Going about!" he cried, the bosun joining him to turn the wheel and the sluggish ship onto the opposite beamer. The ship gave a massive lurch, men, tackle, anything not nailed down sliding across decks to the opposite, port, side. Luckily, nobody was swept overboard. Sean held onto Lurch and Peggy – and 'Lee' – with all his strength.

At last he noticed a thin smile of satisfaction appear for a fleeting moment on the captain's lips. In spite of the sudden movement somehow, through strength or shear willpower, he had barely moved, standing motionless, grasping the rail in front of him. So far he hadn't said a word, leaving his trusted crew to figure out the best way to overcome the otherwise deadly onslaught of the storm. Finally he spoke: "Well done lads. Keep 'er steady."

Just as the bosun and helmsman thought they could hold on no longer, they were relieved by Davey, ignoring his own safety and fighting his way across the deck to join them, adding his weight to the task. Both the seasoned mariners nodded their thanks and approval. Then Sean, handing Lurch and Peggy to the safe hands of 'Lee', who was squatting down at the base of one of the broken masts, took over from the bosun, who was laying prone on the deck, totally exhausted.

Satisfaction spread over the weathered face of the captain once again but, this time he remained silent. Even with the remaining small sails, fore and aft, they made good progress until they finally slipped into the lea of the towering cliffs to starboard. And safety. The boys had helped save the day. It hadn't gone un-noticed.

Mercifully, the vessel was now more stable and in calmer seas so the helmsman turned The Ellen into the head-wind. They lost way, but resisted dropping the sails in case they began to drift too close to the cliffs, and more danger.

Captain Jan Brewer returned to his cabin, nodding to the second mate as if to say, *You know what to do next.*

He did. He waited. Waited for the storm to blow itself out.

Chapter Seven
Rescue comes at a price – for the captain

It was another three hours before the winds dropped, the clouds growing lighter, parting to reveal glimpses of blue sky. Only then could they see the mainland. They could just make out Hartland Point – and lights.

"Damned wreckers!" muttered Brewer, returning to the bridge. He knew that their drama was being noticed by those on shore once visibility improved. Taking out his telescope he searched the Devonshire coastline for movement, sweeping across from the Point towards Appledore, and the mouth of the River Taw. He swept back, towards the Point again then checked. His second worst fear proved true.

"Curses," he said as he turned to his second mate. The watch-keeper had now joined them with a report on the status of the merchandise. To them both, Captain Brewer confirmed what he'd just spotted. "It's a schooner coming out of Clovelly. No. Three of them now. They'll be out for salvage, but deep down they're no more than pirates. Wreckers."

Brewer called down to the bowman. "How bad is the split in the hull? What chance do we have to make it ashore?"

The bowman took another look. "It's not good, Cap'n. We've already taken on too much sea. Unless we bale all of our cargo overboard to lighten her, she'll sink for sure. Bow first. I reckon we've got seven hours, tops."

Brewer was seething. First at his own stupidity at not giving Lundy a wider birth during the storm, then at the mere thought of the shame and embarrassment of surrendering up cargo to those he regarded as no more than opportunists. He could jettison cargo now to save the ship – but that would mean total loss.

His only option was to strike a reasonable bargain with the

schooners from Clovelly, perhaps saving three quarters of his cargo – and his ship – and his crew! The schooners were fast, but it was still a head wind for them so it would take them all of four hours before they reached the Ellen – as long as they could close-haul most of the way.

All he could do now was wait and hope. The hours passed slowly.

"They're here, Cap'n," called the watch-keeper, tapping on his cabin door. Brewer had taken a power nap, preserving his strength and wits so he was alert and ready to come out of this mess the best he could. "Four of them. One more than we thought. You might know one of them."

"Not Chanter?" Brewer's heart sank. He and the brigand Chanter went a long way back. Before he took to the high seas, Chanter was reported – although it was never proven – to be behind a series of highway robberies in North Devon. He always claimed this was a myth, and slanderous, just because it was claimed he was a descendant of Tom Faggus, the blacksmith turned highwayman. Tom actually became a bit of a Robin Hood figure, who later married into the Doone family.

Brewer emerged from his cabin, fastening the last three buttons of his coat, climbing up the steps to the bridge to join his next in command. "You start the bargaining, Jed," he said to the second mate. I want to see what his worst offer on salvage and rescue is before we strike a final deal.

His fears were realised when Ben Chanter himself spoke first. "In a bit of a sorry state, are we?" he called, grinning with satisfaction as he spoke. "How bad are you holed?"

"Bad enough," replied the second mate. "But we might make it into Appledore for repairs."

"Not in these seas I don't reckon." Chanter had already spotted the hole. From where he was looking, head on, it was more than the split the bowman had first reported to Brewer. "Unless you lose some of your cargo I reckon you'll only last probably two hours more – even if you stay here. Less if you try to move her."

"What do you propose, Chanter?" It was Brewer calling from the bridge, barely able to hold his temper.

"Ah... Jan! Jan Brewer. How are you, my friend?" Chanter recalled the days when they were both hell-raisers, from Bristol to Barnstaple, at sea and inland. They might still be friends now were it not for Polly. She had been Brewer's 'intended', until that cold winter night when he called on her at her parent's house in town – her father was a local merchant, supplying the grain ships – only to find she had run off with Chanter that very morning. He had sworn revenge ever since. But now was certainly not the time.

"Well. The way I see it," Chanter continued," if you do nothing you stand to lose your cargo, the ship, *and* your crew."

"Take us back to Appledore for repairs and I'll give you a quarter of the cargo."

"Half!"

Damn his eyes, whispered Brewer under his breath. He was seething, much to angry to respond.

"Any livestock on board?" It was the captain of one of the other of the four schooners who joined the bargaining.

The quartermaster from Ellen replied this time. "Just a few sheep and pigs – a dozen of each at most." *If they're still alive*, he thought.

"OK," it was Chanter again. "I'll tell you what we'll do. You keep the livestock, we'll still claim half of the rest of the cargo, but – and you'll like this - I'll pay for your repairs."

What? Brewer thought. *Why so generous? What's the catch?* Then he found out.

" - in return for part ownership of the Ellen. A fifth."

Brewer turned away in disgust. First Polly, now his ship! "OK, you've got a deal," he muttered.

"What was that?" asked Chanter. "I couldn't quite hear."

"I said you've got a deal!" yelled Brewer, fuming. "Now let's get on with it." He went back to his cabin, searching for his best bottle of rum before he lost that too.

The words were hardly out of his mouth when Chanter and his fellow captains and crew set about unloading the cargo into their own schooners. By now the sea was calm, at least in the shelter of the island, although it was still choppy in open water. They had to move fast to make most of the journey into Clovelly before nightfall. Chanter's schooner was the first to move alongside the Ellen.

The process was simple and they had come well prepared. A makeshift chute was constructed to transfer provisions from the merchant ship to a schooner, one at a time. It was made from an eight foot wide by twenty foot long length of sailcloth, tied at one end to the side of the Ellen, whilst the other was pinned to the deck of the receiving schooner.

A line of crew members at each end, one line on the Ellen, the other on the receiving deck, ensured that goods were passed safely down the line onto the chute, then stored on each schooner quickly and without loss. It was clear that Chanter was well practised.

He boarded the Ellen himself, quietly relieved that Brewer had already disappeared below decks. He, Ben Chanter, would supervise proceedings personally. First he took a very quick count of the cargo. He could only make a rough estimate, guessing the volume by the amount of hold space used for the storage of each category of merchandise.

He would try to take most of it whilst deliberately leaving some of the heaviest cargo in the rear storage areas. That would allow the bow of the Ellen a better chance of keeping her injury to her bow *above* the water line. *After all, no need to be greedy*, he thought, *the main prize is the ownership share of the good ship Ellen herself. Don't want to lose her now.*

She would be towed to Appledore, that very act itself a total embarrassment for Brewer. Due to the failing light by the time they would reach the mainland, and because the stricken ship needed to be booked into the Appledore repair yard, the plan was to sail back to Clovelly first, and anchor off for the night. Relieved of most of its cargo, the Ellen should remain afloat sufficient to make the rest of the journey.

Once sufficient cargo had been transferred from the merchant vessel to the four salvage schooners, Chanter discussed towing arrangements with Brewer's second mate. Chanter was not really keen to meet Brewer himself head to head, and Brewer was still too incensed to even consider being within ten feet of Chanter.

They would run two lines from either side of the Ellen, to two schooners. They had deliberately kept two of the four rescue ships fairly light on cargo to compensate for towing the larger vessel.

They had considered towing the Ellen aft first to reduce the risk of taking on too much water but the bowman deployed his crewmen to make temporary repairs to the hull, now that the damage was sitting above the waterline. It wasn't perfect, but it would be enough to withstand the choppy seas of open water until they reached Clovelly.

They were also fortunate to have a following wind back to the mainland. That allowed each schooner to take a dead ahead straight course with mainsails and spinnakers deployed fully, and without the need for tacking or beam reaches. They set off confidently.

Chapter Eight
For Sean and Rosalee, their real adventures begin.

As they approached Clovelly they were greeted by the local lifeboat. It was totally unnecessary but the crew had been briefed by Chanter to take all precautions. Local inhabitants had come out in force to witness the drama. Some might have expected spoils but the only winners on this occasion were Chanter and his fellow crewmen and schooners. It was dark and now well into the evening, with the local taverns – the Red Lion and the New Inn – already lively and in full swing.

Each crew had to appoint shifts to guard the new found bounty, otherwise there were plenty of would-be wreckers who had arrived during the day from nearby villages to Clovelly, ready to relieve them of their cargo. For most – including the local taverns – it was a time for celebration and rejoicing.

But not for Captain Brewer. He remained in his cabin throughout, trusting his seconds in command to oversee operations without further loss. He would stay on board the Ellen until they reached Appledore the following day, where he would sign all the necessary papers, including the signing over of a fifth ownership of the Ellen to Chanter.

That's if he didn't kill Chanter first.

Most of the crew of the merchant ship Ellen were now, of course, unemployed. Some would continue on to Appledore where they might join another outbound ship from Barnstaple or Bideford. Despite the blow to his fortunes and profitability, Brewer honoured at least some of his pledge to his crew. Along with Sean and 'Lee', Davey also decided to sign off at Clovelly, receiving three shillings each – considered more than fair, given that they had 'worked' for barely four days.

Neither were really used to the boisterous nature of taverns plus, of course, Sean had the added responsibility for the safety of Rosalee. The less they mixed in general company, the less chance there was of people discovering she was a girl.

They collected their belongings from Cook, bade farewell, and by early morning were setting out from Clovelly. As a 'thank you' for helping the helmsman to save the ship off Lundy, Captain Brewer instructed Cook to make sure all three of them were well rewarded with plentiful provisions for their onward journeys. He had also made a special mention of their initiative and bravery in the ship's Log.

Davey was bound for Exeter, so they shared the road with him for just a few miles until they reached Higher Clovelly, where Davey took the road for Great Torrington. They had started out early but it was still a fifteen mile stretch for him which, if he was lucky, he would reach by mid afternoon.

Their friendship with Davey was brief but he proved to be a godsend. Sean took down the name of his relatives in Exeter with a promise to look him up, but they kept to their plan to locate the Sercombe family in the Tavistock area, or thereabouts. Davey advised them to stick to the main roads as much as they could, taking the route first to Bradworthy. It was just under ten miles away but would still take three to four hours to get there.

Davey also suggested that they look out for small farms on the fringe of any village or town they travelled through, offering to cut wood or a half a day's work in exchange for a night under cover and a simple meal. It always helped to explain who they were and what they were doing, that way it allayed any suspicion that they might be up to no good. Country folk were naturally suspicious of strangers.

It was also possible that locals from any of the remote villages might have heard of the Sercombe family, even the actual relatives they were hoping to find.

For the first night they decided to fend for themselves. They arrived in the large village square in Bradworthy just after noon, having been walking continually. They quenched their thirsts at St Peter's Well and filled their water bottles. Although the three shillings they had received from Brewer could have provided them for a room for the night at the Bradworthy Inn, they decided to forgo the luxury and try the next farm outside of the village. They were heading to Chilsworthy, some five miles down the road.

They felt at ease with the Devonshire countryside, it being not so different from County Clare. The mix of arable land and moorland made them feel at home, plus the Devon Red cattle grazing in the fields told them there was civilisation nearby and perhaps a friendly farmer's wife who would supply them with a quart of fresh, warm milk. The road they were on was well maintained, suggesting that they were on the right road – or at least on the road to somewhere of reasonable size.

They had been walking less than an hour when Rosalee's eyes lit up. "I bet there's some lovely trout in there," she said, leaving the road to climb down the bank to the River Waldon, without waiting for Sean.

"Come on, you dogs," he called, as the three of them followed her down to the water's edge. "Fancy another competition?" He was challenging her to another session of trout tickling.

They dropped their belongings, telling Lurch and Peggy to look after them and not move. They had been given ample rations by Cook the night before, enough to keep themselves fed for a day or two, but the memory of Sean's culinary skills with trout came back to her in a flash. She and Sean went their separate ways, up and down-stream, looking for the perfect spot. They also looked out for fresh dock leaves – young leaves, otherwise they tasted bitter – and, hopefully, sorrel.

Some half hour later they met back to where they had left the dogs, the jubilant Rosalee brandishing two small fish – about a pound and a half each, to Sean's... nothing. "I'll go and make camp," said Sean despondently, but anxious to prove he was of at least some use.

Davey was keen to point out that – compared with Ireland – the danger to travellers was a lot less. Even so, they were careful to choose a spot to spend the night that was away from the the road. They stayed next to the river and therefore in lower ground, sheltered from any bad weather that might pay them a visit. A half an hour later they had found the ideal spot, with food in preparation and dry kindling collected and set by, ready to be lit as soon as it became dusk.

With dusk there came an eerie silence. The sun hovered low over the horizon towards the coast from which they had just come, bathing them in a soft, warm evening glow. Skylarks had ceased their celebration of yet another warm spring day after two days of storm and rain, with blackbirds signing off the evening from the nearest hawthorn.

The air was cooler the closer they came to the river, and a light mist formed a mere three to four feet above it – mapping the course of the water as it gurgled down to eventually meet the River Torridge.

As Sean and Rosalee settled for the evening waiting for supper to cook, Lurch and Peggy drew closer, making up for the time they felt they had been neglected during the short ocean voyage from Ireland. Sean passed his palm over Lurch's bony ribcage just as Rosalee did the same to Peggy. Their fingers brushed lightly and unexpectedly. They remained there, fingers entwined, with no word spoken.

Lost in thought they could have been anywhere. It was their first night in England and a new beginning - in more ways than one?

Chapter Nine
Sean and Rosalee grow closer

The 'red sky at night' from the previous sunset proved prophetic, as they woke up to a true 'shepherd's delight' of bright sunshine, bathing their overnight shelter in a warm glow. Sean arose first, stretched and yawned, noticing how the early warmth was evaporating the dew that had settled on their tarps overnight, causing it to steam. He would leave the tarps until last when they were packing up after breakfast, to ensure they were fully dry and not so heavy.

"Wake up, sleepy head," he said as he nudged the still 'pretending to be asleep' Rosalee with his foot. She looked even more beautiful with her eyes closed, safe in the comfort of her slumber. A world away. He wondered what she might be dreaming about. He was soon to find out.

"Can you smell fish?" she asked, bouncing up and out of her bedroll. Lurch and Peggy jumped up too in surprise, before nuzzling in for an early morning fussing.

Indeed she *could* smell fish, probably, although the aroma from the the two trout wrapped in dock leaves was still well buried in the dying embers of the fire. Sean took out his Bowie knife, carefully disturbing the remains of the embers to reveal their still warm breakfast. The 'package' was unbroken, with only the outer dock leaves charred leaving the trout moist and cooked to perfection. They helped themselves to one each.

Rosalee added a few dry sticks on the embers, revitalising the fire without creating any smoke. They were still wary of strangers and attracting attention. "Cook gave me a small packet of tea," she said, sitting down to finish her meal. "I thought we might treat ourselves to some Earl Grey."

"Earl...?"

"...Grey," she said, in reply to Sean's unanswered question. "Earl Grey. It's a type of tea favoured by the gentry, and by the captain it would seem." She poured the equivalent to two cupfuls of water into their one cooking pot. "Cook said to add a few leaves of sorrel to bring out the lemony flavour more. Have you got some left?"

Sean dropped a small handful into the brew, watching the leaves wilt before the heated water took on a brown tinge. "Have you used your handkerchief recently?" he asked.

"Not for a few days," she replied.

"Give it here then. I'll give it a quick rinse. It'll have to do."

With that he took her not-too-grubby handkerchief, poured water over it, and squeezed it dry. It would act as a sieve. She understood why. The mixture had to be strained otherwise their tin mugs would be filled with soggy tea leaves and a sorrel mush. The linen would leave a clear brown liquid, still hot, but not so hot as to scald their mouths.

Sean took the first sip. His face said it all. "Would you like sugar with that, sir?" She was already reaching into her pocket for yet another small bag of treats that Cook had forced on her before they said their goodbyes. She sparingly laced each mug with a sprinkling before stirring them vigorously with a stick.

"That's much better," said Sean. Tea had been a rarity in his household but sometimes available after his Dad had come back from Ennis market – and only then if he had found a good price for his own produce – enough to treat them.

"Do you always slurp?" she asked, grimacing at the unusual sound coming from his lips.

"A little shot of poitin might help to quieten it down."

"Don't push your luck, cousin," she said, but with a hint of a smile showing him she wasn't really offended. "That's for real emergencies only."

He mused for a while over what she'd just said, then ventured a question, just a little cautiously. "So. You're *quite* sure we're cousins, then?"

"I suppose so."

"But we're not really *related*."

"She paused. "Perhaps not. But we *are* in a way. I mean we couldn't..." She didn't finish the sentence. She was afraid to.

After a while he timidly came to the rescue, "Marry?"

It wasn't what she was actually thinking, but she was relieved he had said what he said, and not the 'other thing'.

"If you want to put it like that, 'yes'... I mean 'no', we can't."

"But my uncle was not your Dad, nor was your mammy my auntie. So we're not blood relations, anyway." he concluded, and she knew he was right. "So we could... ."

"Marry?" she whispered, more to herself rather than for his benefit. He was trying to catch her eye, to gauge her reaction, but by now she had turned away, her cheeks bright red.

Sean had started down this road but was now unsure where all this was leading, although he had taken the part of main protagonist in the argument, as well-meaning as it was. He considered it as more of a discussion.

To take the steam out of the situation he finished packing everything up for himself and for Rosalee. He found the tea a real pick-me-up even without a lacing of poitin, and was soon ready to hit the road. It was still dry and good walking weather. They were heading south west, and into the sun.

The last conversation was already a memory – at least for now – so they speculated on what they might find when they got to Tavistock, and what they might have to do if his family were *not* to be found. Of course, as they had just established, it was her family too but only by marriage. They really needed a map or at least a drawing of the area, because they had no idea where they were in relation to Tavistock, nor how far.

The landscape was made up of rolling hills and wooded valleys which, again, reminded them of their homeland. The more they ventured away from the coast, the less the prevailing westerly winds had it's impact on the trees and hedgerows. Rather than being bent over and giving in to the steady winds, they now grew straight and true.

Sheep and cattle grazed freely together, with some field put to vegetables for market, corn, as well as hay for cattle. They watched as buzzards wheeled overhead, giving out their occasional plaintiff cry, or even being mobbed by crows and rooks if they strayed too close to their nests of young. The land seemed productive and fertile, and would be different from the moorlands they encountered later when they came close to Tavistock and the mining areas.

But Chilsworthy was their next landmark. After two hours of steady progress they were expecting it to appear around the next corner, but first they came upon something else. Lurch sensed it before Peggy's nose could engage; he growled, standing stock still for a moment, his keen eye fixed on movement partially hidden in lower ground by the roadside. Then he wagged his tail; Peggy copied him. And waited.

Up bounded two rough-coated hounds nearly *twice* the size of Lurch. Identical to each other in height and markings, their friendly welcome put them (Lurch and Peggy) at ease, as well as Sean and Rosalee. They were long-dogs.

Given that Exmoor and deer country was just a few miles away they were possibly sight-hound cross breeds – between a Greyhound and Deerhound. As surprised as they were at such a rare encounter (Sean saw they were both male, guessing they were from the same litter) he was less surprised when their owners emerged. In dress, they were a sight familiar to him.

They were a family of Romanies.

Sean and Rosalee were initially curious and then relieved at coming across a family of gypsies here in England. They were certainly a familiar part of rural life in County Clare. Often relying on casual work they were an essential part of farm life, always ready to take on short spells of work at sowing and harvesting time, as and when needed by local farmers and country estates.

Back in Ireland they suffered from lack of food and work alongside the tenant farmers during and after the Potato Famine. Like farmers, they were a casualty of the strategically planned evictions of small tenants, who were already pushed to the margins of the breadline.

Seeing that their sight-hounds had already made firm friends with Lurch and Peggy, it was no surprise when the head Romani invited them into the camp. "Fancy a brew?" he said, his outstretched arm guiding them into the centre and the focus of their attention – the pot of fresh spring water just coming to boil over the open fire.

"Thank you," said Rosalee, sitting down on the offered seat but making sure Sean stayed close by her. Sean had enjoyed his first draught of tea earlier that day, but he was looking forward to his second.

"My name's Django, by the way. This is my wife, Mercy. Where are you two bound?" He asked.

"Sean. And Rosalee," replied Sean, pointing to himself then Rosalee. "We're heading for Tavistock... to find our relatives."

"We've travelled all these parts since we arrived from Ireland," said Django." What's their surname? I may be able to help you find them."

"Sercombe. Baker Sercombe to be exact. My Dad said they started as farm labourers, but then his grandfather and Dad went to work in brick kilns," said Sean.

"I don't recollect the name, but if he's still in brick making you should find him. There's a lot of brickworks all around here, especially in Calstock and Tavistock, and down to Bovey Tracey.

They're building new kilns for clay-works, lime - and bricks - because of the new railway."

Sean was filled with a sense of excitement at the prospect of being so near to his family, even a family he had never seen. He felt a sense of belonging again.

"Are you young fellows hungry?" asked Mercy. "We've got enough for all. It's a pot of hare. Our boys – Jamie and Jarvis – are down in Holsworthy at the fair, so they won't be needing any. You're more than welcome."

Sean and Rosalee looked at each other before nodding in agreement, thanking Mercy for her kind offer. Neither of them had eaten hare before.

"She's been stewing overnight," said Django. "They can be tough, so we let it hang for several days before cooking."

"I guess your dogs come in useful for hunting hare, then? Lurch is OK with rabbits," said Sean, "but a hare can easily out-run him, unless we corner it in a field so it can't turn."

"These two work together," Django said.

"Brothers?"

"Yes. From the same litter actually. Easy to tell, eh?" said Django. "It's the Deerhound in them from an estate on the Moor. They're perfect for the chase out in the open moor where they can pick up speed on a straight line."

The hare tasted superb. It had a stronger flavour than rabbit, but Mercy knew how to tenderise it with slow cooking and a mix of herbs, leaves and all sorts of hedgerow finds.

Apart from a fine meal, they found Django and Mercy to be good company. Apparently they had been part of the general migration of Romanies from Ireland into England seeking seasonal work, but Django originated from Spain, coming over with his family to Ireland as a young boy.

"So what's *your* family name?" asked Rosalee, quite taken by the romantic notion of them coming from a foreign country.

"Flores," replied Django. "Mercy was less exotic. She was a 'Lee'." Rosalee could hardly believe it.

"But my mother was a 'Lee'." She said. "Maureen Lee."

"From County Clare?" asked Mercy, grasping Rosalee's arm, gripping it extra tight as if to demand a quick answer. "Did she have dark auburn hair? Like mine?" She ran her free hand through her hair, pinning it behind her ear. She was searching Rosalee's eyes for a 'Yes'.

"She did. It was..."

"She's my sister!" Mercy broke in. "Where is she? *How* is she? Why isn't she *with* you?" But she half-guessed the reason. "She's not...?"

"I'm sorry," said Rosalee, softly, catching hold of Mercy's hands now. "She died... murdered. By the English. Our cottage was burnt to the ground. My Dad told me... forced me... to run out the back door and leave before the soldiers came. He said to never look back."

She was now fighting back the tears as she remembered again the events of only a few days earlier – the tragic story that was so real and fresh again in her memory. Sean moved closer now, laying his arm across her shoulder to comfort her. "I didn't realise what was going to happen. Not until I heard the shots. Two of them."

"Mine two," said Sean. "The same soldiers and constabulary. They just swept up the valley of the Fergus and the Shannon, burning and killing as they went."

Mercy slowly recovered from the sad news – the shock of finding and losing a sister in a heartbeat. Django brought her a small glass of clear liquid. It was poitin.

"Slip this very slowly," he cautioned.

Finally she was able to speak. "So you must be my niece. God *bless* you, child." She leaned forward, kissing Rosalee on the forehead, then on each cheek, adding, "you're *so* brave. And now I see it. You have your mother's good looks."

"She has. She is. She's... " but Sean couldn't finish what he was going to say, what he wanted to say – in case it was something she didn't want, or didn't want to hear. At least not from him.

She was now facing him, looking deep into his eyes through the tears she was desperate to hold back. And she knew.

She knew what he felt, *how* he felt... about *her*.

It was so much to take in for all of them but Django and Mercy knew it couldn't end there. They needed to know more, especially as they still missed the Ireland they had to leave, the Ireland before things started to go so wrong.

"You must stay for supper now, and over-night. We have so much to talk about," said Mercy. "The boys won't be back until morning, and you *can't* go without meeting your cousins. I want to hear more about my dear sister.

"We were married off when we were barely sixteen. Maureen first, then this big lug swept me away a year later. Perhaps you'll help Django gather some dry wood, Sean, while Rosalee and I talk some more." The men did what they were told, followed by Lurch.

"What is Rosalee to *you*, Sean?" It was a subject that had yet to come up, but Django deserved to know who he was playing host to that evening.

"Her step-Dad was my Dad's brother," he said. "So we're sort of cousins, but not blood relations."

"Don't let that stand in your way," replied Django with a smile to himself.

"Oh, but we don't... we haven't... "

"Don't worry, son – or should I call you 'nephew', now? If it's going to happen it will, and if it doesn't... well."

That made about as little sense to both of them, but each knew what Django meant, or was driving at. They decided to leave it at that, saying little more before returning with armfuls of dry wood to the camp.

They were both glad of the exercise after such a substantial mid-day meal. Django explained how the life of Romanies evolved month by month with the seasons – strongly tied to the needs of local farmers or country estates. Django had developed many rural skills, from hedge laying, dry stone walling, through to lambing and animal husbandry. It made him more valuable to a variety of farmers in the district. They were able to tap into his skills as and when they needed him. Sean was impressed.

Mercy learnt embroidery and needlework from her mother, making gloves and socks, quilts, aprons, shawls and decorative tableware to be sold at the nearest market. She was also an excellent cook, making a range of jams, chutneys and preserves according to whatever wild fruit were in season.

The boys took after their dad, learning from him and with him – apart from the excursions they made on their own to local markets, fairs and festivals. Django and Mercy had long since come to the opinion that the less they knew of James and Jarvis' escapades, the better they would sleep at night.

In the very few hours that Django had known Sean he instinctively saw the difference between him and his own boys. Although they were older, he felt that they didn't yet possess the maturity and level-headedness with which Sean was blessed. He was looking forward to knowing more about the young couple that evening over supper, seeing some similarities between them, and himself and Mercy.

Chapter Ten
So far, England appears to be full of promise.

Rosalee found great comfort in discovering she had an aunt. She *did* recall her mother mentioning she had a sister, but that was all. Her mother, Maureen, had never filled in the details – perhaps because she didn't have any to give. Rosalee never asked.

Now they had they found each other it all meant so much more. In the few hours since she had met her aunt, Rosalee felt she had almost, but not quite, found her mother again. In turn, Mercy treated Rosalee like a daughter, becoming the one she never had.

"Here they are," said Mercy as she heard voices approaching. "We can start supper soon."

The mid-day meal had been filling – and nourishing. The main meal of the day. In comparison, supper was a light meal. That's to say, 'light meal, gypsy style.' "How does some fresh, brown trout sound?" Mercy asked the two of them.

Sean and Rosalee managed to hold back their laughter, but only just. "Trout would be fine," they agreed – but with a fair degree of enthusiasm so as not to give the game away.

As it happened, whilst it was still trout, it was totally different from the way Sean had prepared his speciality on the two previous days. The only similarity was the way it was baked in embers. Instead of wrapping the fish in leaves, Mercy used clay. The trout was gutted, but otherwise remained whole. The other difference was that Mercy laced the fish in fresh, young garlic leaves. That, plus the slight dusting of salt and other herbs, sweetened the flesh so that it simply dropped off the bone, helped by the slow cooking.

None of them was hungry just yet. There was one two-pound fish each so the long cooking time worked well for all of them, given that the abundant servings of hare at lunchtime still needed digesting. To help things along, Django opened a new flagon of Devon cider, liberally sharing it with Sean, but not the girls.

Eventually, thirsts gave way to hunger. Supper was served.

"You really eat well," said Sean. "Is this how you normally live?" He secretly slipped Lurch a morsel of trout.

It was Mercy who replied. "When we can. We vary what we eat with the seasons and always seem to manage."

"Everyone pitches in," added Django. "The boys normally work in return for the food we cannot kill ourselves or forage. The hounds – Jake and River – usually catch more than we need. If we can't preserve and store it, we can always sell or barter with it in the local innkeeper."

"Django sometimes gets the villagers going with his guitar," said Mercy. "He's not any old gypsy boy, he's a Gitano – that means he has flamenco running through his veins."

"And you provide the dancing?" Rosalee asked Mercy, her expression begging for a demonstration.

"Used to," Mercy replied, waving any invitation away with her free hand. "I make a few shillings reading palms now and again instead. Or sell my embroidery."

Sean was fascinated at the idea of having his fortune told. "Will you read mine, please?" He had beaten Rosalee to it.

"Are you sure you want to?" asked Mercy, quizzically.

"Yes, why not?" Sean couldn't see the problem.

"First, there are two conditions," said Mercy. Sean leaned forward in anticipation, as did Rosalee.

"What *are* they? She asked, jumping in first this time.

Mercy smiled at their enthusiasm and their naivety. "You have to accept what I say, without question."

They agreed.

"And it will cost one of those shiny new silver threepenny pieces you have in your pockets. It's a Romani tradition I have to abide by, otherwise the reading is void."

"Threepence each?" asked Sean.

Mercy smiled. "I can probably bend tradition a little. I'll read both palms for one silver coin. Come into the vardo."

They followed Mercy into the Romani caravan and took their places opposite her, palms outstretched. "Do you want to know answers to what has *already* happened to you in the past? Or what to expect in the *future*?" she asked.

"The future," they replied together, without deflecting their gaze away from Mercy.

"Are you right handed or left?"

"Right." Again their replies matched.

"Good," said Mercy. Now don't speak or interrupt unless I ask you a direct question."

Mercy took the right hand of each of them in turn, first of Rosalee, then of Sean. The very instant their hands joined, completing the circle, a sudden shock coursed through their bodies, first Rosalee, then Sean. Mercy, too, sat bolt upright as she felt the surge...

For Sean and Rosalee everything went black. They dropped their heads and slumped forward. They lost consciousness. *In* their subconscious state the two youngsters experienced a kind of dream where they were both now joined - Sean's left hand grasping Rosalee's right. They were walking through a dark forest hand-in-hand. The path was green and verdant, a broad swathe over which the deciduous trees on either side met overhead, blocking out most of the light and creating a natural cathedral. The light dappled through intermittently from above, but was more like stars against a dark night sky.

In the distance, but not too far ahead, they could see the contrasting brightness of a sun-kissed clearing opening up before them. They emerged from the edge of the dark forest and the rustle of the leaves from the gentle breeze overhead, to be greeted by a beam of light from above, searching for and following them as soon as they took their initial steps into the brightness. Then they stopped.

Standing before them was a woman, a dozen or so years older than they were clad in a shawl, headscarf, gold earrings, and a richly woven full length skirt made from a coarse woollen Tavistock Kersey cloth. It turned out to be Mercy. After a few moments she spoke.

"You are gradually coming out of the darkness and into the light on your journey though life. The grave sadness and tragic events of the past will always be hard to bear and remain with you for your lifetimes. For that purpose, and for the purpose of facing up to what has befallen you - but most of all so that you can face the future with hope - you have been drawn together through circumstances over which you have no control. But now you must accept without question your joined destinies.

Support each other at all times, trust in each other even when reason might say otherwise, and never allow anyone else to come between you. My blessings will always go with both of you, and may God protect you."

With those final words the vision of Mercy was shrouded in mist and it dissolved before them. The stark brightness of the sun softened into a warm glow as a gentle mist surrounded them. Gradually they returned to full consciousness, back in the vardo. Mercy began to speak once more.

"How are you both feeling?" She turned first to Rosalee. "Describe what you saw, child."

Rosalee gave a full account starting with the blackness before emerging into the light, their encounter with Mercy in the clearing, then returning to where they were all now sat.

"And for you, Sean?" she asked.

"Exactly the same," he answered. "Down to the last detail. What does it all mean?" He slipped his hand in Rosalee's just as he had in the dream, turning to look for her reaction. With his free hand he rubbed the back of his shoulder, responding to an itch that demanded to be scratched. It worked.

Mercy noticed all these gestures, first Sean's and then her niece's reaction. She saw immediate change between the two of them compared with when they first arrived. She reached for their right hands once more.

They braced themselves for a shock but thankfully, this time, it was not to be. They were now emotionally drained, but their thirst for answers kept them fully attentive.

"Let me look at each of your palms now," she said. She scrutinised each palm in turn, first their right palms, then their left. Then she spoke.

"I see great similarities in both your hands. Uncanny. In general you will both have interesting lives with strong family roots. You will be successful in what each of you do and enjoy some privileges, without carrying them to excess. You will both enjoy good physical and mental health your whole lives. But there is something unusual about your heart lines."

Sean and Rosalee looked at each other for the first time since Mercy had begun to speak, sharing the same thought.

She continued. "It says you will both have issues with future partners and relationships. Look," she pointed to a triangular shape forming from below each heart line as they inspected each of their palms. "They appear on *both* your hands, and at the same spot along the line towards your index fingers. Be vigilant in case something, or someone, tries to come between you. It may be that a guardian will rescue you."

Her face took on a more serious expression as her eyes switched first from one, then to the other. "You are destined to have parallel love lives but, above all, respect the prediction and pronouncement each of you received in your dream. The dream you shared."

Mercy released hold of their hands and sat up, bringing the session to a sudden end. She gestured for them to lead the way down the steps ahead of her. Then she followed.

She appeared uneasy, unsettled – worried almost – and she was definitely left ill at ease by the reading. Mercy avoided making eye contact as they re-joined Django by the camp fire.

The one prediction she did not reveal for fear of worrying them, was that the life – at least of one of them – would be cut short before its time.

But of which one? Or would it turn out to be both? Or was it all just Romani superstition?

Chapter Eleven

Rosalee's family provides comfort, but Sean seeks his own.

The end of the evening was crowned by a few more draughts of Devon cider, shared by Django and Sean. Rosalee and Mercy were again content with tea, although she did suspect that Mercy had dropped a splash or two of poitín in both their brews, judging by the taste. It guaranteed a good night's sleep – for all of them.

Sean set up the lean-to shelter off the vardo; their hosts retired to the warmth of their caravan. Lurch and Peggy deserted their master and mistress to join their new-found canine friends, the long-dogs, all four of them snuggling up together close to the fire. It was dawn before any of them stirred, roused by the excitement of the two long-dogs welcoming home the two boys, back from Holsworthy market and fair.

Jamie and Jarvis were also twins just like Jake and River, the two long-dogs. A couple of years older than Sean and Rosalee, they shared the dark good looks of their father as well as his tall, angular build. Their noisy return was earlier than anticipated by their parents, given that they were a good three miles from Holsworthy and it was unlikely that they would have got on the road before dawn.

"We didn't expect you back for another hour at least," said Mercy, making her way to boil a good pot of water for a strong brew of tea. She knew the boys would need it after a boisterous last night at the fair.

"We had a lift to Chilsworthy, then we walked," explained Jarvis, drawing up a makeshift bench by the fire.

"How come you left so early?" Django asked, knowing a heavy night in one the inns often led to a late rise the next day.

"We stayed over in the Old Market Inn – least-ways one of us did," said James, giving Jarvis a rye look, "and we felt it only polite to leave early for fear of waking our hosts."

"Or the host's daughter I shouldn't wonder," said their father. "Quite smitten by the landlord's daughter, aren't you?" It was Django, wise to what was really going on. "About time you made an honest girl of her. One of you, at least."

"I'm too young for marrying" Jarvis replied, "you know that, don't you mother? I wouldn't want to leave you." He gave Mercy a bear-hug of a squeeze, knowing she loved having her boys around her. She was not ready to lose them yet.

"Say hello to our guests," Mercy said, pointing to Sean and Rosalee. They were just climbing out of their night's shelter.

Sean was the first to come into the circle and reach forward to shake their hands, first Jarvis, then James. "Sean," he said, simply. "This is Rosalee."

Smiling, James gave Sean a warm welcome before turning to Rosalee. Django stepped in quickly, seeing that his sons were clearly smitten by her. "Rosalee is your *cousin*, your aunt Maureen's girl," he said. Sean was relieved, a fluttering of jealousy was quick to rise as he noticed their attraction to her.

"They're over from Ireland, arriving just a few days ago," said Mercy. "They're on their way down to Tavistock to find their relatives."

It could have been a tense moment, but Django broke the ice. "Who's for a brew?" he said, passing round four tin mugs.

"You haven't lost your magic touch for making tea, Mam," said Jarvis. The atmosphere had now eased as he turned to Sean. "That's a handsome lurcher. How old is he?"

Jarvis and Sean compared notes on hunting sight-hounds, whilst James filled his parents in on their recent escapades in Holsworthy over the past couple of days.

"Was it worthwhile this time?" asked Mercy, eager to know if they made any money from selling their wares at the fair.

James handed over a leather purse heavy with silver coins. "The ladies loved your embroidery work, mother."

"And we won a few bob to swell the purse," said Jarvis.

That was the main worry for Mercy. Her boys loved to gamble so it always kept her awake at night when they were gone for a few days. If they started to lose, sometimes they would try to make up their losses with bare-knuckle fighting. But that was a hard way to make a living, even though they grew up with it.

"Let's have a look at your hands," she said, holding out her own so she could grab hold of theirs. "Not the palms, turn them over. Both of you." To her relief there were no injuries.

"And we have something else." It was Jarvis, dipping into the depths of his overcoat and taking out another purse – made of silk this time, it's neck tied in a blue ribbon. Mercy gasped in real surprise, opening it carefully barely able to hold in her excitement. It revealed a gleaming bead necklace.

"Goodness," was all she could manage. "It's beautiful."

"Let me put it on for you," offered James. "They're made of pure Murano glass, all the way from Venice."

Mercy was clearly moved, close to tears, kissing first James then Jarvis before showing herself off to Django. "You're good boys," she said. "I always knew it, even though you frighten me sometimes with your ways."

"Well, I'm famished," said Jarvis, reaching in his sack for yet another surprise. "We found these on the way." With that, he pulled out a supply of morel mushrooms, enough for all of them. "I hope you've got some eggs to go with these, mother."

Unlike common mushrooms the morels did take a little longer to cook, but they were worth it. Django had bartered for some fresh duck eggs with the local farmer the previous day. Before long they were tucking into one of Mercy's special breakfasts. It was good to have the boys back home.

Almost apologetically Sean and Rosalee announced that they really should be on their way, but with some regret. It was comforting to be part of a family again. It helped them to cope with the loss of their own parents, if only for a while. It was a particularly emotional time for Rosalee and Mercy, and comforting for Rosalee to know she had a relative she could call upon, as long as she could find her.

Django and his family were staying camped in the same site for a few days more. He had more tasks to complete for the local farmer, ably assisted now by the boys. Mercy was glad as it meant they would be around for a few days more before heading down towards Launceston, where they expected to pick up more work. That was a shame. If Sean and Rosalee had stayed with the family a little longer then they, Jarvis and James could have all travelled part-way together.

Their goodbyes were warm, with promises to look out for each other again. The family travelled in a familiar pattern throughout the year, from month to month, usually picking up work and visiting fairs and markets at the same time each year. Mercy, tearful, followed by Django, hugged both Sean and Rosalee, wishing them luck and good fortune. Then it was the boys' turn.

"You're absolutely sure you *are* my cousin, aren't you?" asked Jarvis as he kissed Rosalee lightly on each cheek before shaking Sean's hand. But he was only being playful this time.

With a full stomach, rested, and with plenty of energy, by mid-day Sean and Rosalee had made good time, soon passing through the village of Chilsworthy. They stopped only to fill their water bottles at the well before heading straight off towards Holsworthy.

Their journey was filled with reflections on Romani life in general, and Mercy and Django in particular. It also threw up questions about Rosalee's mother.

"They were a really lovely family. Unbelievably kind, all of them" sighed Rosalee, breaking a long silence.

Sean agreed. "Did Mercy say why she lost contact with your mother?" He was curious to know.

"I did ask her - because it didn't make any sense. They were clearly very close, until she married Django."

"So what happened?"

"It was all down to their gypsy origins. My mother was a Roma gypsy, as was my Dad – my real Dad. Then when Mercy married Django – a Gitano – it didn't go down well."

"What's the difference?"

"To us it may mean nothing, but Gitanos were initially from Egypt. Mercy said Django's people were originally called 'Egiptanos', whereas my mother and my real Dad originate from Northern India. So did Mercy. That's why I'm so..."

"...beautiful?" he broke in.

Rosalee flushed, not expecting such a bold compliment. "I was going to say 'dark skinned'. You shouldn't say that to me, Sean." Then she lightened up, seeing the funny side. "Even though it's true." She laughed.

"I'm not the only one who thinks so," his jealousy surfacing.

"You mean the boys?" She meant James and Jarvis.

"You noticed, then?"

"Hard not to," she said. "But I would never be interested in them. Not that sort."

"Why not? What do you mean by 'that sort'?"

"I want more in a person than just good looks and charm."

"So you're saying I'm ugly and boring..."

"I won't answer that," she laughed again. "Either way I lose." It was a good way to ease things between them and to have everything out in the open.

Lurch and Peggy had gone ahead foraging. For a while they were out of sight, having disappeared around a bend in the lane. As Sean and Rosalee reached the corner they came bounding back, apparently excited at finally arriving at the small town of Holsworthy. It was so much larger than Chilsworthy. Sean and Rosalee were not expecting to see so many people going about their business during a normal day.

Holsworthy was the largest place they had been to since leaving Kilrush. They were amazed at the number of places where you could buy everyday essentials, even though the market was a few days ago.

Most of the people sold food and household goods from no more than front windows to their small cottages, opening onto the main street as you walked through the town, or by the roadside. They picked up half a loaf for a penny and, another penny bought them a wedge of cheese. The simple fare would make a refreshing change from the lavish diet of trout, hare, rabbit - and more trout.

By now the sun was at its full height so they allowed themselves the luxury of a rest in the market square – partly to enjoy a quick bite, partly to take in the unfamiliar sights of a typical Devonshire village. They could hear the occasional laughter and raucous behaviour coming from The Golden Fleece. It reminded Sean of his thirst for cider at that moment, after the pleasant time drinking a few jars with Django. But he was content with spring water, still preferring the company of Rosalee to a bunch of rowdy locals, as well as acknowledging the responsibility he felt for her now. It has quickly become more than a sense of duty. He needed it.

They were unsure of the best route to take to their (they hoped) *final* destination, Tavistock, so they asked a passer-by. "What's the quickest way to Tavistock," they asked.

He was a fresh-faced boy, a little younger than he and, noticing that he was covered in flower dust, they guessed he was an apprentice at the local bakery. "Are you walking or going by horse and cart?" he asked.

"Walking."

"That's the slowest," replied the boy, hardly resisting a large grin from ear to ear. "Oh, I got you that time," he laughed.

Rosalee stifled her own laughter at Sean's embarrassment, using her shawl to cover her face and drawing Peggy nearer as further camouflage. "Shut up, Lurch," Sean told Lurch, seeing him wag his tail as her heard the laughter. "Traitor!"

Sean stood. Silent. Waiting for them all – especially Rosalee - to contain themselves until the boy was ready to give a serious answer to a serious question.

Finally he calmed himself sufficiently to answer. "Seriously," he said. *Really* seriously, I wouldn't walk. It's a good twenty five miles and a long day's journey. There are some stopping off points on the way, but there are also reports of thieves and brigands at the moment. You may not be that safe, just the two of you. You certainly wouldn't get there by nightfall, but there's a coach leaving in the morning – at eight o'clock. That's what I'd do." Then he paused, having second thoughts.

"Come to think of it, better than that go see Jack Jarrett. He's usually loading up round about now, just behind The Bickford Arms. He's taking a cartload of cabbages to Tavistock tomorrow. If you catch him and offer to help him load and unload, he may only charge you a tanner each for the journey."

"Thanks," said Sean, then waiting for the boy's name.

"Baker's the name. Robby Baker," he said. "Couldn't you tell?" He laughed, showering them with flour dust as he patted himself down. Then he sneezed all over them. Lurch and Peggy copied him. "Mention my name when you see Jack." With that, Robby was on his way again.

Sean and Rosalee looked at each other to see what the other thought, then agreed to follow the road to The Bickford Arms in search of Jack Jarrett. They had only been on their journey from Clovelly for a few days but the novelty of a ten mile walk every day was beginning to wear off a little. After all, they had a spare shilling – which had been hard earned – to pay for a ride. But most of all they felt they deserved it. It would be a welcome change from walking – especially since Sean had been carrying *both* tarps during the past few miles.

"The only thing we have to do now, if this works out, is to decide where to stay tonight." Rosalee was also feeling travel weary, seeing that they had barely stopped to draw breath since they were evicted back in Ireland. Until now. Even gathering kindling and, foraging for and preparing the evening supper – especially outdoors – was becoming a bit of a strain.

A few yards down the road they remembered the last thing the baker's boy had said to them. It was about the dangers that may be lurking along the highway. So far, Devon seemed so calm and peaceful – and safe – that they had forgotten how the world could be a cruel forbidding place.

As they saw The Bickford Arms and the prospect of finding Jack Jarrett in the stables behind, they felt glad to have chosen to have company for the final stretch of the journey.

Chapter Twelve
Making friends on the way, as Tavistock looms closer.

A dray-man was delivering casks of ale to the Bickford Arms as they arrived. He paused as Sean approached, curious as to who this stranger might be. "Could you tell me where to find Jack Jarrett?" Sean asked.

"Round the back, in the stables," the dray-man replied.

They found Jack harnessing his mare, Bonny, to the cart, cursing as the nag wouldn't keep still. She knew when she was going to have to work for her supper and was playing up, just like she always did. Rosalee approached. "Mr Jarrett?"

"Who's asking?" Jack didn't look up, more concerned with getting his mare ready to pick up his next load than being interrupted.

"Robby Baker said you might be able to take us to Tavistock tomorrow," began Rosalee.

"Could do. For a price."

"How much?" she asked. "The two of us. And the dogs."

"Tell you what I'll do," said Jack, at last giving up battling wills with Bonny. "If you come with me - now - to load up the cabbages I've got to deliver, then if you stay to help me unload at the other end ready for the Saturday market, I'll only charge you a tanner."

"Sounds OK to me," agreed Rosalee.

"Each."

"Fine," said Sean.

"Oh," Jack turned to Sean, "so you speak, do you? Or do you always have your wimmin folk speak for 'e?" He laughed.

"Sometimes it's best," Sean replied, not really knowing what answer Jack was expecting. "Let me help you with that harness."

That was the answer Jack was really looking for and he was surprised when Bonny became so biddable under Sean's coaxing. *He's got a way with horses, at least*, thought Jack.

"Up you get," he said to them both, once the last buckle was fastened. "It's only down the road." They turned into a farm courtyard surrounded by a dairy and cheese rooms. They drove to the rear of the outbuildings where the cabbages were waiting. In the barn. "You chuck 'em up, and I'll stack 'em." Jack pointed them both to the pile of vegetables.

It took barely twenty minutes, round trip, but Jack had clearly wanted an easy time of things all along, and secretly appreciated their help, seeing that he was now past his sixtieth year. They arrived back at the stables, Sean helping to take the harness off the old mare. He laid a heavy sheet over the cabbages for the night.

"Where are you two staying?" Jack asked, warming to them, and enjoying their company as much as the help they both provided. He liked their willingness, especially that of a fit young chap like Sean. Plus, he wanted to know where to find them if they were late for morning parole.

"We'll probably find a place to camp on yonder common," Rosalee chipped in, "and pitch there for the night."

"Tell you what I'll do," said Jack, now that he'd had time to think about it. "There's an empty stall next to Bonny with fresh dry hay. You can sleep there the night and keep an eye on my cart at the same time. If you keep your end of the bargain I won't even charge you for the journey."

"That sounds perfect. Thanks," said Sean. They shook on the deal. Jack made his way back to his cottage, a few doors down from The Bickford Arms.

"I'm just down the road if you need me. Otherwise, I'll see you at seven. Sharp. We need to be on the road before eight."

Sean and Rosalee explored their overnight accommodation. There was an iron stove at the far end of the stables where they stored the tack, safe and out of the way of the straw and hay bales and the risk of fire. Rosalee filled their pot with water before adding what scraps of meat they had left, plus a couple of potatoes, a turnip, and few cut-up cabbage leaves. Mercy had given her some of her 'special herbal mix' which she added, with seasoning.

Lighting a few pieces of tinder dry wood the stove quickly gave enough heat for the pot and its makeshift contents to be soon bubbling away. They ignored their hunger for barely an hour before they could wait no longer, tucking in with a couple of chunks of bread ready for the juices. Lurch and Peggy enjoyed the remains of the meal, which was bolstered by a handful of horse feed each.

With all stomachs full they settled down for the night next to the mare, Bonny. The stables were cosy enough but Rosalee stoked up the stove with small logs and coal, an attempt to keep it in until morning. If there was still a bed of embers, and if she could manage to get up in time, she would hard-boil a couple of eggs each for breakfast with another chunk of bread, and what was left of the cheese. She had some Earl Grey and a small jar of honey that Mercy had let her have as a sweetener.

She, Sean, and the two dogs had become used to sleeping together now, all under the one blanket. It made sense, and Rosalee knew she could trust Sean - with her life if she had to. Soon they were all fast asleep. It was no surprise, therefore, that it was the appearance of Jack – now accompanied by his wife – that seized her with panic as she heard them open the lower half of the stable door.

"Wakey, wakey you two lovebirds." It was Jack, rattling his stick on the door to their stable. Rosalee was not quite sure of how he arrived at his definition of Sean and herself, at least not their relationship. She arose quickly, flustered.

It was barely seven o'clock according to Mrs Jarrett so there was no time lost. The cart had been loaded the evening before. All that was needed was to harness Bonny and they could be on their way. Sean was busy helping Jack, so Rosalee would have just enough time to boil the eggs before wrapping then in a cloth, one for each of them together with bread and cheese.

"Would you and Mr Jarrett like a mug of tea?" She hoped so. It would delay the fact that she had still to prepare breakfast. She found two extra mugs hanging in the stables and washed them quickly, hoping they had not previously been used for anything noxious.

"You'll have to ride with the cabbages," said Jack. "The Missus will be riding with me up front." He joined them for the welcome cup of tea, after which they took their places ready for the journey to Tavistock. "I just need to load something else from the house first," he added, making his way to the waiting Bonny and her precious cargo.

Jack led the horse while Sean got into the drivers seat and pulled the cart up to the house. Jack disappeared inside. "Jump down and give me a hand with this, will you, Sean?"

Sean entered the house, listening for the room where he believed the voice was coming from. It was the front parlour. Jack was wrestling with a black metal box. "She's a bit heavy," he explained, breathless. "Grab the other handle."

He was right. It took the two of them to carry it, Jack having filled it – with whatever 'it' was – in the parlour that very morning. He'd padlocked it then found he could not lift it.

"If it's to go in the back I'd better clear a space for it," suggested Sean. He jumped back up onto the cart, clearing a space about two foot square, ready to receive the mystery box. Whilst up there he decided to clear extra room so that he, Rosalee and the two dogs could lay out comfortably without sitting *on* cabbages, and to avoid cabbages falling *on*to them during the journey. "Ready," he said shortly.

They had to drop the tailgate, but even so the box took both their combined strength to get it safely secured among the cabbages. Jack drew the cloth sheet back over the vegetables – and the box – leaving enough room for his passengers to sit, or lie, in relative comfort. The highway was never smooth going, even though the county authorities had a duty to maintain major roads between large villages and towns.

"What's in the box?" she asked once they were underway.

"No idea," Sean replied. "None of our business."

"But why is it so heavy?"

Jack, despite his advancing years and the constant noise of the cartwheels making conversation difficult, heard every word. It was he who answered this time. "It's metal ore," he said." From one of the local mines. That's why it's so heavy. We have to take it to the assay office in Tavistock to be valued." Neither of them knew what an assay office was and didn't ask in case they sounded stupid.

Using their bags and belongings as pillows Rosalee and Sean were reasonably comfortable, possibly more so than Mrs Jarrett. She had to rely on a crudely sprung passenger seat to cushion each and every bump in the road. Luckily, Jack took it at a pace that suited them all, including the mare.

It was a good twenty five miles or more which a swift horse could manage in two hours, but they allowed themselves the whole day. There was no bad weather slowing them down or to encourage them to hurry. Time to relax and enjoy the view.

The young travellers basked in the morning sunshine and admired the unfolding countryside, festooned with spring flowers and the tender new leaves of bracken as well as spring blossom on the trees. The leaves were taking on a light green before they would turn a richer, dark colour with the advance of summer.

Lying on their backs and facing directly upwards they could hear – and see, against a blue sky – skylarks in full song, marking their territories.

As soon as they left the more open countryside, narrow lanes took over which provided almost total shelter from hot sun or cold winds. The trees either side from high hedgerows joined in the middle, created more of a cathedral than a country lane. For a moment, it reminded them of their dream when Mercy was reading their palms. They drifted in and out of sleep, it was so peaceful.

Mrs Jarrett seemed very quiet, perhaps tired and dozing after such an early start. It was Jack who woke her with his first pronouncement of the day. "I normally pull in for half an hour at Halwill, so as Bonny can have a drink from the trough."

"So you can have a drink at that there cider house 'trough', more like," snapped back Mrs Jarrett, seemingly not as asleep as she was first making out.

"What a splendid idea," he agreed, casting his wife a knowing look which she returned – but in good humour.

Although Halwill had started as a typical Devon village it was now undergoing a huge change in circumstances. The railway system in Devonshire continued to advance. It now scarred the landscape where it could not be hidden by tunnels and valleys. A new junction was under construction, bringing an unwelcome disturbance to the peaceful village life, but hopefully it would be matched with prosperity as it opened up cheaper routes to market.

They dismounted to take some exercise whilst Bonny took a drink (as did her master). Mrs Jarrett's time-keeping proved immaculate. They were back on the road within her allotted half hour. The road ahead proved arrow straight for long stretches, enabling them to see well ahead in anticipation of other travellers – or dangers - they might encounter. Their pace was little more than a walking pace, apart from downhill gradients where they asked Bonny to make up some time.

Surprisingly, in the middle of nowhere, they came across an ancient Roman marching camp located on the summit of a high ridge. It was known as Broadbury, which explained not only the quality, but also the regularity, of the highway.

Jack and, indeed, his wife were both looking forward to stopping for an hour at Bridestowe. The White Hart Inn had been a favourite hostelry and watering hole for merchants since the 17th Century. They relished the thought of their splendid speciality meat pie with lashings of gravy and mashed potatoes.

The inn was a traditional Devon Long House dating back to medieval times and, it was believed, had offered hospitality to travellers way back, courtesy of its being a major north-south route through the centre of the county - ever since Roman times.

In particular, the stretch of road they were on was popular with merchants bringing essential goods from the North Devon ports down to the towns, as well as sea ports on the south coast, and vice versa. But, because of that, it was not unusual for thieves to lie in wait for the unsuspecting traveller, including coaches carrying passengers as well as bullion or currency.

"The railways are going to change everything," said Jack, acknowledging the latest developments in Halwill. "I'm glad I've only got a few more years left of this business. Cabbages will be carried by rail in future, and most other things that use coach and horses at the moment – including people. But at least it will be safer."

His last words were almost as if he had a premonition of what was about to happen. They had encouraged Bonny to adopt a faster pace in the anticipation of the slap-up meal to come when they reached Bridestowe.

Because of this they were caught off guard and hardly saw the danger that lurked ahead, at least not before they had a chance to avoid it or retaliate.

But it was the beginning of an adventure that would change the course of their lives – for all of them.

Chapter Thirteen
Sean shows his mettle on the final leg of the journey

"Stand and deliver!" yelled the masked rider, spurring on his horse from the cover of the roadside hedge. Startled, Bonny jumped sideways in fright, tilting the cart and unbalancing Jack and his wife. Bonny soon brought them to a standstill, before Jack could even think about pulling up or urging Bonny to drive forward and away.

"Oh, how I love saying that," the masked rider chuckled under his breath. But Jack could see it was Dan Chanter, brother of Ben Chanter, the wrecker who had towed the stricken Ellen a few days earlier.

"Damn you, Chanter!" cried Jack, steadying Bonny as he and his passengers suddenly realised what had just happened. "I'll see you on the gallows for this."

"Oh dear, Jack," he replied, lowering his mask. "Such bad humour. Now you've recognised me I'll have to kill you - after I've got what I came for, that is. Hand it over."

"A cart load of cabbages? You're welcome."

"Ah, Jack, Jack!" he said, taking on a bored, condescending tone. "You know we're talking about much more than that. We *both* know." He hadn't yet see Sean or Rosalee. They were fully aware of what was happening, but still lay hidden below the sides of the cart.

"I've no idea what you're on about."

"The box, Jack. The box. The box with all the goodies in it. The silver from Wheal Betsy. Open the box, Jack."

"What box?"

"The box I'm not supposed to know about. That box, Jack." He rode round to the back of the cart, his pistol still trained on his passenger. Only then did he see Sean, Rosalee, and the two dogs. "What have we here, Jack? More precious cargo?"

"They know nothing about it," blurted Jack. "Any of it."

"You, boy," said Chanter. "Draw back that sheet." Sean didn't move. Lurch growled.

"Now, boy. If you think anything at all of your pretty little... friend," he said, now pointing the barrel at Rosalee.

"OK, OK," Sean said, through his teeth, "but if you hurt her..."

"...you'll what?" asked Chanter, cocking his pistol. Sean pulled back the sheet revealing the black box. "Ah, perfect. The key, now, please, Jack. Hand it to the boy." Jack complied. Sean moved over to the box. He opened it. It was full of gleaming silver ingots.

"The mother lode!" cried Dan in sheer delight. "Here boy, fill these saddle bags." He threw two leather bags onto the cart. Sean began to fill them for fear Dan would harm Rosalee. Dan's pistol remained cocked, aimed directly at her just inches away from her face.

"You'll hang for this," shouted Jack. As every minute passed he was getting poorer and poorer.

"Jack, me boy. I'll tell you what 'll do. I'm now in such a good mood, I won't kill you after all." Dan was watching Sean with every turn, first in case he made a false move, second in case Sean didn't fill his bags with every ounce of silver. "But I will need something from you - as insurance."

"And what might that be?"

"Her." Dan said. He meant Rosalee. "She'll be coming with me until I'm safely away on my brother's schooner 'Pretty Polly'. I'll be on my way to 'The Indies' by this time tomorrow if you keep your mouth shut. If you don't, and you raise the alarm, then you don't even want to know what I'll do to her."

"If you do so much as..." began Sean.

"Just hand over the bags, boy, or this first bullet will have your name on it," snarled Chanter. "Hand them over. Slowly."

"I can't. They're too heavy."

"Curses," mouthed Chanter, then, "Jack! Give him a hand."

Jack climbed slowly down from his seat at the front of the cart, making his way over to the back where Sean had two bags filled with silver. Chanter backed his horse so that its flanks were pressing against the side of the cart, and at the same height to allow them to be passed across easier. First one, then the other.

"Tie them onto the saddle, Jack. One at a time," he instructed. They would make a heavy load, but Dan's horse was well-muscled, and nearing seventeen hands.

Jack obeyed, begrudgingly. Chanter's horse was a fine solid-boned Hanoverian stallion. Even so, it gave slightly under the additional weight before steadying itself.

"Now you," barked Chanter, pointing at Rosalee. She was to get astride in front of him, and the saddle.

"He'll never take the weight," warned Jack. "You won't get more than a mile." He was right, but what he didn't know was that Dan had a pony and trap tethered just a half mile further on, ready to make his escape.

"Let me worry about that," he replied, You and the boy step away. Get round to the front near the Missus so I can keep an eye on you." Jack and Sean did as they were told, mindful that Chanter still had his pistol trained on Rosalee.

They had only just walked round the cart to join Jack's wife when Sean saw Chanter reaching across for Rosalee's hand. It was just the moment Sean was waiting for. Chanter had tucked his pistol into his belt long enough to reach across for Rosalee's hand. The reins were held in his left hand.

In a flash Sean drew his Bowie knife and, with a clear shot at Chanter's head, he let fly.

He had practised his knife throwing for hours during his idle moments, honing his technique. Based on the distance he was from any target, he could judge the number of revolutions the knife would take spinning through the air, till it stuck firmly in the post, tree trunk, or... .

He had measured it to perfection. His aim was true and straight, taken well before Rosalee had the chance to reach for Chanter's outstretched hand or obscure Sean's target. There was an audible 'Crack'. The knife, the animal bone handle of the knife, connected with the human bone in Chanter's skull.

Rosalee shrieked as the horse reared. Its rider fell back, stricken, but he was still holding onto the reins. Chanter dropped in a heap on the hard road, the saddle bags following him, spilling their valuable bounty as they burst open. Jack had deliberately used very loose knots when tying them to the saddle, in the hope that they would loosen at some stage as Chanter made his getaway.

Chanter was out cold, either from the bone handle of Sean's Bowie knife, or from the hard road, or both. Grabbing a length of stout rope, Jack quickly tied the highwayman - securely this time - before he and Sean loaded him onto the back of the cart. Jack then calmed the horse, while Sean comforted Rosalee.

"Don't worry about me. None of you. I'm perfectly fine," complained Mrs Jarrett. In the excitement they had all but forgotten about her, but not for long. Handing the horse's reins to Sean, Jack went over to help his Missus down from the cart, finding a tot of brandy in his waistcoat pocket to soothe her jagged nerves. She downed it in one.

"I thought you were going to kill him," began Rosalee as she marvelled at Sean's knife throwing skills. "How come you were so certain it would be the knife *handle* that hit him?"

Jack and Mrs Jarrett were thinking the same, stopping what they were doing to wait for the answer to Rosalee's question.

Sean paused... "I wasn't *certain*. It was just luck, I guess."

"You are *such* a liar, Sean Sercombe," she said, as he burst into fits of laughter, more out of relief than anything. They all did, Jack and his Missus sharing the joke, and the relief.

"We'd better get all this cleared up," began Jack, after they had all collected themselves and realised they were stuck out in the middle of the countryside, miles from anywhere, and had barely escaped with their lives. "I don't know about you, but I'm famished, and we're still a few miles outside of Bridestowe." He checked Bonny's harness.

Chanter was still unconscious, lying in the back of the cart surrounded by cabbages, his head resting on the saddlebags now full of silver again, for which his ambitions had become his downfall. So close, yet so far.

Jack helped his wife back to the front seat of the cart before making sure Rosalee was comfortable, and at a safe distance from Chanter, but now hog-tied so tight he could hardly move.

Chanter's horse – a Hanoverian stallion, rare in that part of the world – had now been gentled by Sean, calmer now that he was relieved of the burden of Chanter, not to mention the heavy bags of silver. But it was more than that.

Sean felt immediately drawn to the stallion, as did the stallion to him. As he turned, he could still feel warm breath escaping the horse's nostrils, gently disturbing the long hair resting on his collar. Clearly, the stallion was drawn to Sean.

Now facing each other, man and horse stood eye to eye, the deep brown eyes of the stallion meeting those of Sean, and piercing his very soul. He was lost for what seemed a long time before noticing the most singular feature on the horse's noble head. Below the stallion's ears, now pricked forward in total absorption into the one who would soon become his new master, Sean was drawn to the the pure white star on his forehead. But it wasn't a *star*.

Although its edges were precisely defined, and it *was* a sign, It was not a star sign, but a *rose*. It was the shape of a rose with which Sean was only too familiar – it matched the birthmark carried by his father. *Remarkable*, he whispered to himself, before bring brought back to the present by the voice behind him.

"I reckon you'd best ride him yourself the rest of the way," said Jack, climbing up beside his wife and grasping the reins to get Bonny ready to go. Sean was again aware of where he was, and what had happened. He mounted the stallion, squeezed his flanks lightly, and they were on their way.

But yet another surprise was in store for them, less than a half mile down the road. This time it was much more welcome. It was the pony and trap, tethered by the roadside where it had been left waiting for the return of Chanter.

"Hold," cried Jack, but softly, as they drew up to the waiting rig. Sean dismounted, loosened the girth, secured the stirrups, then tied the Hanoverian to the rear of the pony and trap. Untying the Dartmoor from where he was tethered, he boarded the rig, engaging the pony ready to follow Jack the rest of the way to Bridestowe and a slap up meal at The White Hart Inn. Ben Chanter still hadn't stirred.

They arrived within the hour, a crowd soon collecting at the sight of two carts, a magnificent stallion following. The news that a wanted highwayman had been captured had travelled ahead of them as if by magic. They were greeted by young Phil Guscott at The White Hart who took charge of both horses and carts, taking them to the rear of the inn to be fed and watered.

Within half an hour of arrival it was meat pies all round, with a jug of cider for Sean and Jack. Chanter was left in the back of the cart, conscious but still hog-tied. He was fed bread, cheese and a mug of water by the charitable innkeeper. The highwayman would have to remain secure until they arrived at Tavistock.

There he would be tried in the Stannary Court and sentenced later in Exeter, probably to hang or at least sent to a life of hard labour in Princetown's Dartmoor Prison, along with remaining French prisoners of war who helped build it.

With thirst and appetites fully satisfied, they set off again by mid afternoon with over ten miles still to go. They forced the pace this time, needing to get to Tavistock before the Chief Constable left office for the day. The sooner they could hand over Chanter, the better. They did make one detour, however, at the request of Sean. By chance they discovered that a Sercombe, albeit spelt Surcombe, was the village blacksmith living at Cross Lanes - a mile out of Bridestowe.

It was slightly out of their way, but their curiosity got the better of them, just in case he was related to Sean. However, the blacksmith's attention was mainly drawn to the stallion. He was far less concerned at meeting a prospective distant relative, but he was intrigued by the question.

"Don't think we'm from the same family, Sir" said Samuel Surcombe. "I be from the Dunsford Surcombes. My cousins have the saddlers in Bovey Tracey, but they spell their name a bit different. Don't think we go quite as far as Calstock. That be Cornwall, b'aint it?"

Sean thanked him but with a modicum of disappointment. They carried on to Tavistock, heading straight for the Guildhall and the Chief Constable's office. They were still open for business and were met by the bailiff. He took a weary but non-repentant Chanter to the cells. Soon the Constable joined them, heartened by the news, ready with another surprise.

"Who's to claim the reward?" he asked. Jack expected some kind of reward and turned to the unsuspecting Sean.

"We'll split it, shall we?" asked Jack. Then to the Constable, "How much is it?"

"£200, the notice says." He was pointing to a poster on the wall. "And I'm sure the courts would also grant you title to his pony and trap. And his stallion."

"Sounds fair," answered Jack, but Sean was speechless.

"You'll have to wait until after the sentencing before you see the money, but there shouldn't be any problems. You might as well take charge of the horse and the pony and trap."

"Thank you Constable," said Sean. Jack shook the Constable's hand. "Is the assay office still open?" he asked.

"It should be. It's down the road next door to The Bedford Hotel. Book yourselves rooms there for the night. You can charge the court. You're witnesses, so we need to know where you'll be staying. They've got stables there, too."

They made their way to the assay office where Jack lodged the silver, then arrived at the hotel for their night's stay. It was a unexpected bonus, but no less appreciated.

Maybe fortunes were changing for the better.

Chapter Fourteen
The two become three as their fortunes really change.

The inside to the hotel all seemed *so* grand to Sean and Rosalee. They had never been *inside* a hotel, let alone stay. It was even a treat for Jack and his Mrs Jarrett (they were never told what her Christian name might be), who normally would make do with a room at a village inn at best.

As a general rule the hotelier and his staff might treat such low-born guests with suspicion and indifference, but Jack and his party were considered celebrities, having rid the area of a notorious criminal and a scourge of the local countryside for merchants and travellers. They were given a warm welcome.

Being a last minute arrangement, their rooms were not the *best* in the house, overlooking the stables and the rear courtyard. But fresh, clean linen, exotic soaps and tea served in their room made up for that.

The maid who showed them to their rooms did notice that her strange guests were smelling a little 'ripe', only to be expected after such a long, and eventful, journey. Politely she suggested that she run two baths in the bathrooms along the hall. Her concern was as much for the benefit of other guests, they thought, rather than for themselves.

But they would have to share, the ladies taking the first bath, followed by a reluctant Jack and Sean.

Lurch and Peggy would be tolerated in their room on the promise that they would be well behaved, or they would be confined in the stable block. However, they were glad to be spared their turn in the bathroom. Hotel staff arrived in a sequence of several trips bringing pales of hot water heated on the kitchen stoves, and soon Mrs Jarrett and Rosalee were each soaking up the luxury, quite literally – and separately, of course. They indulged themselves as long as possible before the men were to take turns.

In truth, neither of the men were that bothered about bathing, but the ladies insisted. A few more pales of steaming hot water arrived between the two sessions, and added to the now tepid water. That was enough to ensure all four were suitably sanitised. It was a marked improvement.

To reduce further embarrassment to other guests, Jack and his party were booked in for dinner for eight thirty that night, after most of the more conventional clientele had dined. But it suited them, given that their knowledge of dining etiquette was, understandably, lacking. Confined to a separate booth in the hotel dining area, it also helped preserve further privacy for them, and for other guests.

That said, because the maids and waiters were mainly local people and of a similar rank to themselves, they all found themselves well looked after. This included ample servings of mutton, with local vegetables (perhaps some of Jack's cabbages) and lashings of ale for Jack and Sean. The ladies were offered French wine, which they took in small quantities – largely so that they could remain alert and keep the men in check while they set out to enjoy themselves.

As the clock struck ten o'clock they were all fully replete with sufficient food and drink inside them to ensure a good night's sleep. They made their way upstairs to two separate double rooms next to each other, one for Jack and his wife, the other for Sean, Rosalee, and the two dogs.

"Goodnight, you two," said Jack, as he and Mrs Jarrett retired to their room, " don't make too much noise." His wife chastened him whilst Rosalee and Sean coloured up in embarrassment.

They entered their room, Rosalee first. For the first few moments they simply stared in amazement at such luxury. The maid had left bowls of lavender and other pot pourri on the dressing table, providing a heady fragrance that was almost intoxicating, and a small bottle of perfume. The bed – a four poster double bed – waited with the linen turned back at one corner upon which rested a small bouquet of wild flowers. Attached to it was a small note.

It simply said 'Thank you'.

Rosalee picked up the flowers, smelled their delicate aroma, and turned to face Sean. "You'll have to wait outside – or stand behind that curtain and promise not to look. I have to get changed."

She pointed to the large window overlooking the rear courtyard where the curtain draped to the floor. Hanging up from the wardrobe there were two nightshirts; one for him, and one for her. Sean did as he was told.

For Sean, such precautions to preserve his modesty were not so necessary. He could take off his shirt, slip the nightshirt over his head, then divest himself of his boots and lower garments. Even so, he felt more comfortable if he turned to face away from her.

"What's that mark? On your shoulder?" she asked. She pointed to a small red mark on his shoulder blade.

"It's always been there, apparently. But I've never seen it," he said.

"Look in the mirror," she told him, tilting it so that he could see it, if he looked *over* his shoulder. He did so, his brow wrinkling as he stared at it for the first time, trying to make out what the shape really was. Slowly, tentatively, she reached forward with her delicate fingers. A sensation, a kind he had never felt before ran through his body as she touched his flesh. "It's beautiful," she added. "It's almost like a rosebud. The sign of a rose."

Now flustered and unsettled by such unusual attention and intimacy, he hurriedly pulled the nightshirt over his head.

"Well, it's been there a long time, and it doesn't hurt. So I suppose it's nothing to worry about. My Dad has... had... one too. He said it was a birthmark. A family birthmark."

Rosalee was intrigued but said no more about it, attending to the bed now and their sleeping arrangements. "I could sleep in the chair," offered Sean, noticing how shy she was, but not really meaning it.

"No. It's alright, Sean," she replied. "There are enough pillows. Take the bolster and place it lengthways between us, that will make sure we don't... disturb each other."

It seemed the best way to explain it, although her meaning was quite clear. They slid under the starch clean sheets, first Sean, then Rosalee, careful not to make further contact. Tiredness, plus the wine, ale and copious amounts of food, took its toll. They were both sound asleep in minutes.

It was the gong downstairs calling for breakfast that awoke them. They had slept a full seven hours without stirring. Peggy yelped, then settled again, unused to such a rude intrusion. Lurch moved towards the bedroom door, wagging his tail to attract their attention.

"I'll take the dogs out to the back courtyard," Sean said, shooting out of the covers sideways to avoid his nightshirt riding up. "I'll be back in ten minutes or so. It'll give you time to get up and dressed." She hid her face under the bedclothes, feigning sleep, but ready to leap out as soon as she heard him close the bedroom door.

He had slipped on his trousers, then boots and finally his shirt, initially not noticing that Rosalee was peeking at him from under the sheets to catch another sight of his birthmark. "It's still there," he said, taking the dogs outside.

He could hear movement next door in Jack's room as he passed, but merely tapped on the door lightly. "See you downstairs in about half an hour, for breakfast?" he called. Jack said 'yes'.

Sean let the dogs loose on open land behind the stables while he stretched his own legs, taking in the surroundings. The hotel was becoming a recognised coaching inn, named after the Duke of Bedford. He stopped to watch the loading up of the trunks onto a carriage and four prior to its departure to Exeter and beyond.

"We'll be a lot safer now thanks to you," called out one of the coachmen. Sean was surprised their capture of Chanter had spread so quickly.

The sight of the carriage horses reminded him that he needed to check on the stallion. However, he was pleased to see that the stable lad had already fed and watered him before turning him out into the paddock. Calling the dogs to heal, he returned to the hotel, making his way to the stairs and his room, only to find the three just coming down. They went straight in for breakfast.

"I've always wanted that kedgeree," said Jack. "Who'll join me?" He explained what it was to the rest of the party. They all decided to give it a try, along with toast and marmalade – made from oranges from an orangery in London – and coffee.

The coffee was a luxury too. Thanks to Brazil investing in satisfying the European's growing thirst for the drink as an alternative to tea, it had progressed from a privilege for the elite to becoming more widely available and affordable. However, recent increases in taxation made it more expensive again for the common man, so the four took advantage of a rare opportunity to taste the exotic.

They were relishing their second cup of the rich brown liquid when a waiter came in with a note. Jack opened it. Squinting to read the elegant script. It read:

Booked you in for a second night. Make your way to the Constable's office at the Guildhall tomorrow morning (both words underlined) *at nine o'clock, ready for the court hearing.*

"Relax, people," he said, handing the note for Sean to read too, "we have a free day today, and another night of luxury here it would seem."

It was smiles all round.

Chapter Fifteen
They take to Tavistock, and Tavistock takes to them.

The two couples decided to spend their free day separately. Jack and his wife had their own acquaintances in Tavistock to look up, mainly busying themselves in the Pannier Market. Sean took the opportunity to get to know the stallion more. After grooming him, he carried out basic schooling in the rear paddock. He found the stallion amazingly intelligent and a very willing pupil. They were beginning to bond well.

Afterwards, Sean and Rosalee sought out the Registrar. He could look up births, marriages and deaths in the public records in the likely hope he might trace at least *some* family members. Tavistock was the central authority for quite a large area in that part of Devon, and might even include some families just over the county border into Cornwall. It did.

The birth of his aunties Mary Alice Baker Sercombe and Florence were down as Albaston near Gunnislake, just over the Devon border in Cornwall. Both were younger than his father or the older uncle Billy. They may still be there in the family home, as long as neither had yet married.

I could be there in little over an hour on the stallion, he thought. But first there was the court hearing for Chanter. His family would have to wait.

Even so, it was in a lighter mood that Sean left the Registrar for them both to explore Tavistock. *They were getting closer and closer*, he thought. His grandfather came from farm labouring stock, but was now a tile and brick maker, the family having moved up in status, just as he suspected. If he was someone of means he should be easy to find. He hoped they would take him in – he hoped they would take them *both* in.

It was the first day they were able to relax, able to relax properly since they had fled Ireland. At last they didn't have to be somewhere else, or have food to find and cook, or have to find a place to stay. The town was bustling and thriving thanks to the mines and the railways, recovering well from the wars with France. It was also still a centre for the wool trade, even though it had been declining in recent years. This ensured that they had good rail services to the coast (Plymouth), to Exeter (North) and on the London, or down to Cornwall.

Townspeople seemed prosperous, even those engaged in trades and lower ranks. As Rosalee walked along, taking in the unfamiliar sites and goings on, she did notice that they seemed to be attracting *some* attention. After a while it dawned on them. It was all down to their capturing the infamous highwayman, but initially they felt subconsciously and that it was down to their simple dress.

Whatever the real reason they decided to treat themselves to new clothes. They had some money still, and a lot of money coming if the court hearing of Chanter went as predicted. The reward money was enough to buy a farm, to buy fifty acres and still have money to spare if they wanted to. But first they would treat themselves to new clothes.

Rosalee was still wearing Sean's trousers, her dress having been torn up and adapted to serve as an additional blanket for the days they camped out. That certainly caused some locals to stare, not to mention the fact that her hair was yet to grow out. At first sight they could be forgiven if they mistook them for two boys walking along arm in arm until, as they drew closer, her beauty became so very apparent, especially her flashing dark eyes and engaging smile.

And so it was that they were arm in arm now, Rosalee using it to show her friendship and trust in him. Sean was hoping for more of a commitment, more than mere friendship, but he remained patient. Now that a lot of the uncertainty had been taken out of their current circumstances - how they felt about each other - they allowed themselves to open up and share their thoughts more freely. They had become closer and more at ease. More of a couple.

Catching her reflection in the window of one of the shops, Rosalee was reminded of how awful her hair looked. She first noticed it in the mirror in the hotel, and vowed that she would do something about it fast. Sean really had hacked it to pieces on that last day in Ireland before they arrived in Kilrush. But then it had the desired affect. Unkempt.

Having found a hairdressing salon in the High Street (they didn't know there even was such a thing as a salon before), she arranged for an appointment in two hours time. That would be plenty of time to find shops where they could both buy new clothes.

Rosalee was first to find a suitable ladies outfitters, for functional but not too ostentatious and impractical occasions. The more upper class ladies wore Crinoline dresses with lace ruffles and fine embroidered detail stitched into the material. Rosalee wanted to fit in with those of a more modest means, and chose a dress, skirt and blouse to fit her station – whatever that might be.

Sean saw her as a complete vision whatever she wore, proud to have her on his arm – and even more so in one of her new outfits as they made their way through the busy streets.

Then it was Sean's turn. His priority was a pair of new boots, the soles and uppers of his own now quite worn down. He had his father's as a spare pair, but he indulged himself in a fine two-toned knee-length leather *riding* boots, worthy of when he was to ride the handsome Hanoverian stallion confiscated from Chanter. He wanted to look the part.

By mid-afternoon – suited, booted, hair trimmed and shaped, and armed with the latest fashions - they found themselves quite exhausted. They returned to the hotel with a view of taking a nap before dinner. It was approaching three o'clock. This time Sean saw it was the daily mail coach bound for London that was in the courtyard behind the hotel, preparing to leave, via Exeter.

They found Mrs Jarrett in one of the drawing rooms reading the local newspaper, the Tavistock Gazette. She smiled as they sat down with her, glad of their company. She had also come to like them in the last few days.

"Jack's still probably in The Cornish Arms," she said. "He should be... he'd better be... back here soon. I've just had another note from the Constable about tomorrow." Sean and Rosalee sat down with her, ordering a pot of tea for them all.

"What's the news, then?" he asked.

"Seems like we're quite famous," she said. "But then, you probably already knew that. I'm told that the Stannary Court is being held at Crockern Tor. Outdoors. It's about an hour or so just outside of town, past Merrivale."

"Do we still meet at nine o'clock?" he asked.

"Yes. That's not changed. I think half the town is going to be there judging by reports. But there won't be nobody hanged round here. If it's found that he *was* guilty of highway robbery by the Stannary Court, he then has to go to Exeter Assizes for proper sentencing. Once that's done we should get our reward tomorrow afternoon. I do hope so, 'coz Jack's already spent half ours." She chuckled at the irony of it all.

They sat with Mrs Jarrett until Jack arrived back. He was not sober but still coherent after celebrating - and with good reason. With his share of the reward at last he could retire. They reflected on the differences between themselves and Jack. The reward enabled Jack to retire and put his feet up, now past his sixtieth year; on the other hand, Sean and Rosalee were just about to begin life's adventure – with an excellent start – at a mere sixteen.

But it just went to show how fortunes in life often balance up – with joy cancelling out despair, good luck matching bad, and vice versa. Right now they would give all up all their new-found wealth just to have their parents alive and well, and with them again.

Chapter Sixteen
Sean is called upon yet again to prove himself.

Sean rose early the next morning – the day of the Stannary Court. Rosalee preferred to lie in and build dreams for the future. It was still two hours before breakfast so he had enough time to feed, water, and groom the stallion. In the short time they had been together, they had already bonded.

Sean had noticed how harsh Chanter had been in handling the stallion - using brute force and a painful bit to control such a powerful animal. But it was not *his* way. His motto was that '*the kindest bit is the one used by someone with the softest hands.*' It had not escaped his notice that ladies were often able to communicate with their mounts as well as, if not better than, many male riders - even though they might possess just a quarter of their strength. It led to a softer mouth.

For Sean that was the whole point of horse riding - effective communication *with* the horse. At the horse sales in Ennis, back in Ireland, he saw that some Romani horsemen even employed a bit-less bridle. As long as it was not misused, with rough hands, or poorly fitted so as to cause discomfort or pain to the nose and jaw, it improved performance out riding, as long as it was fitted in a way not to interfere with breathing.

Sean had bought two bits the previous day, the first of which he was about to try out before breakfast, in a small paddock behind the stables. Realising that the strength and the spirit of the Hanoverian was always always present below the surface - after all he was a well-bred stallion - he fitted the bit-less bridle. He could measure the stallions' response in the paddock before taking him out on open moor, where there was a risk he would be just a little too much to handle.

After just a half an hour of 'training' - again, based on tips from, and watching, Romani horse dealers at the market - he was delighted to find his new horse respected the softer approach and responded well to the new bit. He was also recognising a small vocabulary of voice commands. This was a real bonus. There was a dialogue building between them.

In less than an hour, after flat work exercises involving trotting poles and small jumps, the stallion had developed more of a sweat on his neck than he would on a three mile canter. *That shows he's listening to me*, said Sean to himself. The horse was thinking about what he was *being asked* to do, and what his master wanted from him – delivering results out of respect, replacing instinct.

After his 'work-out' with the stallion Sean was famished, hoping that everyone else was now awake, dressed and down for breakfast. But it still left him wondering. On the ride to Merrivale he was of a mind to fit the Egg-butt Snaffle he had bought - much kinder than the one Chanter had used which he had already traded in. It was perhaps a 'safer bet' than the bit-less, but then he had second thoughts. Maybe he would be fine with the bit-less bridle as long as he stayed close to other riders, and kept to the road behind Jack on his pony and trap. He had an hour to make up his mind

As he was grooming the horse he was also thinking of a name for his hard-won prize. After due deliberation and consideration of all the factors he settled upon... *Hans*. It had a certain... *German*... ring to it, in a corny sort of way. He was also teaching the stallion to come to his whistle. The Hanoverian – Hans – had been in the back paddock when Sean initially made his way towards the stables.

He had rattled a handful of feed in a bucket as he called – whistled – for Hans to come over. Snorting, his tail swishing back and forth in greeting, Hans had obeyed. But it was more than that. In the few short hours since they became 'acquainted' on the road to Bridestowe, Sean and Hans had formed a trust. All the more so because Hans knew that Sean would care for him in a way that Chanter had not.

When he first inspected Hans, Sean noticed the red half-healed scars left by Chanter's cruel application of spurs to the stallion's flanks. They were easily addressed by the healing salve applied to calm the horse's wounds, but the wounds to the stallion's soul and trust in human nature, or ill-nature in this case, required more than a soothing balm. It needed love.

On the previous rare occasions when he had gone to the market at Ennis with his father, Sean had always headed for the horse sales arena first, spending most of his day with the auctioneer if he had the chance. In that short time he learnt that kindness ruled over the whip, if it was a matter of gaining trust rather than domination.

He applied the same principles of kindness to nurturing his relationship with Hans, not only in 'joining up' after a lunging exercise, but also in grooming and discovering the affectionate nature of what might have otherwise been a sour and potentially aggressive stallion.

Walking Hans back to his stall, Sean was deep in thought before going into breakfast – about Hans. But his yearning to meet his lost relatives and, most of all, confusion over his feelings for Rosalee, left him bewildered. The gong for breakfast sounded, breaking his spell.

With final strokes of the curry comb he led Hans back to his stall, with his saddle and final choice of tack ready and nearby so that they would be at the Guildhall early. Lurch gave a 'yelp', reminding Sean that *he* existed too and to hurry, just in case he had not heard the call for breakfast.

He was greeted by another hearty meal. Sean had already accomplished so much that day even before his companions had got out of bed, so he took them through all that he had achieved so far, including gaining approval for his new name.

With breakfast despatched and ablutions completed, it was time for the four to bid farewell to their hotel hosts. They were well in time to join the Constable at the appointed time of nine o'clock, at the Guildhall. Sean would be riding the six or seven miles to Crockern Tor on Hans. Rosalee was to go with the Jarretts on their newly-acquired pony and trap.

Sean had decided on the bit-less bridle after all, but he kept close behind the pony and trap, or at the side - where the road was wide enough. They were joined by a whole collection of different townsfolk, excitedly chatting about the proceedings to come. There was quite a festival atmosphere in the air, and it was all down to the four strangers who had first come into town only a few days previously.

Jack took the opportunity to rest Bonny for the day, as well as grabbing a chance to get to know the Dartmoor pony and how she handled. As a mare, and with good confirmation and true to the local breed, she would be a good match for the right Dartmoor stallion. That was as long as she kept well away from the opportunist and random breeding that was creeping into the husbandry on the open moor. But that was not the only reason. The cart was still full of cabbages because Jack had not yet delivered his supply of cabbages to his buyers at the Pannier Market!

Once away from the town Sean and Rosalee, were struck by the relative wildness of the moorland landscape compared with the traditionally managed farmland of the rest of North and Mid Devon. It was *so* exhilarating. The sight of distant hills and even the coastline towards the Tamar, the smell of the new growth of bracken, the heather and gorse forming its own varied patterns, were all matched by the local stories, myths and legends that abounded. In the main they were to attract the curiosity of tourists rather than fuel the fears and imaginations of locals.

It was for Merrivale – the location of a granite quarry - that they were filled with accounts of ghostly and mystical goings on. They focused on the mysterious stone rows, circles, and burial cairns. Their origins stretched back several centuries and even millennia to prehistoric times, and the truth was therefore lost in the many speculative accounts that survived until the nineteenth century.

Crockern Tor was just under two miles the other side of Merrivale, lying north of the main road and some half a mile into the moor - a six hundred feet climb from the road to the tor itself. But the view across to Wistman's Wood and out towards Plymouth was spectacular.

Locals used to say that Crockern Tor was the home of the ancient pagan God of Dartmoor, Old Crockern, whose face profile was reputed to be set into the rock formations facing to the south-west. As a Parliament sitting primarily for stannary (tin miners') disputes and crimes, it comprised a table and seats made of moor stone, hewn from the rocks. Specifically they were the warden's (President's) chair, seats for the jurors, a corner stone for the crier of the court, and a table. Apparently it had been the seat of British justice going back before the Roman invasion.

As they reached the site for the court they could make out the south-western outcrop of stone. It was in the shape of a natural amphitheatre known as Parliament Rock.

Jack, who had been carrying his wife and Rosalee in the pony and trap, had to tether the little Dartmoor by the side of the main road, given that the gradient and the rough ground made it only accessible by foot or on horseback. But Sean also dismounted to walk with them, leading Hans up to the court where he was able to leave him tied up in a holding area.

The court officials and twenty four jurors – mainly made up of tin miners – were already assembled. They, too, had caught the festival spirit, with a feeling of self-importance at being chosen for 'the trial of the decade'. Although it was a serious and official occasion, many had brought along flasks of rum or local Dartmoor whiskey, distilled using the local, peaty spring water, and infused with secret herbal ingredients gathered from the open moor.

After a ten minutes or so the bailiffs arrived with Chanter, in chains. Taking his place - with a guard on either side - he stood defiant, still arrogant and self-assured as the charge was read out. He was non repentant. He answered only to his name and the proceedings began.

He was representing himself. He was so confident even though the testimonies – first by Jack, then by his wife followed by Sean and, finally, Rosalee – sealed his fate. Chanter shot her an evil glance as she completed the last account of the attempted robbery, but she managed to hold her nerve, unfalteringly giving her evidence.

The twenty four man jury reached their verdict which the Lord Warden announced unflinchingly.

Daniel Gordon Chanter you are hereby found guilty as charged of the capital offence of highway robbery. You will be taken from here to Exeter Assizes for sentencing," he said. *"Do you have anything to say in reply to this verdict?"*

Chanter was still defiant, even with probable death staring him in the face. After a long silence, he spoke.

"Just this! You'll not hang me and, if you do, you'll wish you hadn't. I'll come back to 'aunt ye all!"

The Warden turned to the guards. *"Bailiffs, take him away."*

Before those final words had barely reached the ears of the assembled court, Chanter threw back his head, roaring with laughter then, with a broad sweep of his arms sprang forward, free from his shackles.

Quick as a flash he snatched a pistol from the belt of an attendant bailiff, shouting, "Stand and Deliver!" followed by a shot over the heads of the surprised jurors. "Oh, how I love saying that," he added, then ran the short distance to where his horse was tethered.

Somehow, and from someone, Dan Chanter had managed to get hold of a key to his chains, waiting until he was out in the open before making his move. Undoubtedly it was the work of his brother, Ben. He must have known someone local who could bribe Dan's jailers. Typical of the Chanter clan, he waited for the right time until his escape would have the greatest dramatic effect. After being found guilty.

Hans was more shocked than any of the crowd gathered round as Chanter untied him, threw the reins over the stallion's neck, vaulting into the saddle. The girth had been loosened by Sean as he tethered Hans - but only slightly - so the saddle remained in place as Chanter's weight pressed down on his broad back. Slipping his booted feet into the stirrups, he gave the horse a couple of sharp digs with his heels, spurring Hans into action.

They sprang forward, both horse and rider parting the astonished spectators. Dan had decided beforehand to head towards Wistman's Wood. He would cut across the open moor rather than take the road via Two Bridges, but it was still a four mile ride. The terrain would be rough, but all the better. It would deter more nervous (and less desperate) riders from following him.

He would be safe there for a while, as long as nobody guessed where he was going and took the main road to catch up with him. Once in the wood he would lay low under the cover of darkness. His plan was to pick up the Devonport Leat and follow it all the way to Plymouth, to the place where it finally drained into its reservoir, serving as the Devonport water supply.

His logic, at least, was sound. The open moor was laced with bogs and unsound ground, especially hazardous at night or when unpredictable moorland mists descended. Using the Leat as his 'road map', his going would also prove flat, straight, and a guaranteed route to the docks. There he would look for the vessel that, again, his brother Ben had arranged to take him to France.

That was the plan and, in less than a minute Dan had nearly crested the high ground. The crowd gasped. At that point he would have vanished from sight. But his master plan was not to be. He hadn't reckoned on Sean.

Trusting in his close, but brief, connection with Hans, Sean placed his thumb and middle finger to his lips and tongue, and blew. His shrill whistle pierced the air, cutting through the light warm breeze like an arrow. A second later it reached the ears of one highly charged, fully alert, Hanoverian stallion.

Right on cue, Hans dug his hind hooves into the moorland earth to check his stride. With the softer, bit-less bit, Chanter didn't have the same control over the stallion's mouth as he would have with the D-Ring he was used to. He lurched forward over the mane, now unbalanced. Hans did what all stallions always do best when engaged and wanting to take over. He reared – so high that he was almost vertical - to unseat the totally disorientated highwayman.

Chanter crashed onto the hard moorland turf, cracking his head on one of the many pieces of granite clitter that lay on the rough animal track. He didn't get up, not even when three court bailiffs finally reached where he had fallen. He was unconscious. Again. They had to carry him back to the court.

The gathered crowd and court officials cheered, tossing caps in the air, applauding Sean for yet another example of his initiative. He was the hero of the hour once more but, this time he was helped by his faithful – for he had proven his faithfulness that very day – stallion. Hans virtually danced and pranced back down the hill behind the tor to join his master. It was his new master, Sean, the one who had gained his faith within three short days, thanks to love and kindness - qualities that would always win over the loyalty of even the most feisty stallion. Not brute force and cruelty.

Sean and Hans rode back together triumphant. The crowd were jubilant and delighted to see the highwayman overcome twice in a matter of days, again rendered harmless. The boy had done it again without even throwing a punch let alone a knife, this time. Most of all they were relieved, as it sent a clear message to other would-be thieves and vagabonds that the people of Tavistock were not to be messed with.

The applause from the crowd that was bestowed on him on

Chanter's recapture was still ringing in his ears when he, Jack and Mrs Jarrett - and Rosalee - arrived back at The Bedford Hotel, emotionally drained.

They had decided to stay a third night. They deserved it!

Chapter Seventeen
Sean is still impatient to track down his grandfather.

If they hadn't decided to stay the extra night then it would have been arranged for them anyway. Sean's celebrity was now so well established and documented. It had even made the national newspapers. The manager of The Bedford Hotel insisted they stay on, upgrading their rooms to the best in the hotel. A telegram of congratulations from the Duke of Bedford himself was waiting for him. It contained instructions to the manager that no expense was to be spared. Their stay was to be a memorable one.

Before they had even returned to Tavistock, news of yet another act of bravery by the young man had already reached the ears of the townsfolk. They made their way to the hotel in droves, locals lined the main street to welcome their return, shouting congratulations as they passed. The festival fever seemed to have no end to it. The throng of well-wishers reached its peak as they arrived at the hotel.

"Let's shoot round the back to the stables before they see us," said Jack. He and his Missus took off, leaving Sean and Rosalee to face the admiring crowds. Eventually they forced their way through and were safe – almost – inside.

The Bedford Hotel was packed, not only with overnight guests but also locals drinking in the lounge bar, or having coffee in the restaurant. Their conversations were all about what had happened that day at Crockern Tor. Jack and his party entered through the back entrance but were still hardly able to get to their rooms without being besieged with questions from well-wishers and town officials.

The Tavistock Gazette had sent a special reporter to record every detail of the day from witnesses and bystanders but, most importantly, from Sean himself.

He had also brought a photographer with him. They held up departure of the coach so that photographs could be taken. It normally left The Bedford Hotel for London at three in the afternoon but it was ordered to delay departure by the owners of The Times newspaper. That way a photograph of the hero could be delivered for the next days' London edition.

The professional photographer, Arthur Morey, had been despatched urgently from Exeter at the request of the newspaper. Daguerreotypes – one of the first photographic processes at the time - could be taken and the plates carried for developing the next morning on arrival at The Times' London offices in Queen Victoria Street. Having a professional photographer from the newspaper in the town was a talking point in itself.

Due to the long exposure time needed when the photographs were actually taken – the subjects had to keep stock still for several minutes – Arthur was only able to take three studies for The Times. One was a group shot to include Jack and his wife, and the dogs; one was of Sean and Hans; a third was of Sean on his own, given that it was nigh impossible for the horse to remain still for so long. The stallion was as excited as the crowds around him.

With all the trial formalities now over, the final – and most important part according to Jack – was the collection of the reward. They were only too glad to be away from the crowds that had assembled around The Bedford Hotel so, once the last photograph had been taken, the Chief Constable took them back to the Guildhall. After the cheques had been handed over they were taken to Gill's Bank for the safe depositing of £100 into each of Jack and Sean's new accounts.

It was afterwards in the lobby of the actual bank that another surprise awaited Sean. A more unexpected, welcome one he couldn't possibly hope for as a tall, well-dressed man in his late fifties approached him.

"I'm sorry," he said apologetically, "but I believe we may be related. I couldn't help overhear your name being mentioned. My name is 'Sercombe' too. William Sercombe, from Calstock - Albaston to be exact. May I ask where you hail from?"

The blood drained from Sean's face as he realised that he had at last found his relatives, his grandfather, William Senior.

"I... I'm originally from Ireland," he said. "Near Ennis. My father is... was... Francis Sercombe."

"Frankie?" queried William.

"Yes," said Sean. "I think he was your son."

"Francis John Baker Sercombe, to be precise," said William Senior. "he took my first wife's name as part of his." But then William faltered. "You said... was?"

"Y-yes, sir," said Sean. "I'm afraid he died. Was killed."

"Where? How?" His grandfather was shocked, his bloodline found - and lost - in an instant.

"Murdered. By the English. During the evictions."

"I'm so sorry, boy. What name did Francis give you?"

"Sean, sir." He reached to shake William's hand. "I'm so glad I found you. In was my Dad's dying wish, in a way."

William grasped hold of Sean's hand in a hearty hand-shake, equally delighted to rediscover his lost family.

"If only we hadn't had that disagreement, he would still be alive. Such is the price of love, I suppose." William was thinking about the sacrifices he made, and the price his sons had finally paid when he married his second wife so soon.

"And your mother? Anne? He married a local gypsy girl – a McGowan from Ireland, I heard – years ago."

"Dead, too, I'm afraid. They died together. Shot."

It was more bad news than William could cope with, but there was more. "What about your uncle, his brother, William Junior - Billy?"

"His farm was burned down alongside ours," said Sean. "The same day. He and is wife were also shot. Murdered."

"Oh my god," sighed William. "What on earth *is* going on over there?" Visibly shaken, he sat down to collect himself.

Sean sat down with him, wondering what to say next. He had already, in the few short moments since meeting his grandfather, reported enough bad news to last a lifetime.

"His daughter... step-daughter... is outside," he said. "We escaped together. About two or three weeks ago."

They walked out into the Tavistock main street, Sean taking his grandfather over to where Jack and his wife, and Rosalee, were waiting. "This is my grandfather – your Dad's father – William Senior." He introduced him to Rosalee.

"I'm so sorry to hear about your family," said William. "I can't imagine how you feel." Rosalee caught hold of Sean's hand. Two young ladies came over to join them. "These are my two daughters, Mary and Florrie... Florence." William then proceeded to explain the family connection to them. They were only small children when Frankie and Billy left for Ireland and scarcely remembered them. They were only a few years older than Sean.

"Where are you staying?" asked William.

"At The Bedford," said Sean, gesturing to Jack. "all of us."

"Very smart. We're in a small guest house just off Market Square. We often come for the market, when we can." William then went on to explain how he was now a brick and tile maker, designing and building a new kind of kiln and had come to the town on business.

The growth of the railways had brought wealth and opportunities to the region, alongside a shortage of capacity to produce enough bricks for the construction of bridges, warehouses and storage. In addition, the local copper mine was booming. The South West was especially rich in raw materials. Apart from agriculture and cattle, the demand for tin, copper and granite further north and west continued to expand, meaning the need for greater transport links.

A local company had even managed to carry granite quarried at Haytor on Dartmoor all the way on a granite railway – drawn by a dozen or so horses – down to Teignmouth Docks and from there on to London. It was to build The London Bridge.

Rosalee was fascinated that Sean had new-found aunties who were only just a little older than he was. But it all worked out well because, at last, she had some similar age female company who she could hopefully call as friends. Seeing how well they were dressed in the latest fashions for young ladies of some standing, she realised how she must have appeared as a simple Irish 'colleen' with no breeding whatsoever.

But she need not have been concerned, Mary and Florence were courteous and gracious, the Sercombes having also risen from very humble beginnings – granddaughters of a simple farm labourer – to a more respected status since their father rose to the ranks of businessman, industrialist, and inventor.

After the introductions were over and each had expressed delight in discovering the other, the two parties went their separate ways; William and his daughters to their guest house; Jack, his wife, Sean and Rosalee returning to The Bedford, hoping it would be a little quieter with the crowds now dispersed.

It was, and dinner in the hotel was a civilised affair once again after the crowds, drawn to the court hearing at the prospect of seeing a real highwayman in the flesh, had finally made their separate ways back home.

The next day was market day. Friday. After breakfast Jack and his wife bade farewell to Sean and Rosalee. Jack aimed to take in just half a day at the market before returning to Holsworthy, and home. Sean and Rosalee were sad to see them leave. For one thing, it meant they had to decide what to do next. They had so much to think about and were on their own again... but were they?

Suddenly they had a *new* family. They had arranged to meet up with his grandfather and aunties at ten o'clock at the entrance to the Pannier Market. Something to look forward to... but before that they received an unexpected visitor at the hotel. It was the brother of the photographer.

Albert Morey was a tailor, but one with a keen eye for new business, always looking for ways to promote himself and his father's clientele. He had joined his father straight from school as an apprentice tailor's cutter, based at his father's tailor's shop on The Parade in Exmouth. But he was ambitious.

Not content with sitting and waiting for customers to walk through the door, he ventured far and wide on his pony and trap, seeking out custom with personal fittings in the country houses of rich landowners, providing a bespoke made-to-measure service. He was young and it also gave him the opportunity to meet new and exciting people. Starting out before dawn that day he was looking forward to meeting a local hero and, hopefully, furthering the reputation of his father's business as to 'go-to' tailor for leading citizens in the area. He had travelled all the way from Exmouth.

He took after his father for spotting an opportunity. Henry Morey had already become well-known for providing bespoke tailoring services for none other than Chief Sitting Bull and some of his braves. They had visited his actual shop at 10, The Parade, Exmouth, where Arthur had photographed them.

The great American Indian Chief was part of the Buffalo Bill Cody Wild West Show when it was in the area. He called in for a new waistcoat to be specially made. The Native American Indian had adopted this European fashion item as part of their uniform, ever since they had stolen them as booty on their raiding parties on settlers in the American West. It gave them a new identity but they especially liked to have their arms bare, wearing it without a shirt. Patronage by the great American legend became quite a talking point for Henry.

Now the son, Albert, had turned up in in Tavistock in the hope of fitting Sean out with the latest fashion. It was to be free, in return for being allowed to feature Sean as one of his celebrity customers. After some deliberation Sean agreed on the basis that it *would* cost him nothing. Not only that, he felt somewhat flattered to have been placed on the same footing – almost – as the famous American legend.

The only catch, if you could call it that, was that he agreed to have his photograph taken in his new suit by the tailor's brother, none other than (guess who!) *Arthur* Morey. It was he who had tipped Albert off to capitalise on the opportunity.

The fitting took nearly an hour. With ten o'clock fast approaching, and in order to keep the promise to meet up with his grandfather at the Pannier Market, they would have to hurry. Albert had a pony and trap waiting to take him to the railway station, which they shared, dropping Sean and Rosalee off on the way to where William, Mary, and Florence were waiting.

After short introductions, longer because he seemed quite taken by one of the sisters and engaged her in conversation to a greater extent than Sean's other relatives, Albert went on his way back to Exeter and then Exmouth, by train. But it was a chance meeting that was to lead to an outcome that nobody could have predicted.

The last Friday of the month was usually the largest of the weekly markets in the town, attracting buyers and sellers of farm produce as well as livestock for auction. It was also the day when the Duke of Bedford himself could be seen mingling with the crowds, and enjoying the company of friends in his adopted community. Previously, as part of the expansion of his copper mining interests in the area, he had invested in dozens of miners' cottagers for his workers. He was very popular with them as well as businesses in the town.

The main mission for William today was to arrange an appointment with the Duke to discuss the supply of bricks and tiles for future building projects. Rising from farm labourer to brick maker in local brickworks in Callington, William had now become proficient in the technology of the industry, recently inventing a new patent based on the Hoffman Kiln. He was also looking for an investor for building those kilns in the area to meet the increased demand for building materials.

"I will have to leave you all at noon," he said. "I have a meeting with the Duke at the Guildhall. Perhaps we can see each other back there at two o'clock?"

They agreed and the four of them went inside to browse the many craft and food stalls. Sean was outnumbered now by females. Even Lurch and Peggy clung to them rather than him, mainly for the attention they gave both dogs. As soon as he spotted the auction ring Sean decided to remain there for the horse auctions, while the girls resumed exploring the rest of the market. Rosalee was getting on really well with her aunts.

The horse auctions began with smaller ponies – mainly Dartmoors - before progressing to the more expensive mounts favoured by the hunting fraternity. In particular, Sean was fascinated by the sale of, and the prices fetched by, the larger Hunters – mainly bought by members and followers of the Spooners and West Dartmoor Hunt.

It was the conformation and stature of the Hunters, that fetched the highest prices, that he noted most. Many were full-thoroughbreds or based on thoroughbreds, some were even ex-racehorses used as brood mares, and he recognised some cross-breeding with what he thought were Connemara ponies.

Barely fifteen hands at best, this traditional Irish breed added sturdiness and temperament to an otherwise flighty pure thoroughbred. This suited moorland riding as they were hardy, resistant to many of the harsh winters that prevailed over some winters. With the right pairing, a suitable Hunter approaching sixteen hands could often be produced.

But this gave him a better idea. If he were to cross his *Hanoverian*, Hans, with a reasonably sized thoroughbred, it should result in temperament, sturdiness, *and height* – perfect for the more 'substantial' or taller rider. Few of those for sale actually were seventeen hands, so he saw opportunity and higher prices in scarcity.

Sean's mind was now racing with the opportunities that lay before him. He could put Hans out to stud – perhaps for ten guineas per visiting mare – or he could buy his own brood mares. With Newton Abbot and Exeter racecourses not so far away, as well as some point-to-point stables nearby, he could hope to pick up ex-racehorses for little or no cost initially.

Ironically, the modern Hanoverian was bred by introducing the Cleveland Bay imported from England into Germany as one of its foundations. Now he was looking at applying that new breed to the English thoroughbred to produce a *new* breed of Hunter. The more he thought about it, the more he discovered ways to achieve his dream. First and foremost he had the capital to begin his own venture. His £100 reward money could buy a reasonably sized farm with acreage - sufficient to begin his own breeding programme. He couldn't wait to tell Rosalee.

That very thought – the mere fact that he suddenly and instinctively realised that his first reaction was to share his idea *with* her – intrigued, delighted and, finally, worried him. His first thought was *always* of Rosalee when considering his own future. It was *so* natural. He didn't *have* to think about it. It seemed second nature to include her in his every thought. Did she feel the same about him? She had never said.

And what if she didn't *like* the idea? More especially, what *did* she want? She had joined him willingly in Ireland and now remained with him to face all their challenges over here in England, without question or considering any other options.

Nor did he think about any kind of life *without* her. Was it *just* because she, in a way, was *already* family?

Or was there more to it? Then he doubted himself. His plans. He had never *asked* her about anything, such as '*did she want to go with him to find his family?*' He *assumed* she would buy into whatever plans or direction he chose, the ones he chose for them both. His mind was filled – cluttered – with all these concerns and possibilities as he left the auction ring to join the family at the Guildhall. He needed to clear his mind.

The girls were so engrossed they hardly noticed his arrival. Even Rosalee virtually snubbed him, she was so wrapped up in her new friends. They were so interested in their gossip and own opinions of all the sights and sounds so new to them in Tavistock. *They're like a flock of starlings chattering together*, he said to himself, as he compared them with the host of birds that had congregated on the Guildhall roof.

In the end it was William rejoining them after his meeting with the Duke of Bedford, that gained their attention.

He was of a buoyant mood and greeted them all in good humour. "Who's for a proper Devonshire Cream Tea?" he asked, taking hold of his daughters, one on each arm. "On me!" He didn't even wait for an answer before whisking them all off to a tea house he had found a few yards past The Guildhall.

"How was it with the Duke, father?" asked Mary, after they had sat themselves down at a table they could all fit around. William ordered cream teas for five before answering.

"Very promising," he replied. "The problem is the families around here seem to serve each other. It's a closed shop and hard to break into the 'club' unless you have influence."

"Well, father," said Florence this time. "Thanks to Sean and his recent escapades, the Sercombe family name seems to be on everybody's lips these days. Surely that will help. Perhaps we should start our own 'club'."

"No disrespect to Sean, but things go a little deeper. The family connections we're talking about are so ingrained they go back decades, even generations I'm afraid," said William. "My only way forward is to influence someone of some standing who has the Duke's ear, and to come up with a better price. I may have to look much further afield for investors – perhaps Exeter or even Dorset."

William then went on to explain how he needed to focus close to where railways were not yet so well developed. That could mean remaining in Devon and Cornwall. Branch lines were springing up everywhere, connecting small villages and towns, especially if there was mining activity in the area or tourist opportunities. That's where the potential arose.

He had even heard of a wealthy publisher from London who was taking on the locals, fighting to get permission to lay track over open land to enable Barnstaple to be connected by a new branch line to Lynton, Lynmouth, and also Ilfracombe. In turn that would make the whole area accessible to tourists and holidaymakers from as far afield as London.

Journey time could be cut to less than six hours, effectively one day's travel. That would bring wealth and prosperity for all in North Devon. It was that kind of project – and that calibre of entrepreneur - that William wanted to work with. He wanted to break new ground ahead of the competition.

Sean was quite taken by his grandfather's knowledge and vision of how the wheels of business and commerce turned. In some ways, it made his earlier ambitions of horse breeding somewhat less exciting, even mundane. He also saw the effect William's dynamism had on Rosalee. It was a whole new world to her, although Mary and Florence were used to it by now.

"So you may be moving?" she asked.

"Perhaps, Rosalee," he replied. "With my boys gone and now

never coming back I have to build a dynasty for my two girls to inherit. As you can see they aren't getting any younger and it looks as though they're not marriage material. So I may be stuck with them." The men laughed; the ladies abstained.

"Father!" cried Mary. "That's so cruel. How do you know if I haven't caught someone's eye already?"

What a giveaway! This was a new revelation for them all, except for William. So far, Florence thought she was the only one who had spotted the way the tailor, Albert Morey, and Mary had exchanged glances, even though hardly a word had passed between them. Mary was blushing profusely. Usually she gave her father as good as she got.

"And who might that be, young lady?" he asked. "Anyone we know? Some new acquaintance, perhaps?"

Sean could see this was not going well for Mary and came to her rescue. He changed the subject.

"Are you going back today or staying overnight until Saturday?" he asked. His diversionary tactics worked.

"We travel back tomorrow," William replied. "Although I was considering a trip to Exeter to get a feel for the place and its potential. It's on the main line to London Waterloo and those areas can only get more prosperous. They also tell me Exmouth is nice this time of year." He chuckled as he shot a glance to Mary. "Full of nice young men."

"Father!" It was Mary taking the bait and storming off to the Ladies Room. Florence followed her sister, in support.

"I think it's time we went back to our hotel," said Sean, getting up to pay the bill.

"I'll get this, young man," broke in William and signalling to the waitress. Sean protested, but gave in as William insisted.

After saying their goodbyes they returned to their respective lodgings. It had been another exhausting day and Sean still had

Hans to see to before retiring for the night. But it was not a chore, more of a pleasure as he became more and more closely connected with the stallion with every training session.

Just grooming his equine friend was a relaxing experience in itself. Sometimes Rosalee joined him, overcoming her initial fears of the size of such a splendid animal.

The two of them had a lot to think about - mainly how to shape their futures. But that was for another day. As the days wore on it looked like a future they might well be sharing.

If only one of them plucked up the courage to talk about it.

Chapter Eighteen
The couple have choices to make about their true feelings.

With Jack and his wife having left for home they felt 'on their own' again, but meeting his grandfather more than made up for it. Not only that, his capturing of the highwayman, Dan Chanter, *did* give him *some* standing in the town. He had a good reputation now and one upon which he could build to his advantage. That became evident soon after they arrived back at The Bedford that evening. It was a visit from the Chief Constable on official business.

"You have been impressive once again, Sean. I have a proposition for you," said the Chief Constable Mark Merritt. "Can we talk in private?"

Sean led the Constable into a quiet booth in the lounge. "Is it alright if Rosalee sits in with us?" he asked.

Merritt agreed and opened the conversation. "I have to create a proper police force," he said. "The government, in particular the politician Robert Peel, wants all counties to have a network of law enforcers throughout England.

"Sean, you've shown a natural sense for law and order, as well as displaying courage and initiative to tackle problems instinctively and with success. I would like you to consider signing up as a Junior Police Constable for the town's force. What do you say?"

Sean was so amazed at the offer, he did not have a quick answer at all for such an unexpected approach. "It's something I've never even considered. I'd have to think about it and discuss it with Rosalee first. What would be involved?"

Merritt saw Sean and Rosalee exchange quizzical glances, but continued to explain. "I would deputise you to enforce the law and order in our district along with three other more senior deputies. It would mean settling minor civil disorders where necessary but, most of all, curbing criminal activities and keeping the peace. You'll learn as you go along."

"And you think I'd be able to do all that?"

"Quite sure," replied Merritt. "I know you'll be the youngest on the force, but you've already demonstrated your bravery. Most of all, you have a cool head on your shoulders. You don't panic in a crisis."

"I always feel safe with him," Rosalee chipped in.

It was a comment not lost on Merritt, who agreed that it added to his qualities. "It pays 20 shillings a week, your uniform is paid for, and it comes with a cottage in the town – in the new Fitzford Cottages built by the Duke's son – at a special rent of two shillings a week.

Your position replaces the old Parish Constables who were unpaid. You will have to work regular hours and be 'on call', and be based in The Guildhall. If you are happy to use your own horse on public duties, the town will provide you will stabling and full livery costs."

Rosalee was already smiling before Sean looked to her for approval. "If Rosalee is happy with it all, and it looks as though she is, then I would be happy to accept the position," he replied. He and Merritt shook hands.

"I look forward to seeing you at eight o'clock Monday morning at The Guildhall," said Merritt. With that he left, leaving a totally astonished Sean and Rosalee.

After the Chief Constable had gone they hardly spoke for a while, astounded at how their future was shaping after so little time in England in general, and Tavistock in particular. Once they were sat down for their dinner at The Bedford they ran though all that had happened in the last two hours.

Rosalee was first to express her joy, her delight of having a place to stay. "We'll have a permanent roof over out heads again" she enthused. "A place of our own. I must find a job now, seeing that you have such a bright future before you. I don't want to be seen as a kept woman." The look on her face showed she was joking, but he knew she wanted it to be an equal partnership.

Of course, there were other things to consider. Thanks to the reward money he was now a man of means. He had yet to discuss with her his ideas about putting Hans out to stud but, with this latest offer, that seemed less urgent. It was a venture that could succeed, or even fail. Compared with that his post as town constable offered more security, and accommodation. After all, he had to think of Rosalee as much as himself.

But then he began wondering again, the same old doubts and insecurities coming to the surface. *How did she feel about him? Really feel?* In the little time they had been together they had been inseparable, thrown together by circumstance and his father's wishes rather than by choice. *His* choice. Was it *her* choice too?

"What did you think of that Morey fellow?" he asked.

"Which one?"

"I think you know." Did Sean have an edge to his tone? "The tailor chappie. You seemed to be getting on well?"

Was that a statement or a question? She mused. "We *all* did," she shot back at him. "He was very charming. To *everyone*."

She was curious. Was he jealous? Just a *little* bit? She had noticed it before at the gypsy camp with Mercy's boys, but he never really came out with how he felt. How he felt about *her*. "He seemed to look at you a certain way," he said.

Ah, so that's it, she thought. *It's all coming out now.* "I think you're confusing me with your aunt. Mary." she said, coldly.

He had pushed her too far. He knew it, and had to make amends. "Yes. I suppose you're right," he   replied. Or should he had said 'hoped'?

"Is that an apology?"

"Yes. I'm sorry. Will you forgive me?" he asked.

"Just this once," she replied and, with that, she excused herself.

But there were still unanswered questions, and unanswered feelings, for them *both* to mull over.

True, in many other ways it was remarkable how life was falling into place so quickly. The subject that seemed so easy to avoid and which never came up in conversation, was that they were assumed to be a *couple* without being married, or showing any obvious relationship between them.

Normally, in this strict Victorian society, a man and woman living together and unmarried would be frowned upon as immoral. But they had arrived in Tavistock as a couple – being accepted as such with no questions being asked - and they were reticent about discussing the subject. So they didn't.

Rosalee had just taken herself off to the Ladies Room in a huff and returned, somewhat cooled down and calmer.

"This package has come for you, sir," said the porter as he handed Sean a large envelope. They were just finishing dinner.

"What's in it?" Rosalee wanted to know. Sean looked at her with a *How do I know?* expression.

Sean opened the package carefully. It was a legal document containing the outline of his new position as constable and its terms, a rent book for a cottage by the canal, and its key. A note confirmed that they could move in on Sunday.

Rosalee forgot their tiff, threw her arms around Sean, hugging him so hard that he could hardly breathe. She was so beside herself with happiness, she very nearly admitted what was in her heart – how she had fallen for him so deeply.

The next morning they were still so excited they both woke up and dressed before dawn. There was little to pack but Sean needed to water and feed Hans before transferring him to the constabulary stables and paddock. They had breakfast early, making their way to their new cottage by nine o'clock.

The cottages were relatively new and purpose built for local workers and residents. Due to the expansion of the copper mines and influx of labour for them, the availability of good accommodation was only just about catching up with demand. Prior to these new builds, some families were having to live in one room. The over-crowding had led to subsequent outbreaks of disease - typhus and cholera - reaching epidemic proportions.

Sean and Rosalee moved into one of four cottages reserved for the new police constables. He would have work colleagues nearby. "Am I supposed to carry you over the threshold?" he asked, bending down to put her into a fireman's lift.

"Don't you dare," she replied indignantly. "We're not even married." She was now whispering, in case neighbours were listening. Which of course they were!

The terraced cottages that were rented to all public officials were furnished with bare essentials which, in their case, was necessary and welcome. Compared with the one-room thatched farm cottages in Ireland in which they had grown up as children, it was luxury. They even introduced Thomas Crapper's popular invention into most modern homes: the flush toilet. They were already recently acquainted with such an appliance in the hotel, much to their initial amusement. In this instance, however, it was situated *outside* in an adjoining outhouse. But it was no less appreciated.

Once their few belongings were put away and they had enjoyed their first cup of tea in their new house (made with milk borrowed from a neighbour, and water boiled on a stove in the hearth). As much as they were loathe to leave their new found comfort, they realised they had to buy provisions. The previous tenants had left *some* basic non-perishable foods and household needs, but otherwise their larder was bare.

With light hearts filled with optimism they ventured back into town to shop for the next few days' meals. They also sent a telegram to Sean's grandfather, telling him of his new position, including their new address. William had promised to visit the town on market day in two weeks' time, partially to follow up on his meeting with the Duke. But now he had another reason, enjoying the company of his new family.

After their shopping expedition Sean and Rosalee took the dogs on a walk to explore the outskirts of the town. Fitzford Cottages lined the banks of the Tavistock Canal itself that stretched nearly five miles from The Bedford Hotel to Morwhellham Quay.

The Quay was a hub from which goods bound for export, minerals, heavy loads – principally copper from the mines at Mary Tavy - could be taken all the way down to Plymouth on the River Tamar. The waterway route to the seaport was a good fifteen to twenty miles long, but navigable, and easier going than the roads which were rough and not very well maintained. They were both slow. That was another practical reason why they needed the railway which was quicker, cheaper and more comfortable than road or canal.

As soon as they left the bustle of the town the quiet of the countryside took over. Perfect for Lurch and Peggy to go off on their own, Sean and Rosalee could amble slowly across flat, flower-strewn meadows, reflecting on the similarity with the landscape they left behind in Ireland. But those reflections also brought back sad memories, ones that Sean was keen to mask with happier thoughts for their future.

"What will I do all day whilst you're busy at work?" she began. "The other women in the terrace have families to bring up, they'll think I'm lazy."

"For now I just want you to make it into our home, *your* home as much as mine. It could do with a woman's touch. That will keep you busy for a while."

"You won't be in any danger, will you?" she added. "There are some rough places and taverns in areas where the miners live. Don't get into any fights, will you?"

"I can take care of myself," he replied. "That's why they gave me the job. Plus, I'll have other constables with me."

"I'll have to make friends with the neighbour's wives, I suppose," she went on. "What shall I say if they ask if we're married? Or if we're starting a family ourselves?"

"You'll just have to lie," he said. "Tell them that I'm a horrible person, that I beat you, and that I'm the last person on earth that you'd marry."

"Oh, I could never do that. It's so untrue."

He saw his opening. "So you *will* marry me, then?" He stopped, turning to face her. He was now serious, searching her eyes for an answer. The suddenness of it all was a shock, and one that reached into her deepest emotions.

He could see her eyes moisten. "Of course I'll marry you. Who else could love you as much as I do?" then laughing, "And who else would have you?"

With that she reached forwards and upwards to kiss him, the first time ever they had shared such an intimacy. He held her so close for the longest time until the 'yelp' of Lurch interrupted their moment. Life was starting to make total sense. For both of them.

The palm reading by Mercy should have provided enough clues, but they had been blind to the obvious so far, or had been unwilling to accept that they were to spend the rest of their lives together. "I've never wanted anyone else other than you, Rosalee," he whispered. "And I never will."

They walked back to the cottage slowly – breaking up their silence with occasional thoughts and hopes they might share in future plans.

In reality they had known each other for a mere matter of weeks, but it felt like a lifetime together.

Chapter Nineteen
The couple are first settled – then unsettled...

And so it was, within the month, the two became man and wife. The first person to hear about their intentions was his grandfather the next time he was in town. He was delighted not only at that news, but also of Sean's new position of constable.

He had similar news himself concerning Mary, his eldest daughter. Despite his teasing he *had* taken them to Exmouth for a few days after they last left Tavistock. He had put on a pretence that he needed a new waistcoat – from none other than Morey's the tailors on The Parade.

Of course, his ulterior motive was to give Mary a chance to meet young Albert once more. It was a Saturday afternoon before their train had finally reached the seaside town and the shop. They had already booked accommodation at a hotel near the railway station. With some reluctance, and after a feigned shyness, she and her younger sister accompanied their father to the tailor's shop on The Parade.

"I'm so pleased your train connections from Tavistock worked well," said Morey Senior, Henry, showing William into a fitting room. The girls sat together chatting in the main shop, conveniently so that the young Albert Morey could join in the conversation and become better acquainted with Mary.

"I'll be back in Tavistock next week," he said. "It's the first fitting for your... nephew is it not? *Sean* Sercombe?"

"Yes. He's my older brother's boy," Mary answered.

"A very *brave* nephew," he added.

"Yes, indeed."

"My own brother, Arthur, was sent down by The London Times and The Tavistock Gazette newspapers to take his photograph. Have you seen them yet?"

"No. Do you have copies?"

"I'll go and fetch them. He certainly cuts a dash. Arthur will be taking more photographs of Sean in his new suit of clothes when they're finished, to display in our shop window. He'll be next to the picture of Chief Sitting Bull. I just hope he doesn't mind." He laughed nervously. "Or get scalped."

After twenty minutes or so William emerged from the fitting room. Measurements had been taken and material chosen, with the waistcoat due to be ready Monday morning.

By that time, Albert had charmed the girls sufficiently to coax them to join him on a Sunday morning drive after church, along the promenade. Of course, for the sake of propriety, Florence would have to accompany them, but she would be discreet enough to allow them some time on their own, albeit always in plain view.

So that was the beginning of a new romance and one that resulted in the marriage of the two of them – eventually.

As for Sean and Rosalee, theirs was a simple wedding held at St Andrews Church in Calstock. Sean wanted to celebrate the most important day of his life in the birthplace of his father, Frankie and of Rosalee's step-father, Billy. His grandfather and the rest of the family helped with most of the wedding arrangements. Due to William's influence they were able to persuade the local vicar to allow the ceremony to go ahead at such short notice on a special licence.

The guest list was limited mainly to family, with Jack and his wife added to their friends, as were Django and Mercy. It was only by chance that they came. Sean had spotted their boys in Tavistock on market day and passed on an invitation. It was an added bonus for Rosalee to have relatives from her side of the family. Of course, Mary invited Albert Morey!

The ceremony took place on the Saturday – the soon-to-be happy couple arriving at the church in a horse-drawn open carriage drawn, of course, by Hans. The stallion had never looked more handsome, decked out with colourful plumes and ribbons. Jack did the honours as driver. Sean sported the new outfit specially made for him by Arthur Morey – the one he was wearing in the new display in the tailor's shop window. As for Rosalee, her aunts – Florence and Mary – made sure she was fitted out in the latest lady's fashion.

As Rosalee's aunt Mercy's husband, Django was the closest male to qualify as 'family' to Rosalee, he was duly appointed to give her away. The honours fell to William as Best Man to Sean, in the absence of his son, Frankie.

In the short time since they had set up home in Tavistock, Sean and Rosalee had made *some* close friends, but largely neighbours and those with whom Sean worked. A small, but enthusiastic, 'Guard of Honour' was comprised of the Chief Constable and Sean's fellow assistant constables – proudly raising their truncheons to form an arch into the church.

Most of all, at least for Sean, it was a special moment to see his marriage confirmed and recorded in the community in which his close family had been born and raised. It was also a proud moment for William.

They had decided upon the Tamar Inn for their wedding breakfast, it was on the Quay at Calstock. Ironically, up to the previous century it had a reputation as a haunt for smugglers and highwaymen, which made Sean feel *so* much more at home. Once speeches were over they snook away to board the carriage for the local station, catching the late afternoon train to Plymouth. Even Hans had a final chance to see them off!

The city was yet another new experience for them. Ever since the defeat of the Spanish Armada by Drake, not to mention the Pilgrim Father's sailing in the Mayflower to settle in America, Plymouth had continued to expand as a principal port – commercially as well as militarily. It was quite a culture shock for them compared with Tavistock, but seemed a good choice for the start of a new life together.

They had decided to explore all of life's opportunities, as they came along plus, William was determined to treat them to a taste of 'the high life' of the new luxury Duke of Cornwall Hotel. Meanwhile they simply enjoyed the journey through the Tamar Valley. The train took them through the stunning countryside bordering the river and, ultimately the estuary, as it opened out before them when it reached Saltash.

Arriving at Plymouth station, they found that the hotel had sent a carriage to meet them for the short trip through the city streets to where they had been booked in for the next five nights. Much of the flavour of the old town was reminiscent of the port of Kilrush, an immediate reminder of how far they had travelled in such a short time.

The carriage rattled slowly through cobbled streets where they noticed a similar *kind* of poverty and poor living standards of ordinary working people, but not nearly as bad as those they had left behind in Ireland.

Some areas were quite pleasant in contrast, consisting of tree-lined avenues opening out into lush green space where recreational 'squares' had been created for the more well-off to enjoy. Thinking back, in some ways it all seemed like a dream when she compared this to her old life.

It was just as Rosalee was casting her mind back to Kilrush, and in particular the shipwreck off Lundy, that something caused a cold shiver to run through her body. The vision of a face from way back then brought her back from her dream state. It was the profile of a face she recognised, of the captain of the wrecker's schooner, Chanter - not Dan the highwayman, but his brother, Ben.

They had turned into North Road West just up the hill from

Plymouth station and were passing The Archer Inn, making for Archer Place before threading their way through the back streets on their way to The Duke of Cornwall.

"What's wrong?" asked Sean, spotting *something* was not quite right. Rosalee had turned a ghostly white. "You look like you've seen a..."

"I think I may have," she answered. "I could have sworn it was Chanter."

"It can't be. He's in Dartmoor Prison."

"No. Not him. Not Dan. His brother. The captain of that ship that rescued the Ellen off Lundy."

"Ben Chanter, you mean?"

"That's what I said. It was only a glimpse, but it was a Chanter alright. Either one is bad news."

"Did *he* see *you*?" The way Sean came out with this question told her he was beginning to get worried too.

"No. I just caught a side view. He was talking – facing away – but arguing with someone by the sound of it. In French."

"French?"

"Yes, Mr Parrot. He looked foreign, anyway by the way he dressed. I'd say he w*as* French. All frills and girl's make-up!"

"Well he doesn't know *us*," said Sean, reassuringly. "It's nothing to worry about."

"You're right,"she agreed. "Even if he did, he wouldn't try anything. Not with *your* track record with his brother!" She held him close, feeling a lot calmer now but still mindful of the dangers that can be out there, that still *are* out there.

It was a brief episode, unsettling at first, but one that didn't spoil the happiness of the next few days at least. Living in luxury again, reminiscent of their first days in Tavistock at The Duke of Bedford, they enjoyed being waited on once more – including the added novelty once more of an *inside* toilet!

True, Ben Chanter had *not* seen her. He was more wrapped up in his conversation with his companion, or was it his adversary? It was certainly a heated exchange verging on an argument. And with good reason.

"I don't owe you a thing!" Ben Chanter had said (but in French).

"I had my schooner moored up for three days waiting for your worthless brother!" the Frenchman was clearly furious, referring to Dan Chanter's non-appearance after his trial. "You have to pay for my mooring and lost cargo to France!"

Chanter argued back. "I'm out of pocket too! It cost me a tidy sum to bribe the guards in Tavistock jail – I won't see that again – and, to cap it all, I've lost that handsome Hanoverian stallion I brought over from Germany..."

"...Yes! You still owe *me* la monnaie for *that*!" broke in the Frenchman. "He was a top bloodline, with papers."

"That was the Irish lad's fault," shouted Chanter. "And *he's* got my horse – my brother's, anyway. We'd better set about tracking him down. *He* needs to pay! Not me."

So the argument carried on, but not before the Frenchman – a certain Count Bonnier – had, himself, noticed Rosalee in the carriage. He was facing her carriage window as she was looking out, at the very moment it passed himself and Chanter arguing in Archer Place. He had looked up and, how could he *not* be smitten by the beauty of such a bride - on her *wedding day* of all days?

As well as being a French opportunist, operating on the fringes of legal enterprise, he was also a renowned libertine. As a womaniser with a sleazy reputation on both sides of the channel he used his charm, wealth and position in society to ruin many a *good* reputation of ladies in Victorian society.

His eyes were drawn to those of Rosalee on that very day. Hers were locked with his and her blood ran cold. As much as the sight of Chanter had unsettled her, albeit a fleeting one, it was the full-on glare of Bonnier that had struck home and filled her with a sense of fear, without her knowing why.

After all, there was no real reason why she *should* be so worried. Unless he had noticed the 'Duke of Cornwall Hotel' insignia on the side of the coach it was unlikely he could find her again.

But had *he? And would he* want *to – to seek her out?* That thought troubled her. Again, it was an irrational assumption which she tried to dismiss as a foolhardy notion.

And she *did* wipe it from her thoughts. Holding onto Sean more tightly as the coach continued on its way, she gained comfort in the knowledge that she knew Sean – of all the people in the world she could think of – was more than capable of keeping her safe. But, little did she know at the time that it was a challenge waiting to face them in the future – both of them. Such matters were rarely resolved without *someone* getting hurt. But who?

That time would not be now, however. Compared with rural Devonshire this was a large city in which it was easy to become lost, and equally difficult to be found.

A week later, with the enjoyable and all-too-few days of the honeymoon soon behind them, they found themselves back into the daily routine of Tavistock as a married couple. Finally, happiness had descended upon them. Sean – in spite of his tender years - proved an excellent choice as a town constable. He soon progressed to a more senior rank, applying a natural dedication well beyond his previous station in life. He was also an excellent choice as a husband!

For her part, as a dutiful housewife, Rosalee busied herself baking and supplying confectioneries to the local tea shops, combined with trips over to see her aunts (by marriage!) in Calstock. It was a real treat for her to enjoy family once again, so it was with some sadness when William gave them his latest news. They were leaving the area to explore business opportunities in Leicester.

Rosalee was especially sorry at the prospect of losing contact with Mary and Florence who had become like sisters to her. They would be separated by two hundred and fifty miles! But William was getting no younger. He needed to make one final effort in building and construction so he could leave a secure legacy for his girls. Secretly, he was also making Sean a benefactor in his estate.

But was all lost? Their life in Tavistock had been good in the two years they had spent in the town, and they were still young. Sean had an idea for their futures, the idea he had before being offered the position as a police officer. They were sat in front of their open fire in the cottage after supper that evening, when Sean broached the subject with Rosalee.

"I know we've been happy here," he began, "but this move by grandfather has got me thinking."

It had been troubling Rosalee all day. "I will miss them all terribly," she said. "Mary and Florence are like my sisters."

"We don't *need* to miss them."

"But we're settled here. We have everything we do need. They'll be *miles* away."

"I know," he replied." But 'everything' is nothing without family, too. They won't be close any more. It's like losing a family all over again. I have an idea that will change all that."

"Tell me," she said. "I need something to cheer me up."

"I see we have two options – but only if you agree."

"What's the first?"

"Hans is still only rising eight and in the past couple of years we have already earned about a hundred guineas in stud fees, without really trying. That is to say *I* haven't had to try. I now *he* has!" They laughed. "Even without a steady income, I'm sure we could get by financially in Leicestershire. It's the best hunting country in England with a lot of wealthy clients."

"And the second?"

"Grandfather has always said there was a job there waiting for me if ever I wanted it. He's keen to keep things in the family, and I know he still misses not having my Dad and Uncle working with him. He said he could train me in the business."

"And then I wouldn't lose Mary and Florence."

It was their innate understanding, intuition and trust between each of them that came to their rescue once again – just as it had in those first days fleeing the English. It was as if they hardly had to *discuss* the issue. They seemed to arrive at the same conclusion, in total agreement without debate.

"Sean," she said after only a short pause. "You've always had our best interests at heart and so far we've made things work. I trust your judgement.

"How much notice do you have to give the police force?"

Chapter Twenty
On the move again – but with family this time.

The Tavistock police received Sean's news with much disappointment. He had rapidly become a favourite of Mark Merritt, who saw the day when he might even take over the force. One day. William, on the other hand, was delighted.

It would be a bitter-sweet departure from Devonshire. They loved their neighbours and were received well in the town, thanks largely to Sean's glowing reputation before he even took up the post as constable.

The cottage had been a perfect home. They would miss that, too. It was modest but they loved it, and the area where they lived on the edge of the town suited them well because was on the fringe of the countryside.

With her skills in crafts, learnt from her mother, Rosalee had made their house their home. It was therefore with some sadness that they boarded the train that morning for the long journey to Leicester, leaving it all behind.

Making several trips to Leicester in advance of their move, William had everything organised – not only for himself and the girls, but also for Sean and Rosalee. He had chosen the city because it offered most potential. Recently it had been voted the second richest city in Europe. He settled on Aylestone to buy a house. At that time it was just a village – but an easy commutable distance of the city. And, because it lay just outside Leicester city centre, Aylestone had enormous potential for residential development.

The house William had bought had enough room for them all. It was also central to several locations that would be good for private and industrial expansion. His ambition was to extend his interests into *building* new houses, rather than merely supplying bricks, as long as he could find investors.

William had thought of everything, or so they hoped. This included livery for Hans in nearby Glen Parva, just a couple of miles from the house. The stallion was to be transported in a special carriage on a goods train. He even had the company of three other horses, thoroughbred racehorses travelling from Newton Abbot to Leicester racecourse.

'Old Aylestone', as it came to be known, was in danger of its community being drawn into the Leicester city conurbation but, for now, it proudly retained its rural identity. William had purchased a large five bedroom detached house, complete with basement servant accommodation, conveniently located on the main Leicester Road.

The village centre was a few yards down the hill, less than a quarter of a mile away and therefore walkable. At the village cross-roads one lane led down to the Grand Union Canal, still an important trade route for coal and heavy materials, given that the nearest *railway* stations were a few miles away in Leicester itself, or Wigston, Countesthorpe and Blaby.

Up to this point, Sean and Rosalee had only taken short local journeys by train – single trips, there and back. On this occasion, however, it was more complicated. There were several train changes to be made further up the country once they had boarded at Tavistock.

William had travelled ahead several days before so it meant Sean was charged with looking after his aunts, Mary and Florence. This was warmly welcomed by Rosalee. She now had female company on the long journey – 'the journey into the unknown' as she called it. In truth they were all feeling a sense of nervousness, but mixed with excitement. Each was glad of the other's company.

One of the most striking differences - for them all - was the change in landscape as they left the comparatively varied West

Country countryside. Leaving Exeter and passing north of Taunton, the flatness of the Somerset Levels was of particular note, before they approached Bristol.

Recent heavy rainfall had flooded the plains so much so, that the waters almost reached the raised embankments of the railway lines. And they could see for miles – west towards the coast, where the towns of Burnham on Sea and Weston Super Mare were still obscured, and east towards Bath, which was also hidden as the horizon rose higher in the distance.

After stopping for passengers at Bristol, their next large city to pass through was Birmingham, where they had to change trains. Bristol had seemed small in relation to the hive of activity that confronted them as they changed platforms for their New Street connection – their *final* connection – to Leicester. From there they were to be – or at least they *hoped* they would be – greeted by William, for the short carriage drive to their new home in Aylestone.

As soon as they reached the urban landscape of the city, they were immediately struck by the different smells from various factories – the sweetness of a biscuit factory in contrast with the acid taste in the air of a local tannery. And they missed the pure air of Devonshire as the inversion layer, like some ghostly shroud, kept the smoke and steam from the gasworks hovering over the rooftops of the city houses.

And they were tired. With time lost between connections on the way, the journey had taken all day. They were a little hungry as well as weary - ready to relax, but also thankful at last to be reunited with William. In the last mile or so as they approached London Road station in Leicester, Florence was hanging out of the railway carriage window, searching the crowded platform for her father.

"There he is," she shouted excitedly, immediately reaching up for her valise to make a quick exit from the train. The others followed suit but less frantic, checking that they had not left anything behind in the compartment.

"There you are!" said William with some relief as his daughters ran along the platform to embrace him. "I thought you'd got lost!"

"No chance of that," replied Rosalee. "Not with Sean looking after us."

William and Sean shook hands, then William hugged his granddaughter in the warmest of welcomes. He loved it that Sean and Rosalee were a constant reminder of his lost sons.

"Come on," said William. "Follow me. I've got a carriage waiting and a lovely hot supper when we get in." He had employed a live-in husband and wife as servants for them.

It was only a few miles from the station before they reached home. They were all amazed at the large houses they had passed on the way. They drove through Victoria Park from which they could see clear evidence of wealthy residents in Leicester itself, an indication that industry was thriving.

On the other side of the industrial coin rural Leicestershire was renowned for its strong agricultural tradition – largely sheep – keeping a balance with a city that had diversified into hosiery as well as boots and shoes. That all led to the growing population alongside wealth and the ability for a middle class able to buy what were, otherwise, formerly luxury items. Light engineering and factory-based knitwear added to this.

Of course, progress meant more residential houses and therefore more bricks - William's specialism. As well as a continuing tradition as a coal mining region, the expansion of factory-based industry and, in turn, the railways for the transport of finished goods and raw materials, meant there were growing opportunities. All that was needed were investors to match and back the entrepreneurship.

Although Sean had *some* capital – he still had the whole of his £100 reward money banked, as well as the stud fees – William did not look to him as an investor. In any case, the sums needed were in the thousands rather than hundreds.

He had chosen the Midlands for his 'new start' because he felt that business further north was a more open affair. Not only was it national, but international in scope. In the West Country, local money remained with local investment groups and investors. They were less keen on allowing 'newcomers' into the fold. This was also true if new money came in looking to find new West Country opportunities.

Luckily, the Duke of Bedford, although he had adopted Tavistock as his own, still retained an open mind and looked upon William as someone in whom he had faith and in whom he might invest. It was with that expectation that William had relocated to Leicester to make his mark, and now he had a grandson to work with him. After a few days spent settling into their home they would begin a new venture. Together.

William had managed to find stabling for Hans along New Bridge Road and further grazing near King's Lock (the latter was named after the long-serving lock-keeper, George King). They also had a small stable block behind the house, but only sufficient for the pony they used for the pony and trap, and an occasional overnight stay for Hans. William used the pony and trap for short expeditions, for pleasure and for business.

He had selected Aylestone village as their base for several reasons. It was still largely rural, which suited them well after living in Devon and Cornwall, but it had good local transport links to the city of Leicester. Aylestone Park was looked upon by many city dwellers as a place to go and relax at weekends.

For that reason, a horse-drawn tram service operated all the way from Leicester Clock Tower, with pick-up and drop-off stops along the way, and a terminus in Aylestone. It was something of which the three girls would take full advantage for their frequent shopping trips to the city.

Sean had been provided with names of the kennel masters at all the local Hunts for the area including the Quorn, Fernie, Atherstone and Belvoir. That was the first task on his list – to visit all of them, on Hans, while it was still early summer and therefore out of season for hunting. Any stud fees he could still win would obviate a need for him to dip into his savings, at least until William could officially put him on the payroll.

Quorn was a good fifteen miles hack from Aylestone, taking him all of two hours at a reasonable pace. On his first exploratory visit he decided to take a diversion around the centre of the main city, heading for Bradgate Park then on through Woodhouse Eaves.

It was Sean's first taste of the Leicestershire countryside so he decided to enjoy it and discover as much about his surroundings as he could. Hans found the going quite easy after the steep hills and gradients he had to cope with across moorland Devonshire. In parts, the Charnwood Forest area *did* challenge him a little, but they arrived at the Quorn Hunt kennels still relatively fresh – a factor that didn't escape the Field Master who greeted them.

"Did you come far?" he asked.

"Aylestone," replied Sean.

"That's the best part of fifteen miles, and he hasn't even got a sweat on. You must keep him in peak condition."

"Yes," replied Sean. "It's easier going for him compared with Dartmoor."

"Dartmoor? What made you move all the way up here?" asked the Field Master.

"More business opportunities, really. My grandfather's a brick maker and builder," said Sean.

"Plenty of call for that around here. Lot's of people getting rich on it. Luckily, a lot of 'em likes to hunt."

Sean and the Field Master then went on to talk terms and how a stud arrangement might work. Sean did not admit to having limited resources for breeding *at his stables*, but the Field Master came to his rescue, providing the ideal scenario without even having to think about it.

"I know for sure," he said, "that quite a few of the Hunt members have mares in season between now and September."

"How many mares might that be," asked Sean, "turned out for the summer?"

"Here? Close on a dozen, I reckon. Of those suitable for breeding, anyway."

"You've got about forty acres here I would guess," said Sean. "Is that about right?"

"Near enough. And we mix a small number cattle and sheep in the pastures, enough the keep the grazing sweet."

"Could you set aside, say, ten acres so that we could let the mares run free with the stallion?"

"Pasture breeding, you mean?" asked the Field Master. It made him think, *this boy knows his stuff.*

"Exactly," said Sean. "I'd be happy to stay here for the first few days to keep an eye on the mares – just in case there was any aggression between them. But Hans is pretty friendly, especially for a stallion. Some say pasture breeding is better than using a breeding shed. It should work well."

The Field Master was impressed. Not only did it mean he could rotate the mares over the three months or so as they came in season - so that *more than* a dozen were covered - but it would involve no extra keep for any of the mares belonging to the Hunt itself. They shook hands on the deal, agreeing to introduce the first mares in a couple of weeks' time.

"You'll find a room reserved for you at The King William," said the Field Master. "Stabling too. The Hunt will pay for it."

Sean thanked him and made his way to the village inn, pleased with himself and looking forward to breaking the news to Rosalee and the rest of the family. He would miss Hans, of course, but it was business. He could 'deliver' the stallion by riding him over personally, as before and, perhaps, agree to have a Hunt horse on loan for the period.

His grandfather also thought it was a good arrangement. The idea of being responsible for a dozen or so brood mares, even though they would have been able to charge livery, did not make any sense. It would have been a tie on Sean when, at that time, William wanted him to learn more about the building industry.

Not only that, the Soar Valley was a flood plain and introduced a risk to expensive brood mares' safety that they did not want to take on. A prolonged spell of wet weather or flash flood – which happened every few years there without warning - could mean disaster to their finances.

On the plus side, the occasional flood meant that the land remained fertile, being constantly renewed of its nutrients. The pasture was good grazing. However, in this case, the risk of losing valuable brood mares by accident was too great.

It was a good start. Sean knew that once the first foals were born a year later, the word would spread to the other Hunts. Referrals and personal recommendations were his strongest advertising tools and he was confident that the qualities of the Hanoverian would soon win favour with his elite clientele, once they saw the foals he could produce.

William was 'investing' in Sean because he knew he could trust him. After all, he was family. Although he had a lot to learn about the business, Sean had already proven himself to be a people person in his job as a town constable. He would easily be able to manage a workforce of tough factory workers and labourers on construction sites.

That said, he would gain a lot more respect if he had more technical knowledge. He was enrolled by William in the Leicester Mechanical Institute, a new adult education centre, to study mechanical arts. It would not only give him authority but he would be able to work with William more closely on the technical aspects of construction plans.

The girls were *so* excited at Sean's news – wanting to know all about the Quorn Hunt as well as details of the journey to get there. They all agreed that they should hire a carriage and pair one day to explore the Charnwood Forest and perhaps arrange a picnic in Swithland Woods or in nearby Newtown Linford.

But Mary was bursting to tell them about her own good news. Albert was coming to stay for a few days, arriving in a couple of weeks. They had courted from a distance most of the time ever since that second meeting. Their letters were exchanged weekly but, since Mary had moved to Aylestone, being *so* far apart was proving difficult - for both of them. His last letter was delivered two days before he was due to arrive.

At the end it read: *Be prepared for a big surprise.*

What could it mean? There was only one thing she could think of. But she was wrong. It was much more than 'that'.

Chapter Twenty One
Sean and Rosalee experience the shock of their lives.

On the morning Albert was due to arrive Mary received a further telegram, simply saying: *I will make my own way from the station. No need to meet me. ETA 4pm.*

Even more strange.

By half past three that afternoon she was waiting at the front gate of their house, looking out for a coach. Albert had been so vague. What *could* his surprise *really* be? She could hardly wait to find out.

Maybe he wasn't travelling by coach after all. He hadn't said, so Mary didn't know whether or not he would be on the tram. As well as looking for a coach, she was watching for Albert walking up from the village, just in case he had used the tram. Florence came to join her as a quarter to four approached. Five minutes later they were followed by William. Sean and Rosalee stayed in the house, finishing off in the kitchen where they had been baking Cornish pasties.

Earlier than expected they caught sight of Albert. It was five minutes to four. He was early and had decided to take a large coach and four after all, riding up front next to the coachman, waving furiously as soon as he saw them. He could hardly miss such a reception.

Arriving at the gate he immediately jumped down and ran to her. Mary kissed him – even though her father was standing right next to her. William cleared his throat. It was not the thing to do, not in broad daylight in a public place. Not to be deterred, Albert wrapped his slight frame around her in the best way he could - a bear hug.

William made sure he was the next to greet him, shaking hands. He turned to the coachman, unloading trunk after trunk, by the gate.

"What's all this?" he asked, noticing that the amount of luggage was *far* more than a single traveller would carry with him. "Are you moving in permanently, Albert?" He laughed at his own joke.

"Ready for your surprise?" Albert replied, walking towards the coach and opening the door. He began his introductions.

"May I present," he began, then paused as the first of his fellow travellers emerged. "Mr and Mrs Francis Sercombe!"

"Frankie!" gasped William, holding onto the gate to keep himself upright. "Oh my God, I thought I'd lost you for ever!"

Frankie ran towards his father, flinging his arms around his neck in a mixture of pure relief and delight. "I love you, Dad, and I'm *so* sorry!" he said, too moved to say more.

Albert continued...

"Mr and Mrs *Billy* Sercombe!"

Frankie's brother ran over now, knocking him out of the way with, "My turn now!" All three of them combined in a group hug. The wives were being left out. Finally, Billy made his own introductions.

"Let me introduce Annie – Frankie's lovely wife," he said. She shook the hand of her father-in-law for the first time ever, kissing him on the cheek before making way for her sister-in-law to approach.

"This is Maureen," she said. "Billy's wife." Maureen took her turn to embrace William. For her too, it was for the first time.

"And who are these little tykes?" asked William, as Annie pushed Seamus and Bridie forward.

Once Albert had been relieved of his compere duties, Mary reunited with him. However, she soon rejoined Florence. The two sisters had not seen their brothers since they were little more than toddlers and were unsure as to who was who.

"This is Frankie," Albert said – bringing him forward, "and the eldest." The girls were in tears, as was Frankie.

"Billy, come forward," said Albert, acting as Master of Ceremonies once more. "Say 'hello' to your sisters – Mary and, this one, is Florence." It was another chance for a group hug, both sisters and both brothers together again at last.

"Where's Sean?" asked Annie, anxiously.

"... and my girl, Rosalee?" joined in Maureen.

"I'll go and fetch them," volunteered William. He ran up the driveway to the house – the first time he had run since...?

They all stood around, chatting excitedly, surrounded by luggage. They had forgotten one important duty.

"Who's paying?" It was the coachman. He had ignored all the goings on whilst he finished unloading all the cases and trunks. As soon as William ran into the house he saw his chance to ask to be paid. Albert obliged. The coachman started for the terminus in the hope of picking up fares back to Leicester.

"Mamma!" Rosalee could hardly see through her teas as she hurried down to where they were all collected outside the gates to the house. Maureen ran to meet her. "I thought you were dead, mother" she shouted. Billy joined them, comforting them both as they embraced each other.

By this time Sean had finally emerged from the house, at first disbelieving his grandfather until he saw living proof that his parents were both truly alive.

Annie was first to greet him. "Everything's fine, now boy," she said. "We're safe."

"You made it, son. I knew you could do it," said Frankie, as he drew Sean to him. "And thank you for saving Rosalee."

Sean was still dazed. He went over to his younger brother and sister, Seamus and Bridie, before noticing someone was missing. "Where's Declan?" asked Sean, running over to look inside the coach in case he was playing hide and seek. "Didn't he make it? What happened to him?"

"He's fine, son," said Frankie. "He's nearly fifteen, now. A big lad, almost as big as you. He works on the merchant ships, to Canada, America... everywhere."

"But I heard the shots!" said Sean, turning to face his parents again, once more remembering that last day on the farm in Ireland. "I very nearly turned back, then I saw the cottage ablaze. It was then I remembered my promise to you. To Rosalee. We're married, you know." He had no idea why he said that, but he was so confused he could hardly think. Everything seemed so jumbled up, confused, just when it had finally started to make sense again.

Annie reached out for him. "We're all together now. That's the main thing. We'll explain later," she said, as they all made their way to the house, each sharing the task of carrying the luggage up the drive.

Finally, Lurch and Peggy sprang out as they reached the main door, bounding across to welcome each newcomer in turn, joining the excitement. They had been going wild inside. William held the door open for his guests.

"Shall we all go inside?" he said, eager himself to hear the full story behind such an unbelievable twist to the day.

"I shall have to go back to the kitchen to bake more pasties," said Rosalee. "Sean – you stay with your family. Will you help me, Mamma?"

She followed her daughter into the downstairs kitchen. It was Saturday and the servants had been given the day off, so Rosalee had been using the opportunity to practice her kitchen skills. She had not anticipated the size of the order when she started out but, luckily, she had enough ingredients.

William always kept a few bottles of local Everard's ale in the house, together with wine for special occasions. Today qualified as such an occasion to beat all others, so he fetched enough for all.

Mary and Albert had escaped. They decided to go for a long walk, partly to allow the expanded Sercombe family to share their stories over the 'missing years' but, mostly, so they could have time to themselves. By now her father allowed her to do so without insisting that Florence acted as chaperone.

They took a quiet stroll along the canal towpath, down the hill and through the village. Albert filled her in on the detail of her brothers' miraculous survival as they enjoyed the relative peace of the early evening.

Back at the house, reunion celebrations were soon in full swing. It had been the best part of twenty years since William had seen his two sons, but the story they all wanted to hear was, *how come they had survived the English military when they were evicted, three or so years ago?* And *how did they find their family again after so long?*

Sean was the first with the questions. He was mystified. "I heard the shots, father. I thought the British had murdered you and Mammy. What happened? How did you get away?"

"It was the other way round, Sean," Frankie replied. "But let me start from the beginning."

He then went on to explain everything, from the time he and Billy had devised their plans, to the day their cottages were burnt down, and the time they boarded the train to Leicester earlier that day.

On the last get together that Frankie and Billy had spent at Ennis market they had hatched a plan. An escape plan. But it was much more than what he had asked Sean to carry out on that last day, more than just rescuing Rosalee.

Frankie and Billy knew that the evictions were inevitable. It was just a matter of time. The food riots in Ennis a few weeks earlier had made things much worse. It was just the excuse the English needed, triggering the order from the British government for troops to sweep down through the valley down to Kilrush, burning and killing as they went.

As soon as Billy knew the British were on their way to their cottage – mainly because he could see the road from Ennis to his village from three miles away, high up on the hillside above the

Fergus River – he would put their plan into action. He immediately called Rosalee, handing her the survival pack he had already prepared for her, and giving her instructions on how to link up with Sean at the stone circle.

There were several other cottages in their small hamlet. Before the troops reached theirs Billy had made sure that Rosalee was long gone. He could not even imagine her getting into the hands of the soldiers, most of whom had been conscripted for cash and were no more than mercenaries, with no discipline or respect for human life, let alone women.

But Billy wanted *some* revenge. He knew they would burn his cottage anyway and almost certainly kill both Maureen and himself if they surrendered. It was the usual mayhem when the soldiers arrived, total chaos with troops and villagers running everywhere, either shooting or being shot.

The platoon was usually split into teams of two, each pair of soldiers deployed to break down the front door of each cottage simultaneously on the order from their captain, before entering and killing anyone and everyone inside. A group of soldiers would remain on patrol in the centre of the hamlet, in readiness to despatch any villager who might manage to escape their cottage in the first foray.

But Billy planned to get in first. They already had an escape plan, in the shape of a sixteen hands cob gelding who could carry both himself and Maureen to safety. She would have him tacked up and ready in an outbuilding behind the cottage, out of sight. All he had to do was wait.

As soon as the troops kicked in the door Billy fired first, killing both soldiers. The look on their startled faces stayed with him for hours later. Revenge was sweet. He left them where they had fallen and set fire to the cottage himself.

Hopefully, it might disguise his crime, but in any case he didn't care. The troops waiting outside in the square would simply assume that the bodies of its occupants – but not of the two soldiers – would be burnt inside the cottage.

He had told Frankie to watch for the burning of his cottage - and those of his neighbours, which he could see clearly from the opposite side of the valley. That was his sign to be ready for the soldiers. Frankie would carry out an identical plan and wait for Billy and Maureen, linking up with them later.

It would take Billy and Maureen the best part of two hours to reach Frankie and Annie, but they could travel faster than the troops – even two up on the cob. They would ride to an agreed rendezvous just outside of Frankie's village, and wait.

After what seemed like much too long, Billy and Maureen finally saw the marauding soldiers approach Frankie and Annie's cottage. They remained out of sight hidden, waiting - watching from a safe distance as they saw the familiar pattern unfold. The soldiers were firing indiscriminately at anything and anyone that moved, friend or foe, ransacking everything they came across, continuing through the village, killing and burning as they went.

By that time, however, Frankie had pushed Sean out of the back door to head for the stone circle and wait for Rosalee. From there the two youngsters were to make their way across the water from Kilrush to Bristol - then on in search of their lost family in England.

Again, just like Billy had done at his own cottage an hour before, Frankie waited for the soldiers to force entry. He killed the two unfortunates brave enough – or foolish enough - to walk through the door. As expected, no more soldiers followed after them. Those shots, the ones from Frankie's pistol, were the shots that Sean had thought had killed his parents. Thank goodness he was wrong.

Frankie set fire to the cottage before he, his wife Annie, Declan, Seamus and Bridie, fled to meet up with his brother, Billy, and Maureen. Their logic had been to get Sean and Rosalee away and as far distant as possible, so they could make a fresh start. They saw no future in Ireland for their oldest children, but Declan, Seamus and Bridie were too young to fend for themselves.

Sean could look after himself and Frankie knew he was old enough to look after Rosalee too. It was a decision well made as he would prove them right. That said, the brothers kept their full plan a secret from Rosalee and Sean. Until now. They were worried in case they wouldn't do as they were told and make a clean break, but would try to stay with them instead.

Billy and Frankie shared the telling of the unbelievable story, aided at times by their wives if a point of detail should be left out. But there were still unanswered questions.

"So the English didn't come after you?" asked Sean. "For the murders of four of their men, I mean?"

"It was *so* chaotic nobody knew who was who and where they had to be. The troops just ran riot, so much so that they didn't even check on the safety of their *own* men. Any unaccounted for on the night were unlikely to be missed until pay-day. And they didn't *know* us."

With that, Frankie went on to tell them about the good fortune they found after their escape. This included life as a Romani and the kindnesses bestowed on them that helped them not only to survive, but to get their lives on track again. Quite literally.

Once Frankie, his brother and families were together, they had headed towards Cork. Maureen knew she had family there – her Romani family – who would take them in and protect them. That way they would be less visible than in a town or other village community. It was one important advantage of being part of Romani culture – looking after each other.

Thanks to the Romani men in the community, Frankie and Billy found work on the railways. It was more regular than seasonal work on the land and the pay was better. As in England, Ireland was expanding its rail network and needed labour – navigators who constructed the banks, built the bridges, excavated the tunnels, and laid the tracks – 'navvies' they were called.

"The work on the railways set us up well," said Frankie. "We earned good money, even enough so the kids could go to school. Maureen and Annie had new friends so it all worked out perfectly. They could tell that Billy and I were English, but they forgave us that transgression because Annie, Maureen and the children were Irish. They were happy times, but we never lost sight of needing to find you both again. We knew it would only be a temporary situation, until we could get across the Bristol Channel to start yet another new life.

"Within two years we had saved up enough to come back over. We weren't the only ones. We got on a ship to Bristol with a bunch of 'spalpeens' – that's seasonal workers to you. Even Declan got a year's work out of it before signing up on one of the merchant ships. He had always wanted to go to sea so we didn't stop him. At least he could look for a life better than the one we had in Ireland. Initially he was cabin boy on the food ships sailing from Ireland to Liverpool.

"As soon as we docked in Bristol our first thought was to try to find Dad down in Cornwall. Calstock. We took the train down to Exeter where we had to change trains for Tavistock. That's where we had a stroke of luck."

"What was that?" asked William. He was listening to every word. They all were.

William took over the story. "I wanted a newspaper so, while we were on the platform waiting for the Tavistock train, I bought the local newspaper."

"The Exmouth Journal," said Annie.

Frankie took up the story once more. "I could hardly believe it. There on the front page was a picture of Sean, dressed in a brand new suit and looking oh, so grand. Like a toff!"

"Then we realised what it was," said Annie. "It was an advertisement for a local shop at 10, The Parade, Exmouth: Morey & Son, Bespoke Tailor."

"As you can imagine, we were on the next connection to

Exmouth, arriving there inside the hour," Frankie continued. "That's when we found the shop – and Albert – and asked him about the whereabouts of Sean."

"What timing," broke in Sean. "Albert must have been on his way up here just a few days afterwards!"

"That's right, son," said his mother. "We left most of our luggage in Exeter, ready for the next leg of the journey – not to Tavistock, but here, to Leicester. With Albert."

"You didn't think to warn us?" asked William, a bit hurt.

"We wanted it to be a surprise, Dad," said Billy. "Sorry."

"It certainly was that," his Dad replied. It was more than a surprise, it was a dream come true.

"Dinner will be ready in half an hour," announced Rosalee. She had been busy in the kitchen during all the storytelling, but her mother had updated her in similar fashion, whilst she helped her prepare extra Cornish pasties for the new guests.

The meal was a joyous occasion with the pasties making it a real homecoming for the Sercombe families. Only Albert was disappointed that the pasties had the pastry crimped on the *side*, whereas he complained it should be on the *top*, in the way that Devonshire housewives finished them. But that was a minor blip, the main thing being that the whole family with the exception of Declan, were present. At least he was safe.

"Florence tells me Kate passed away a few years' back," said Frankie.

She was the second wife that William had lost to illness. His sons expressed their sorrow at their father's loss, even though Kate had been the core reason for the family fall-out. William reflected on his loss, but took a philosophical approach, given that the grieving process had been over a long time ago now.

"At least I have you two for comfort," he said. "My beloved Annie's boys."

Annie had been William Snr's first wife. It was only by coincidence that William Jnr's (Billy's) wife carried the same name, just as he carried his father's name.

After a long evening chatting over the missing years it was time to retire for some well-earned sleep.

"Albert," said William, "if you have no objection I will give you the servants' quarters for a couple of nights. As luck would have it they have two days off and are staying at the wife's mother's place in Northampton. They'll be back late Monday morning. I hope you'll be comfortable."

With that the families gradually dispersed to their own allocated rooms before preparing for the next day. It would be a busy Sunday. The visitors – *all* of them - were to be treated to a grand tour of Aylestone Meadows. William had already booked afternoon tea at the King's Lock Tea Rooms. Living where they were it was in walkable distance.

The day was fine and sunny, enabling the ladies to dress in their finery. Sunday was the busiest day at the Meadows, with the succession of trams bringing day-trippers out from the smoky depths of the city for a welcome day of fresher air and exercise in the countryside, and by the river.

The canal and river waterways were important commercial routes, bringing coal from the mines to fuel the new factories, together with raw materials and finished goods to and from markets all over the Midlands.

Situated in the Soar Valley the whole area was a flood plain with benefits as well as risks, but most of the existing residential houses were built on higher ground, in and around the village.

Whilst waterways provided a dual purpose of recreation and leisure for the city-dwelling factory workers, in terms of the needs of industry in recent years, the railway network had introduced fierce competition for the Grand Union Canal traffic. New railway lines carved their way over meadow and stream thanks to viaducts, as well as overcoming the obstacle of high ground with the navigation of tunnels and cuttings. But today, thoughts of commerce and industry could be forgotten. It was a welcome day of rest - for everyone.

The day out was planned by William days before his surprise visitors turned up from the dead. He already had a table booked in advance at King's Lock. It was going to be a new experience for them all, as well as an unexpected treat. As *was* expected, however, Albert and Mary made excuses to have more time on their own, but otherwise William basked in a full day with his family restored.

Surprisingly – or was it? - past differences were not only forgotten, they were not even mentioned. For years, the disagreement over William marrying so soon after his first wife's death had gnawed away at both parties. The longer the years of separation continued, the more they had each immersed themselves in careers and raising families.

For Billy and Frankie it was the loss of seeing their sisters grow up that ate away at them, as much as the guilt they carried at behaving so rashly. They had challenged their father during a period when, if they had realised, he was still coping with the grieving of their mother, Annie.

For William, of course, he blamed himself. Seeking what he thought would be happiness, salvaged from the embers of grief and loneliness, he had been blind to the effect his actions might have on his boys. So he hit out, only to regret it more and more as he grew older.

How many times had each of them dreamed of a reconciliation? It was countless, but they never gave up hope. Eviction from their farms in Ireland was a sad day for Frankie and Billy. They did not know it at the time, but it was a blessing in disguise, even if they had to flee their adopted country with blood on their hands.

Finally, their determination had paid off, with the look on their father's face as they were reunited worth all the pain and effort spent to get them home again. It was the end of one chapter and the beginning of another.

Life recently had been full of surprises, tragedies as well as pleasant ones, but nothing could have prepared them for the night ahead, or the events in store for them.

In some ways – at least for William - it turned out to be good fortune disguised as a tragedy. It was one of nature's 'hundred year events', that had last occurred in 1795.

Although they could not know it at the time, it would not occur again with such force and intensity until the next century - in 1986.

Chapter Twenty Two
Sean and Rosalee soon see why Hans is part of their lives.

In fact, *nobody* was prepared for what lay ahead, not on such a scale. It had been *so* calm the day before with a soft breeze, very little cloud, and not too hot for July. The storm that hit that night caught the whole city totally unawares.

It began with the deafening clap of thunder that awoke Sean and Rosalee shortly after two o'clock in the morning. His first thought, was "Hans!"

As luck would have it, the Dartmoor pony and William's trap was in the yard behind their house. Even so, as Sean approached the stall he could tell she was traumatised by the storm. But what of Hans? He was stabled a mile or so away in Glen Parva. He knew he had to get there as soon as he could to check on him. There was only one thing for it. He quickly gathered the harness, tacking up the mare, before getting the trap ready to take him down there.

"Where do you think *you're* going?" he asked, recognising the slim dark figure making it's way across the back yard to the stables.

"With you," shouted Rosalee, her voice had to compete with the thunder and howling wind that had suddenly sprung up.

"Get back in the house," he replied, perhaps too sharply.

"If you're seeing to Hans, then somebody has to look after the pony and trap while you do it. I'm coming with you."

He knew it was useless arguing with her and he had little time to waste trying. The rain continued to pelt down and he feared that the River Sence running through Blaby – just below where Hans was stabled – would be in full flood. He had to make sure it didn't rise too far and engulf the stable block where Hans was kept. The little Dartmoor mare had settled down now with the comfort of humans nearby, obediently responding as they snapped the reins urging her forward, themselves tightly clinging to the rails of the trap.

"Wait for me!" It was Frankie, hearing the commotion outside. His room overlooked the stables to the rear. Hurriedly getting dressed and rushing out to help, he leapt onto the cart behind the driver's seat, crouching under the force of the gale.

Further conversation was out of the question as the brave little Dartmoor forced her way against the fierce headwind, powering up the road from the village towards Glen Hills and then Glen Parva. As soon as they crested the hill overlooking the canal and the railway line beyond the River Sence, they could see they were in time. But only just, and as long as they could act quickly.

Hans' stables were just off a road – not much more than a small track - called New Bridge Road, named because it took you down to the 'new' Whetstone Lane Bridge. It had only taken them fifteen minutes, but just as well as they could visibly see the waters gradually rising from the swollen river, threatening the stables minute by minute. They started out along track towards the stables, then stopped.

The stables were still well above the water line but that wouldn't last long. Meanwhile, the track ahead was flooded with a powerful current surging downwards this time from where the canal higher up had breached. It was cutting them off – cutting off Hans, from safety. They could hear the stallion squealing in terror, frightened by the lightning and made mad by the almost continuous thunder overhead. The storm was right above them.

Ironically, were it not for the lightning they would barely be able to see anything in the darkness. That and the thunder together were incessant now, adding to the noise of the rain lashing down. It had reached a deafening pitch. The brave little Dartmoor cried out to the stallion. Hans responded by crashing his hind legs against the side of the stable in panic.

"I'm coming, Hans!" yelled Sean above the din. With that he launched himself into the torrent that had engulfed New Bridge Road, in an attempt to reach the stable, and Hans.

"Be careful, Sean," cried Rosalee.

But she was too late. The force of the water swept Sean sideways, and downwards, down into the field below, flooded by the breach to the banks of the River Sence. She saw his head momentarily rise above the surface of the water. Then he was gone. Rosalee was hysterical. Frankie had to hold onto her to prevent her following the same fate as Sean.

The stallion went berserk, sensing the danger to his master he thrashed away at the door to his stable with his hind hooves. Eventually the screws holding the metal catch gave in, pulled out from their housing The door burst open. Hans was free, knowing exactly what he had to do.

Well out of his depth, Sean was being swept across towards the railway bank, drawn in by the current and into to the heart of the river. For almost a quarter of a mile across all you could see was water. If Sean was dragged into the centre much further he would have been taken under the surface. The river was so deep, and the force of the current so strong it would suck him under. He rose once more, struggling to call out one last desperate time, "Rosalee! Dad!" and, finally - "Hans!"

His last cry struck the heart of the stallion as he crashed out of the stable, plunging fearlessly into the rising waters. With all his strength he ploughed into the flood, his hooves striking out frantically, swimming to where he had last heard his brave master's voice. There was another flash of lightning as Hans caught sight of his master's hand, barely surfacing the waters. Hans struck out again in one final effort, his strength gradually failing after so much physical effort.

But he wouldn't give up. He couldn't give up. Hans was suddenly empowered by an infusion of mental awareness and intelligence - as well as physical strength. He allowed himself to be taken by the current, down, round and *beyond* where he had last seen Sean's arm. It worked. He was treading water now. Waiting for Sean.

Driven by an instinct for survival.

Hans' massive bulk was sideways to the current, it's waters washing over him. But he kept his position steady, and himself afloat. All Sean could see on the last occasion that he surfaced was a dark shape ahead of him. It could have been a fallen tree, a feeding trough swept away - anything. Then he realised. It was *Hans*. Sean made one final push of his own body towards the faithful stallion. He reached out.

Hans responded immediately as he felt Sean grab his long mane. He raised his own head to pull his master further out of the water and, in so doing, lowered his back below the surface so that Sean could sit astride. He slumped forward over the stallion's neck, holding on for dear life as the Hanoverian warmblood made its way back towards the stable block.

Rosalee and Frankie watched the rescue in disbelief, still not ready to celebrate until they could see – as difficult as it was between flashes of lightning - that Hans and Sean were   safe, treading dry land instead of water.

Finally Hans emerged from the dark waters, triumphantly raising his solid seventeen hands stature high above the New Bridge Road, as his master remained barely conscious, draped across his neck. Just alive, safe, but so near to death.

Despite the darkness, punctuated less and less now by lightning from the receding storm, there was another light. Or rather, not so much a light as a glow. It was pulsatng from the forehead of the stallion, Hans. The glow had a shape, an outline – it was a clear mark. It was the sign of the rose, a signal from the stallion that his bond with his master had found further reason to serve. He had fulfilled his duty as guardian, in saving his life.

Frankie rushed forward to check that his son really *was* there, draped across the stallion's back. Was it something he had imagined? He *was* really alive, and he *hadn't* dreamt it?

"I thought I'd lost you again," cried Frankie, still beside himself with anguish, but at the same time finding relief wash over him. As Frankie cradled his son, Rosalee comforted Hans.

"Thank you, Hans," she said, crying into his mane out of sheer gratitude. "You've saved Sean, you've saved us all."

On releasing her hold of the stallion, Hans moved over to nuzzle Sean whilst still being held by Frankie. In all the excitement, the little Dartmoor and the trap had been left free and untethered, but she remained unmoved. She whinnied. It was as if she was seeking an answer, wanting to make sure that her new big brother, Hans, had survived unscathed. Hans walked over slowly to reassure the mare, nuzzling her neck.

Eventually, Sean regained full consciousness and was able to speak. "Rosalee," he murmured, "are you alright?"

"I'm here, Sean, so is Hans, Dad. We're all safe."

Hans was exhausted but calm once more, knowing that his master was safe. The glow, the sign of the rose on his forehead remained, but softer now. Still the storm continued but with lessening intensity that signalled the worst was over.

It was another half hour before the storm finally passed, by which time Sean had fully recovered his senses, but not his strength. Rosalee and Frankie left him to be alone with Hans. The bond bestowed upon them of companionship, loyalty and guardianship had grown stronger and much deeper. Sean owed Hans his life but, if the stallion could express himself, he would say that it was a fair trade - for the better life Sean had given him, after the cruelty he had suffered at the hands of the highwayman, Dan Chanter.

Soon they had all recovered enough to begin the journey home. The little Dartmoor had stayed patient throughout, but was more than ready to head for home – and breakfast. They were all soaking wet, with only the waterproof tarpaulin as shelter from the light wind that still prevailed. It was always kept in the cart, 'just in case', for any eventuality. But the storm had at least now passed and the rain abated.

By the time they emerged from New Bridge Road and turned west onto Leicester Road towards Aylestone, the dawn broke and a bright July sunrise bathed them in its warmth. They were travelling at little more than walking pace.

For one thing, Hans was so exhausted he could hardly raise his head to see the cart in front of him; for another, they wanted to relish in the sunlight and its warmth for as long as they could, allowing it to instil in them enough energy to ensure their arrival back home.

As for the rest of their family back at the house? When they returned they were all still fast asleep. They had not even missed them. It was as if nothing had happened.

Chapter Twenty Three
William Snr. turns misfortune into opportunity.

But what a story there *was* to tell! Frankie and Rosalee ordered Sean to go to bed immediately, for fear he might catch a chill after so long in the water. He was drained, emotionally and physically so, for the first time since Rosalee had known him, he obeyed without question.

She settled Hans in his stall behind the house whilst Frankie looked after the little Dartmoor pony. They made sure they both had clean, warm blankets, given the soaking they had endured, adding extra bedding for more warmth. Sean and Rosalee were also back in their room before anyone else in the household had even stirred.

Frankie crept quietly into his room, but inadvertently woke Annie as he returned to their bed. He explained briefly what had happened during the night but he, too, was exhausted. He slept until lunchtime. Annie also told the others to not let Sean and Rosalee be disturbed until they were ready to face the day.

It was at dinner that evening before they were all sat together, able to share the dramas of the previous night to an incredulous audience. They could hardly believe it themselves.

Given what had transpired, Albert delayed his return for a few days, taking a room at the local inn. There were reports of major disruptions to rail travel throughout the country – especially south to Exeter - mainly due to flooded track and even bridges swept away by the deluge. The Somerset Levels suffered particularly badly, leading to major dredging of the local rivers being necessary to the release the flood waters to the coastal outlets and estuaries.

Ironically, Albert managed to get a room at The Union Inn, located by the canal side just yards from the junction of Leicester Road with New Bridge Road, the scene of the previous night's near tragedy. The canal bank adjacent to the inn had luckily not been breached, and the inn was on higher ground, clear of the flooding caused by the River Sence.

"The stable block where Hans had been kept were still standing this afternoon," said Albert, returning from The Union Inn later that afternoon., "but the pasture below is still under water. It will be a few days before he can go back."

"As long as we have no more rain it will still take time for it to drain away fully, followed by another week before you can let horses and stock back on it. The ground will be saturated for a while."

William had been assessing the full effect of the storm. "I hear that the viaduct at Crow Mill has been swept away."

"That means they'll need somebody to rebuild it," chipped in Sean. His grandfather was impressed by his quick thinking.

"You're absolutely on the ball, Sean," William replied. "I've already sent enquiries to local brickworks to see what supply lead times are like."

"The existing structure was built in wood, wasn't it?"

"Right again, Sean. But the rebuild needs to be steel girders on brick foundations. That should make it strong enough to stand up to another storm, should that ever happen."

"Have you thought about the labour that's needed for such a project, grandfather?" Sean was keen to know.

"That will be your job, Sean, and where your Irish accent should come in useful."

"I'll put the word out," said Sean. Physically he was still very tired, but his mind was sharp.

"I know railway workers in Ireland that would be happy to come over," said Billy, joining in the conversation.

"That's right," said Frankie. "We know plenty of navvies skilled in building the railways from when we worked on the new lines near Cork."

"Looks like we have the tools for the job," concluded William.

"Let's have dinner now, then we can get together tomorrow morning and devise a plan of action."

But for now, they were all content to be together, safe and well. Nobody, apart from Frankie and Rosalee, knew how close they came to losing Sean, so they decided to keep that detail to the minimum. William, his two sons plus his grandson, were currently firmly focused on seeing how they could best benefit from the effects of the storm that nearly killed Sean.

The first priority for the morning was to check on the horses to make sure they were recovering from the ordeal of the previous day. It was clear from Hans' hindquarters that he had lost a bit of condition, which could be down to mental as much as physical stress. But it was less than might result from a day's hunting. Sean was confident that further rest and plenty of grooming would restore him back to full strength.

Both horses were kept in the stables behind the house for the time being. Sean would have to inspect the soundness of the foundations of the stable block on New Bridge Road before taking Hans back there. Not only that, he would have to be kept at the house whilst the fields were still flooded.

The ground would be at risk of being poached too much if horses were turned out on soft pasture. He would also have to postpone putting Hans to stud at The Quorn Hunt until the roads through Charnwood Forest were clear.

Soon after breakfast the men were assembled in the main living room and, led by William, ready to move forward on a proposal to bid for the repair of Crow Mill viaduct.

"I think the first thing I must do," said William." is to contact the Midland Railway to discuss the design of a new bridge. They have an office in the city, so I will go there first to find out who will be overseeing the rebuild. We need a contact."

"I would like to come with you on that, grandfather," said Sean," if only to observe."

"Good idea, Sean," replied William. "We have to establish the scale of the task. I think they'll go for a total redesign and rebuild, but using brick and iron to replace the wooden structures which, clearly, would be a longer term solution."

"That's what they've been using in Ireland," joined in Frankie. "Billy and me worked on the maintenance of the Kilnap Viaduct. It's an eight-arch railway viaduct over the valley of the Glennamought River. We had to inspect and repair the brickwork, so we know how they're built. Crow Mills will only be half that size."

"Splendid, son," replied William. "The ones I've seen in the Mechanical Institute library show metal girders resting on brick pillars. I imagine it will end up something like that. If they're of the same mind we can at least bid for the supply of materials and construction of the pillars."

It was a great start for the new 'team' with everyone in agreement and a different part to play. Sean would very much be the apprentice under his grandfather's wing. It would be good practical experience against the theory he would study in his engineering course at the Institute in a few weeks' time.

But the added bonus – and one that their father could not possibly have anticipated - was the availability of his two sons, Billy and Frankie, already experienced in the kind of project they were hoping to take on. Furthermore, there was every chance they could tap into a ready supply of Irish 'navvies' experienced in the actual construction of the brickwork.

After the meeting of the men, Sean went to catch up with Rosalee to keep her up to date with all that was being planned. Surrounded by aunts, she was now blessed with abundant female company – not to mention being reunited with her mother. It was just as well to have so many ladies in the house. The servants had been employed to cater for William and his family which, at the time, did not include his two sons.

The ladies took turns to help with meals as well as other housework, albeit on a temporary basis. In the meantime, the fact that there were so many branches in the family all under one roof did make life rather fun, if a little chaotic at times.

Sean was due to accompany his grandfather that afternoon on their exploratory visit to the Midland Railway offices in Leicester. Until then, he and Rosalee were free to pay full attention to Hans. After all he deserved it.

Hans stood quietly in his stall, pulling out and chewing hay from a hay net while they busied themselves grooming him. It would ensure he shone like a button but, once the floods had subsided, he had to be ready to travel to the Quorn Hunt for his stud duties and look his best. Immersed in pampering Hans, they hardly noticed Maureen joining them.

"I've brought you a cup of tea each," she said as she entered the stables. "I'll put them over here." She set the cups down.

"Come and say 'Hello' to Hans, Mamma," said Rosalee. "Isn't he handsome?"

She had to agree, but she was more conscious of the aura that surrounded him – visible to her, but not to Sean or her daughter. She moved slowly forward. Hans began to fidget slightly, becoming aware that Maureen knew his secret. Although Maureen was of Romani blood, for whom horses were a main part of their culture, she was normally more used to nothing larger than a Connemara pony.

"He's beautiful," she said, building up courage to stroke his strong neck and crest. Hans snorted softly in response as he relaxed, leaning into Maureen and urging her to continue, which she did for some time before breaking her silence.

"He has a special place in your lives," she continued at last. "It's a place devoted to you both. He recognises the depth of feeling and commitment you have for each other, and has become joined to your inner spirits."

She was speaking as a pure Romani now, using the mystical powers of insight with which she had been handed down from her own grandmother as a young girl. Sean and Rosalee moved closer together, automatically joining hands.

They had already discovered that it was possible to belong to someone before you had even met them.

"The critical point in all this came on the night of the storm," said Maureen. "It forced him to declare himself in his actions. His firm mission is now to keep you both safe, to be a guardian for you throughout your lives. His first real test came when you nearly drowned, Sean. He would have given up his own life to save you. Luckily, you both survived."

Hans' ears were pricked forward as if he were listening to her every word, understanding. Maureen continued with her prophecy. "You must keep him with you always and never be parted from him, or each other. He will look after you and, when it is his time to depart from this world, assuming that is before you, his spirit will remain with you, and in you, until it is your turn to die." She was looking at both of them as she spoke these final words.

Sean and Rosalee looked at each other, filled with a new understanding of why Hans had acted so courageously. Now it all made sense. It also explained their good fortune ever since they had left Ireland, where potential tragedy had been turned into opportunity. The shipwreck on the stormy crossing to England was one instance where they survived, and it placed them on the right road to finding their family, quite literally.

Most curious of all was that Hans 'came' upon them by accident and, again, out of a would-be crisis. He was instrumental in Sean saving the day. Then, as soon as Sean and Hans began their unique connection, good fortune smiled on them once more. The reward money, Sean's position in the Tavistock constabulary, finding his grandfather and then being reunited with his family – all appeared to be chance events, but they were pre-ordained, according to Maureen.

Rosalee was part of that – part of Sean's journey in every way from the moment she found him on that first night by the stone circle. Hans was there *for her*, too.

Her mother had one final pronouncement to make before she went back inside the house. "There is one promise you must make, a vow you must take when Hans eventually passes away and bestows the gift of his spirit on you."

"What's that?" they asked.

"As you leave this world you must pass on that same gift, the mantle of guardianship to another being – whether that be human or, as is the case with Hans, another animal."

"But who to?" asked Sean.

Maureen's answer was simple, but predictable. "When that time comes, you will know."

That afternoon Sean and his grandfather had caught the horse-drawn tram from the Aylestone terminus into Leicester city centre. The Midland Railway offices were in the Campbell Street Station, where they arrived after a five minute walk from the Clock Tower. They were greeted by a receptionist and asked for the Chief Engineer.

"I'm afraid he's out on a field survey until late this afternoon," she said, "but I can let you see his assistant. With that she led them to a small meeting room with a table and four chairs. In the centre they noticed a new device that, so far, they had only seen pictured in newspapers or The Army and Navy Store catalogue. The telephone.

The engineer's assistant, Wilkes, welcomed them cordially by offering them a cup of tea and biscuits. They accepted.

"I think I may have heard of you already, Mr Sercombe," he began, are you the one who patented that new modification of the Hoffman

Brick Kiln?"

"The very same," replied William. He was flattered. It was a good start and they got straight down to business.

"Here at Midland Railway we're always looking for better and cheaper ways to do things, much the same as you did. What do you feel you can do for us today?" he asked.

"I hope quite a bit," said William. "I've spent a lifetime in bricks and tiles. But for the past few years I've also specialised in construction – some residential, but also industrial. As you're the biggest railway company in Britain, I should imagine there are plenty of new branch lines in the pipeline."

"Yes, that's true," said Wilkes. "But most of them have already been put out to tender and contracted out. You're talking about a long time into the future."

"What about repairs and maintenance," said William," like the viaduct at Crow Mill?"

"You're certainly quick off the mark Mr Sercombe, I'll give you that. It only came down two days ago!"

"Thirty six hours ago to be precise," said William. "I've already conducted an initial survey of the general layout – this morning – and I could submit approximate costings in a week's time."

"I admire your speed, Mr Sercombe ..."

"... call me William. And this is Sean, by the way."

Wilkes paused, then continued. "I admire your speed – William - but what capacity do you have? Most of our regular construction companies are fully booked up for months – years even. So much so, there's a shortage of skilled labour."

"I have connections overseas," he said. "Skilled 'navvies' already used to working on railways in general, and brickwork in particular. Or, perhaps that should be the other way round." William laughed at his own joke and, thankfully, Wilkes joined in. "I can bring over special teams ready to start at short notice," he concluded.

"What about plans, specifications, stress levels, and load bearing.

Have you thought of that?" asked Wilkes.

"I've visited completed viaducts in the West Country, which is where I'm from. I'm confident that a combination of broad brick pillar structures topped with heavy grade steel is the way to go. Not only that, my two main foremen have worked on similar structures in Ireland, carrying out maintenance.

"It will last, which is more than could be said for the wooden structures that just collapsed."

"That all sounds wonderful," said Wilkes. "We want to get the line operational again as soon as possible. It serves as a major link between London and the Midlands, so every day lost is expensive. My only concern is the delay I think you will experience in getting materials – ironically, bricks."

"I've already thought of that..."

"... how surprising," broke in Wilkes, whimsically.

"... I have a couple of my new kiln designs coming on stream within the next two months," said William. "They're in Devon – in the Tamar Valley and just outside Exmouth where there's a plentiful supply of Brick-Earth for a nice red brick.

"I've also already contacted Ketley's in Staffordshire to place a provisional order for blue bricks. We'll need them for the foundations for their low water porosity.

"The dissembling of the existing remnants of the viaduct will take at least eight weeks – plus the excavation needed before we even lay one brick," he concluded.

"And the steels?"

"Again, if we can get quick approval of the plans, these can be manufactured – abroad if need be – whilst the under-build is being carried out." William was himself going at full speed now, his enthusiasm was infectious and clearly impressed Wilkes.

"You could have new track laid and be rolling stock over it inside a year – but I would suggest twenty months is more realistic, allowing for unforeseen hold-ups."

"I think I've heard enough," said Wilkes. William and Sean's hearts sank, "...but it's all good. I will report back to my boss, the Chief Engineer, to see what his reaction is. Meanwhile I would advise you to follow up on some of the practicalities related to materials supply – not to mention the labour you will need to employ – before our next meeting."

Sean was about to break in with a question, but William nudged him as a signal to keep quiet. '*To quit whilst they were ahead*' as William explained later. Wilkes had given him the go ahead in principal – on the assumption that the Chief Engineer would grant them a follow-up meeting. It was as much of a guarantee that they could dare expect this early on.

They shook hands with Wilkes, made their departure, and practically skipped along the street to catch the next tram home. Then his grandfather came up with a novel idea.

"That went *so* well, I think we should celebrate!"

"It's a bit early in the day for that, Granddad!" said Sean.

"No! Not the pub." said William. "Let's try that new coffee house on Church Gate. My treat."

So they did, making their way across town and sitting down in the cafe after a fifteen minute walk.

"I think Thomas Cook, the travel chap, is behind this idea," said William. "Coffee is quite the trend again now, what with Cook and other temperance campaigners trying to coax us away from the evil alcohol."

It was a pleasant interlude for them both, for Sean especially, before they caught the tram back home, and back to the family.

Chapter Twenty Four
Leicestershire proves a beautiful choice in so many ways.

Albert Morey was now a regular guest at mealtimes – which was fine and helped everybody to get used to him. By now It was quite obvious that he and Mary would become a permanent feature in the Sercombe family. Within a few days of the storm it was also evident that the disruptions to rail travel would soon be at an end. Soon Albert would be going home to Devonshire.

In all the disruption and excitement that had gone on ever since he arrived, together with the rediscovery of his soon-to-be in-laws, he had yet to accomplish what he had originally come for - to propose formally to Mary, after obtaining the blessing of William. This he did on the evening before he was due to take the train back to Exmouth.

Mary was thrilled, of course, as were all the whole family. They also agreed to have the wedding in Leicester and without too much delay – certainly within the next two years. Furthermore, after a lot of soul-searching and discussion, Albert decided to move up to Leicester. Albert's father, Henry was sorry to 'lose' him, but was able to employ a young apprentice 'cutter' as a replacement. Even so, Henry and his wife, Emma, would of course miss him when Albert relocated.

For her part, Mary would be central to making all the arrangements in the meantime – beginning with selecting a church and a venue for the reception afterwards. Both she and Florence were accomplished dressmakers so it was only natural that they would make her own wedding dress.

Her skills also extended to art, which she used to teach at the local school when they lived in Calstock, but she had a real feel for painting in watercolours. By late summer Sean had enrolled at the Mechanics Institute, where he found he had quite a gift for the technical drawing side.

Draughtsmanship was part of the course. He excelled in it, but he was most proficient on field trips where he had to visualise industrial structures in their natural setting, for presentation purposes. As it turned out, one of his first projects was to create an artist's representation of the new viaduct for Crow Mill. This he completed by drawing from plan, after which he made location studies at the site itself.

Mary assisted him in creating almost photographic effects by injecting watercolours into his illustrations. These became the final set of drawings for his grandfather William's presentation. It was the icing on the cake.

Together with a full schedule of costings and a staged construction plan, including the agreed investments from suppliers and other venture capitalists, he was able to deliver a powerful presentation.

It impressed the Chief Engineer and the Board of The Midland Railway so much, William walked out of the meeting room with a draft contract that very day.

Rosalee loved living with her aunts and was delighted when Mary asked her to help with the making of her wedding dress. She was to be Maid of Honour with Florence Chief Bridesmaid. Thanks to her artistic skills, Mary had even drawn her own designs so she could see what the final dresses would look like. She then transposed them into patterns.

It was a turning point for Rosalee who, although she had previously devoted her free time to cooking and confectionery, gained greater satisfaction from dressmaking. Mary and Florence proved to be excellent instructors, to such a level that Rosalee and Florence started a business from home, offering all aspects of making and mending to the locals.

Sean, too, was inspired by Mary's artwork, spending some of his spare time learning more of the basic techniques in painting as well as drawing. Much of his engineering work was produced as line drawings as well as diagrams. After a while, away from the technical drawing board, he ventured out into oil painting. It was how he relaxed.

But, leading up to that and before the work on the viaduct was to start proper, Sean and Rosalee explored as much of the local countryside as time allowed. It was the best summer they had enjoyed for a long time, and all the more because they had a large family around them.

The two brothers, wives and family, did move out after a couple of months – but only as far as two adjoining houses not far from the gas works in Aylestone. It was on the tram route and therefore convenient for the city, and for dropping down to see their father and family. Some weeks they were virtually daily visitors, working closely with William on preparing the groundwork for the viaduct rebuild.

It was just as well that they had their own houses – albeit rented – because an office had to be created downstairs at their father's as a centre for planning. William even invested in a telephone, which turned out to be essential for chasing up orders for materials, surveyor's reports, and constant contact with the railway company's Leicester office.

During that summer Sean had finally fulfilled his obligation to provide Hans' stud services to the Quorn Hunt. There had been a slight delay due to the Soar Valley flooding. Much of the countryside between Glen Parva and the Hunt Kennels was still soft and the water table remained high. For that reason, Sean decided to hire a horse-drawn horse box in which to transport Hans, rather than ride him. In turn, it seemed more sensible to stick to the main roads. Plus he could take Rosalee.

They started early to make the most of the cooler morning air, as much for their own comfort as the horses'. It worked out a little longer in distance so it took more like three hours this time, plus the fact they kept to a slow pace. They wanted to make sure Hans arrived looking his best and not over-heated. They also had the journey back to consider. On the first trip Sean had stayed overnight, and rested.

They were both sad to say their goodbyes to Hans as they turned away from the Quorn Hunt and home. Originally, it was planned for Sean to stay over for a few days to make sure Hans settled in without problems. But because the Field Master had an extra hand to oversee the pasture breeding programme, and the fact that Sean could now be contacted by telephone, it was decided his stay over was unnecessary.

Rosalee was disappointed not to have a 'mini holiday' in such a beautiful part of the county, so Sean made up for it by arranging a picnic on the way, in Swithland Woods. It was not even eleven o'clock when they started their return journey, plenty of time left in the day not to hurry. They could even take a diversion, perhaps to sit for a while by the reservoir.

" I know we've brought sandwiches," said Sean as they were passing The Griffin Hotel, "but I fancy a Ploughman's Lunch. Shall we stop here and treat ourselves?" Rosalee agreed.

It proved to be an excellent move. The hotel even brewed its own beer. Sean allowed himself two pints, whilst Rosalee matched him with their home-made ginger beer. Luckily there would be plenty of opportunities for comfort stops on the way back home.

"All this wealth, and wealthy gentry able to waste their time chasing a fox around the countryside," said Sean, "yet there are still local people barely able to feed themselves."

In the way through, on both trips, he had noticed how poor people were in many of the village cottages, their children virtually dressed in rags.

Occasionally, they would pass Romanies camped by the roadside. Living mainly off the land as they did and able to fend for themselves by gathering wild fruit, berries, as well as hunting the odd animal, they seemed relatively healthy, if not rich in comparison.

But for those without a regular wage life could be especially hard if any of the family were to be injured, or fall ill. Doctors were expensive and usually had to be paid with a brace of (poached) pheasant, or hare.

"It's a sharp contrast to those in the city," said Rosalee, "where some have even got unions looking after them in the factories. Others are able to pay a little each week out of their wages into insurance schemes, for when they cannot work."

"I still love it out here," said Sean, "as well as where we live in the countryside. I'd like to draw it, to capture what it's like out here, but also what life is like for those not so well off."

"You're good enough, I reckon," said Rosalee.

"I'm getting there, agreed Sean. "With Mary helping me, I can go out into the villages and draw the scenes in pencil first. Then I can go home and paint the scenes in oils."

"Colouring in?" she asked, mockingly. "Like the kids do at school?"

"You're not too old for a slap," he said. But she knew he didn't mean it. He paused. "...but you'll have to come with me."

"I should hope so, too," she said. "Otherwise, who knows what you'd get up to?"

After their lunch they travelled over to Swithland Reservoir, enjoying the sights and sounds around them, as well as the trees providing shade from the mid-day sun. They tethered the horses to graze by the water while they relaxed for an hour.

The Hunt had loaned Sean an old Hunter gelding so he still had a mode of transport until his beloved Hans returned to him in October. By that time all the mares would have been covered, or would be 'off the boil' as it were. 'Out of season' for breeding, but 'in season' for hunting. Some may have even been available for the pre-season 'cubbing'.

Having timed most of their journey for early morning or late afternoon, the cooler periods ensured that the horses were not too fatigued by the time they arrived home. Sean dropped Rosalee off at the house first, before returning the horse-drawn horse box. Then he rode the Hunter over to where he would be stabled – in Hans' vacant stall.

It was only a thirty minute walk home but Rosalee was already there waiting for him, with the little Dartmoor and trap and a ride home.

Love can be so easy some times.

Chapter Twenty Five
Sean develops his skills and makes his name.

And so the year unfolded. Sean found the technical and theoretical side of his studies challenging, but rewarding. His schooling so far – principally in Ireland – had been limited to learning from his mother and father, seated in practical matters rather than academic learning.

It was his grasp of the practical that William found most helpful 'in the field' during the early stages of rebuilding the viaduct. Alongside that, Sean still found opportunities to develop his natural instinct for combining his artistic abilities with the practical and technical needs of his course, more and more.

To develop his painting, Sean fitted in quite a few outdoor drawing sessions during the evenings while it was still light. These sketches he took home then, under Mary's guidance, proceeded to work them up into quite impressive studies. Although principally a water colourist, she showed him a range of techniques covering colour and design, which he was able to translate into oils.

Rosalee loved going with Sean on his sketching expeditions. He took his grandfather's pony and trap to transport his artist materials. *Adding Rosdalee to the 'baggage' was no bother*, he told her. This time it was *she* who threatened *him* with a slap, but only in jest.

"I'd like to take a trip down to The Baker's Arms in Blaby," he said. "Saturday would be good, around lunchtime. Then I can do studies of some of the locals."

"It's one of the oldest public houses in England, isn't it?" she said, more a statement rather than a question. "Apparently you can still take your bread there to be baked in their ovens. I'll prepare some of my pastries – and dough for bread."

Setting out soon after breakfast they were at The Baker's Arms by half past nine. Rosalee didn't want to be too late in case there was a queue for the ovens. Locals used to bake their bread for the week, for about a ha'penny, if they didn't have a suitable oven at home.

In the first hour or so, Sean was able to prepare a couple of sketches of the pub itself, *ready for the colouring in* as Rosalee had described it. By that time the locals began to turn up for their lunch-time session. With the permission of some of them, he was able to work up several portraits before they left for home. It was a signal for them to depart.

Rosalee had gone for a walk around the village, arriving back a little after three o'clock. Sean was ready to leave.

"I thought you'd got lost," he said.

"I did," she said. "Lost in thought."

"What...?"

"I met a lovely family of Romanies."

"Where was that?"

"Just round the corner – a half a mile away – in Mill Lane," she answered.

"So, how come you got lost?"

"Lost in thought," she corrected. "It took me back to when we spent that time with Mercy and Django."

"And now you're going to tell me you're related?"

"Could be," she said. "Their name's Ryan. The same as my Dad's. My real Dad's."

Sean had finished packing up his materials and was now checking the pony's harness. "Jump up," he said. "We're off."

"Can we take a *tiny* diversion via Mill Lane?" she asked. "I want to show you. We don't have to stop."

Sean agreed, turning the cart left as they emerged from the courtyard of the pub, along Wigston Lane and then left again down Mill Lane. A vardo was on the grass verge of the lane as they approached the Romani camp.

"Hello, Rosalee," called the children, waving as they rode slowly past. Their mother and grandmother waved too.

Rosalee waved back, as did Sean, breathing in the aroma of the cook-pot as they drew alongside. "Rabbit stew," sighed Sean. He also spotted two lurchers sleeping between the front wheels of the vardo. Reluctantly he urged the little Dartmoor on and towards The Ford, down the lane to the left again and over the River Sence. It would come out on the Wigston to Glen Parva road that carried them on to New Bridge Road.

The river had receded months ago to it's normal level but they could see the debris left stranded in the hedgerows after the flood. The watermark had crept up Mill Lane towards Blaby village, but not as far as the Romani camp.

As usual, the brook running through the centre of Sycamore Street, below Church Street and along the wall bordering Blaby Hall, had been under water, making the causeway unpassable. Soon they were at the cross-roads and The Union Inn where Albert had been staying. They crossed into New Bridge Road.

With another hunting season over, Hans was enjoying another 'holiday' with the mares at the Quorn Hunt. As before, Sean had a horse on loan so that he still had transport, even though he missed Hans enormously.

"We'd better check on the gelding," said Rosalee, "just to make sure he's OK." He was in Hans' stall. They checked his hay and water, leaving him a bucket of feed, then retraced their steps to the Leicester Road before turning for home.

In a few minutes they would be home, but there was still something bothering Sean.

"What did you talk about?" he asked. "When you spent however long it was with... the Ryans."

"The past. And the future.... and"

".... and?"

"Babies," said Rosalee. She said no more at first, hoping that Sean would open up the conversation to make the subject less hard going. "I wanted to know why we haven't had any." *There. She'd said it. Now what would he say?*

"So you've been talking to total strangers about our family matters?" asked Sean, rather annoyed.

"It's not like that," replied Rosalee. "But I just wanted somebody to talk to and sometimes it's best if they aren't friends or family. Then it doesn't get too personal."

Sean took her view without commenting on it, going on to ask, "So, who did you see and what did she say? I take it that it was a woman you saw."

"Yes. It was Grandmother Ryan. She said sometimes when you go through a lot of upset it can affect your ability to start a family. I explained all we'd been through in the last couple of years and the family history."

"Your own mother wasn't able to have any more children after you, was she?" He was beginning to understand.

"She said we have to be patient, try not to worry, and it will most likely just happen." said Rosalee, calmer now.

She placed her slim hand into his, as a token of reassurance, leaning into his shoulder. They were both glad, in a way, that the subject had been raised. It had been a worry – for them both. Sean had applied all his paternalism into training Hans during the period they had lived in Tavistock. In turn, Rosalee had been 'nesting' by making their humble cottage a warm and cosy place to bring up children.

Sean and Rosalee missed not having Hans with them so, before the second summer ended and days became shorter, while Hans was still at stud - they decided on a day out in Charnwood Forest. From there they were in reach of the kennels at the Quorn Hunt.

Sean had already taken up painting so he decided to take his materials. He could make sketches in advance of working them up into full oil canvases.

Eager to see the stallion again they drove the pony and trap straight there, arriving by ten o'clock that morning. Hans was pleased to see them, racing over the paddock where he had been turned out as soon as he heard Sean's whistle. In spite of his stud duties, he looked well and in good condition. The Hunt had kept their promise again to look after him well.

"Let me make a few sketches of him while he's in the paddock, with the mares in the background." Rosalee agreed.

Sean took his time, making sure he captured the beauty of *both* his subjects! He also took one of the Hunt buildings. By eleven thirty they were ready to head for Newtown Linford, where they would stop for a late lunch. He had made quick sketches, leaving his memory to fill in the detail.

"He looked well," said Rosalee as they headed back through the countryside. They were now aiming for The Bradgate, a local village inn where they could expect another excellent Ploughman's Lunch and a decent pint of ale for Sean.

"Let's hope he proves more fertile than we are," but he regretted it as soon as he'd said it. He squeezed her hand as an apology. "I'm sure Grandmother Ryan is right."

Seeing Hans had cheered them both up. They appreciated the good fortune that had already blessed them even though children was not one of them. They had their family back, which was the greatest blessing. That aside, they had money in the bank, a good home, and both of them were earning a living. To crown it all, it was a beautiful day.

But again, Sean was saddened by evidence along the way that not everyone prospered. He paused to sketch some of the more poignant examples of poverty, hunger, and poor health – sometimes a whole family would be living in no more than a crude shelter -

pitched in the farmer's field where they had managed to pick up a casual day's pay.

They have so many mouths to field on so little money, whereas we are rich in comparison but have no children, Rosalee mused. But she knew she had the love of Sean and, for now, that was all she really needed.

Thanks to further encouragement from Mary, Sean soon had quite a portfolio of art that he had produced in oils. He was even asked to take on private commissions after he had presented the Quorn Hunt with an impressive canvas depicting Hans, with the kennels in the background. The one he had drawn of Rosalee holding Hans was his personal favourite, which he kept for the family home.

He turned down portrait commissions, preferring more rural landscapes incorporating the country houses of the wealthy Leicestershire Hunting fraternity. However, it was the studies of the less affluent rural communities that caught the eye of a local Lord of the Manor, who offered to be his Patron.

If his Patron could get his work shown in exhibitions, that would fulfil his main motivation for concentrating on village life – getting the message out to a wider world about the deprivation that existed within rural communities.

The first institute to support him was Leicester Museum. It had a special section devoted to art, and local artists in particular. Located in the city at the top of The New Walk, it was the perfect outlet for informing residents of the city, as well as visitors to it, of the unfortunate lives of those living within an otherwise prospering and growing city.

Within the short space of less than two years, Sean built up quite a reputation as an important new talent within the art world. It also meant that he had to socialise, meeting people from different backgrounds and levels of society – including those with wealth and rank way above his own. Adaptability had always been his strength but, in the main, he let his talent do the talking, whereas Rosalee found it easy to impress by just to staying beautiful.

"It's ironic, really," said Rosalee one day after they had returned home from one of his exhibitions in Nottingham. "You start out as an engineer, then discover you have more of an artistic than a mathematical or scientific gift. You put Hans out to stud at the local Hunt, then you discover more demand for your landscape painting than for Hans' services."

"Yes," he agreed. "We start out on one path and then find ourselves travelling down a totally different road."

"We even sailed out from Ireland bound for Bristol, then a storm blew us off course and we never got there!" laughed Rosalee, suddenly realising that they had never achieved fully all that they had set out to do.

But there was still one ambition that continued to escape them – to start a family. Was that another course upon which they would embark, yet end up in a totally different place?

Based on their journey so far, that was highly likely.

Chapter Twenty Six
Sean's new-found fame attracts unwanted attention.

Frankie and Billy brought over twenty men from Ireland to work on the demolition of the existing Crow Mills Viaduct. They were joined by thirty or so local labourers to take down the final remnants that nature had been unable to destroy completely. Even so, it was a mammoth task. Although the wooden structure had failed to withstand the recent 'storm of the century', it was made up of stout lumber, requiring some twenty or so men to move some of the cross-members.

It took over a month to clear the site, after which the work of the true 'navvies' could begin. For that, the brothers needed skilled workers – including bricklayers and masonry workers. Another forty experienced craftsmen were employed for that work, to build the pillars necessary to support the iron girders forming a rigid base on which, finally, the tracks were to be laid. Many more of those were 'imported' from Ireland.

William had now employed a senior civil engineer as his second-in-command, leaving Sean to learn on the job under an experienced, qualified professional. Sean also continued with his studies at the Mechanical Institute. To say that he had a busy life would be an understatement so, on the few days he had spare to follow his 'other career' as an artist, he made sure Rosalee joined him.

Going forward, Hans was put out to stud when it suited Sean, and well below what Hans was capable of – partly because he proved to be perfect transport when he was needed on site at Crow Mills. The other reason was that he loved the company of the Hanoverian. When he was not riding him, or engaged in his painting or studies, he spent restful evenings grooming the stallion out at New Bridge Road.

Sean and Rosalee soon adapted well to their new social life beyond the family. This came about by way of his Patron, the then incumbent Lord of the Manor, Sir Clive. Sean's canvases were selling well and there was a constant demand for more, which Sean soon found difficult to deliver. But he was also needed for personal appearances as a celebrity on the 'circuit' of exhibitions and galleries in which his work featured.

That involved the presence of Rosalee as well. She enjoyed the new life, but only up to a point. Moreover, Sean was less happy about the attention she was getting from young would-be suitors. Although they were otherwise happily married it did make him feel uneasy at times. Jealous.

It was something, Rosalee had said, referring to the attention she was receiving, *that he would just have to get used to.* But it still gnawed away at him so he decided to do something about it. Whenever he could he asked Florence to go along as chaperone when Sean could not be at her side!

It worked to an extent until a certain suitor came along – not for Rosalee – but with an eye for his unspoken-for aunt. Rosalee would be on her own again when Sean was not around. Aunt Florence would have better things to attend to.

Florence had caught the eye of Ernest Millhouse, a fellow student of Sean's at The Mechanical Institute, but in a different discipline, mechanical engineering. Ernest's other fascination apart from Florence was the relatively new invention – the motor car. Meanwhile, he continued as a grocer's assistant during the day, leaving him free to attend night school – as well as to 'court' Florence. It was at one of Sean's exhibitions that he was introduced to Florence.

Rosalee was, of course, pleased that Florence had at last found romance but, on the other hand, she would lose a companion and protector at these events. It was inevitable at some stage but they had come to value each other's friendship more now that Mary had left for Exmouth. Although Florence was technically her aunt, there was only a small age difference between them. They were more like sisters.

Thankfully, Rosalee still had her other aunt – Annie, the wife of her uncle Frankie – as well as her mother, as her sole confident. But that was also about to change.

It was the postmark on the letter – 'Tavistock' – that first stirred their curiosity. *Who was left who they still knew in Tavistock?* No-one, as far as they were aware.

But they were wrong. The opening to Maureen's letter – for it was addressed to 'Maureen Sercombe' - at William's address – gave them a clue. The letter started: *My Dearest Sister –*

It was from Mercy! She went on to say that she had found the advertisement featuring Sean 'in his new suit' in the Tavistock Gazette. That led them to Morey's tailor shop, who then gave them William's address in Aylestone.

Maureen could hardly read the rest of the letter through her tears, but it turned out that she and Django were planning to visit. She couldn't make out whether Mercy wanted to come to live permanently in Leicester, or whether it was just to see her, but apparently her two boys, James and Jarvis, 'had found themselves wives' (at last!) and they had no real reason to stay in Devon any more.

It all sounded rather drastic to Maureen, but she was delighted at the prospect of being reunited with her sister – who she hadn't seen since she was a girl, and who she had only just found out was still alive! She wrote back immediately – 'c/o Tavistock Post Office' – inviting her up straight away, and giving her new address.

Rosalee was delighted too, and eager to see her aunt Mercy once again. Although the sisters – Maureen and Mercy – had inherited some Romani powers of perception and intuition, it was Mercy to whom she was keen to turn, to ask her about their fertility. It was something with which she was less comfortable talking about to her own mother.

The letter that came the next day – but not from Mercy - was less welcome. It was an invitation. Sir Clive had invited Sean to an evening dinner at Blaby Hall, principally to meet one of the governors of The National Gallery in London. He could hardly refuse. It was through such high contacts that Sean was going to develop his reputation further.

His paintings commissioned by local landowners were providing him with a decent income, but it was for his collection of social studies – for which he retained ownership – that he wished to build a reputation.

Rosalee dreaded going. She feared – almost knew for sure – that a certain acquaintance of Sir Clive, the French Count Bonnier, was most likely to be there. They had been officially introduced at an earlier function organised for Sean. Rosalee remembered that she had already seen him, and where.

His was the face of the Frenchman she had seen arguing with Ben Chanter on that very first day of her honeymoon, as they were driving through Archer Place. Since that very first introduction more than two years later, Bonnier would not leave her alone. He had become infatuated and, even though it was quite understandable in a way, the fact that she was already *very* married, did not seem to register with him.

"I can't very well say 'no'," said Sean, apologetically. "Sir Clive has gone to great lengths to arrange this for my benefit, and it could be an important step forward."

"I know," she replied, still irritated, "but I cannot rely on Florence to protect me."

"It won't be like other times," said Sean. "It's only a small dinner – no more than a dozen at most, so he can't get up to any funny business. And, if he does..."

"...you mustn't make a scene. It will ruin things for you," she replied. "Just don't leave me alone with him."

"I won't, I promise," he said. "I won't leave your side." But sometimes uncontrollable events take over.

The evening started without incident, apart from the Count continually staring across the dinner table at Rosalee. It sent shivers down her but she did her best to ignore him, as did Sean.

"So you're the celebrated Sercombe Lee-Ryan?" said the governor, introducing himself. "I'm Percival Fitzpatrick. So pleased to make your acquaintance. And this must be your lovely wife I've heard so much about."

"Yes. Rosalee." replied Sean, but not appreciating his last remark. *Here we go*, he thought.

"The *lovely* Rosalee," chipped in Bonnier, lurking in the background. Sean's hair bristled on the back of his neck. He controlled himself, but only just. Rosalee grasped his hand.

"Charmed, I'm sure," responded the governor – to Rosalee, not to Bonnier.

They sat down for dinner. Thankfully Rosalee was placed away from the Count, but in his direct eyeline. She was now skilled at making small talk with the wives of other guests so, for now, she was able to relax. But, with the dinner over, and the brandy and cigars offered, the order of things changed.

The ladies were left to take coffee whilst the men repaired into the billiard room. Rosalee took the opportunity to visit the ladies room. Without thinking, she did this alone.

Sir Clive had a side room displaying a collection of Sean's rural studies. He had left the others chatting in the billiard room, now directing the governor and Sean through to discuss his paintings. It was twenty minutes before they rejoined the main party. Sean noticed that the Bonnier was missing.

Suddenly the door to the billiard room burst open. It was

Rosalee, clearly in distress and making adjustments to her clothing. "Sean, we're leaving," she said through her tears.

"What...?" What happened?" he spluttered, moving across the room to comfort her.

"It's that *monster!*" she burst out, as 'the monster' she had been referring to – the Count Bonnier – walked back in, sheepishly, smirking. Sean was in no doubt what to do.

Smack! It was the sound of Sean's fist connecting with the Count's jaw, just below his left eye. Bonnier went down. He was still conscious, but bleeding and complaining.

"You shtupid Eeengleesh idiot!" he squalled. "Chanter was right. You're an imbecile who doesn't know his place."

"*Chanter?* What's he got to do with it?" Sean screamed. Then he remembered. It all came out after the trial of the highwayman back in Tavistock, where Dan Chanter's brother – Ben - had arranged his escape.

His plan would have been to board a schooner waiting for him in Plymouth. It was to take him to France. The ship must have belonged to Count Bonnier. *That* was the connection.

Luckily Sean stayed alert – not trusting the Frenchman one bit. He sprang forward once more as he saw Bonnier reach inside his waistcoat pocket. He had a Derringer! Bonnier raised his hand, holding the small pistol and cocked ready to fire. Instinctively Sean launch his right boot, catching Bonnier on the wrist, sending the gun flying across the billiard room floor. But it didn't end there.

Before the Count could recover his composure, Sean was on him again. Reaching forward he grabbed the Frenchman by the cravat – even though he was aiming for his throat – lifting Bonnier force-ably so that he was almost on his feet. Sean drew back his fist once more, this time hitting him squarely between the eyes. The Count's nose split like an orange, bleeding profusely all over the expensive Axminster carpet. Luckily it was already a claret pattern.

"Give Chanter *that* message from *me*," said Sean. Then, to his

Patron, "We're leaving. Send him the bill for the carpet." With that, Sean and Rosalee strode towards the main doors to the drive adding, "Sorry, M'Lord," were his final words, "but you need to choose your friends a bit more carefully."

They were elated. It was something that Sean wanted to do – had needed to do – for so long. Rosalee could hardly contain her relief. She flung her arms around her Sean – her hero – and kissed him until her lungs were bursting. "I'm not sure about you, Rosalee," he said, "but I could do with a drink."

They walked – no skipped - down the Blaby Hall driveway, through the jitty running between the rectory and the school, to The Bakers Arms. It was there that Frankie and Billy were waiting. They promised to meet them with the pony and trap to give them a lift home – even though they were both dressed in their finery and over-dressed for a village pub.

"How did it go?" asked Billy as soon as they walked into the main bar.

"You could say it was a thumping success!" laughed Rosalee, turning to Sean.

"She's right," replied Sean. "But we left as soon as the Count was out for the count!" He had to explain both remarks fully before Billy and Frankie could join them in the joke.

"Pints all round," called Sean," and a glass of ruby port for my good lady, please!" It was time for celebration.

But he was still a little concerned that he had been traced by Ben Chanter all the way from Devon. He was no doubt out for revenge after Sean had captured his brother Dan not once, but twice, sending him to a life of hard labour in Dartmoor Prison. *But where was Ben Chanter now?*

Clearly the Count was out to make trouble, encouraged by or even commissioned by Chanter to do Sean harm, directly or indirectly through Rosalee. He didn't seem to mind which.

Perhaps they *should* be on their guard against more dangers that lay ahead. He kept his thoughts to himself as he didn't want to spoil the evening, let alone alarm Rosalee.

And if Chanter was behind it all, and had come *this* far to trace Sean, it seemed logical that he would certainly not leave things as they were, with Sean triumphant yet again.

Chapter Twenty Seven
Sometimes, ill-fortune seeks out even the most virtuous

It had been an unexpectedly boisterous night for Rosalee and Sean, drinking with their fathers for the first time ever, strictly on their own and away from the rest of the family.

Sean recounted again all that had happened over dinner in Blaby Hall that evening. They filled in the events with more detail of the episodes with the Chanter brothers – first the salvage of the good ship Ennis involving Ben and then, later, their encounter with Dan Chanter holding them at gunpoint on the road to Tavistock.

But Sean was still quite concerned that Rosalee had been drawn into the danger now, with the apparent attack on her just hours before by the French Count. It was after they had arrived home from The Bakers Arms and were getting ready for bed that he turned to question her again, this time with a more serious expression on his face.

"He didn't *hurt* you, did he?" asked Sean, as gently as he could. She knew what he meant by 'hurt'.

"No. It was nothing," she answered.

"But you must have been gone a long time whilst I was with the governor. *Anything* could have happened."

"Nothing *did*, Sean," she insisted.

"But I saw how you were adjusting your cloths. And how upset you were. Is there something you're not telling me?"

"I said nothing happened. *Nothing!*"

"So he didn't...?"

"No! Nothing *like* that. Now can we *not* talk about it? I'm tired." With that the conversation ended, but he was still riddled with doubt that she wasn't telling him everything.

And so he let the matter drop, for the time being at least. He was just happy she was safe and appeared to have recovered from the incident. There was a small reference to 'a potential international incident' in the *Tatler and Bystander*, but there was no mention at in any of the newspapers, either locally in *The Leicester Daily Mercury*, or nationally. It was something that, if he truly had nothing to worry about, was best left to fade into a distant memory.

That he managed to do, forgetting the whole affair until Rosalee had a surprise announcement for him.

"I'm pregnant," she said. "I saw the doctor today."

Sean was grooming Hans in his stable on New Bridge Road. It was early evening and she knew he would be at his calmest. It was the right time to give him the shock news.

"That's.....wonderful!" he whispered, kissing her and holding her so close she could hardly breathe.

"Careful," she laughed. "I said 'I'm going to have a baby'. You'll crush me – us!"

"How long have you...?"

"... I'm about six weeks," she replied.

Sean pondered for a while, carrying on with his grooming. Secretly, he was trying to work out how long it had been since the upset with the Count at Blaby Hall. It was two months ago. It started to niggle him again, a renewed sense of doubt creeping in as he went through the events of the evening yet again in his mind. *Was the baby really his?*

Rosalee joined him in the grooming with a curry comb, working the opposite flank to Sean. "You need to look after yourself from now on," he said, softly. "I thought you were looking a bit tubby."

"You're not too old..." she began.

"... for a slap. I know," he finished. They carried on in silence. Rosalee could almost hear Sean's brain working but she said nothing. She knew what he was thinking but what *more* could she do to reassure him, to prove to him once and for all that the baby could *only* be his?

Later that evening they told the family the good news - William first, followed by Florence. Then they took the pony and trap down to the cottages where Frankie, Billy and their families lived. Rosalee smiled inwardly as she noticed how carefully Sean helped her on and off the trap at either end of the journey, wondering *How long will it last?*

"I must let Mercy know," said Maureen as they were leaving for home. "It may be just the excuse she needs to come and visit. She's been putting off coming up for some reason."

Sean and Rosalee reflected on the last time they had seen Mercy and Django – when Mercy gave them the palm reading and her predictions. In a way they were pretty much accurate, certainly in so far as they had remained together then married, and were now about to start a family. Under the guardianship of Hans they were destined to be bound to each other for the rest of their lives.

Their news was received by an equally delighted Mercy and Django, but they would not be able to make the trip until later that year. By that time Rosalee would be just a few weeks from the full term of her pregnancy. On the plus side, the completion of the Crow Mills viaduct was in its final stages. William was already working on something new - negotiating the building of whole terraces of new houses in Aylestone, but closer to Leicester.

If all went to plan, by the time Mercy and Django were due to arrive, the grand reopening of the main line from the North Midlands to Rugby and beyond would have taken place. The immediate pressure would be off William, Sean, Frankie and Billy. They would then be in a much better position to welcome guests.

They had arranged to stay with Mercy's sister's, Maureen and Billy, in their cottage. Django was looking forward to the visit for other reasons. He had heard so much about the annual horse fair in Mountsorrel. Along with fairs at Stow and Appleby it was a major event on the Romani calendar. All things considered it was the perfect time for a visit, to be reunited with a 'lost' relative, and to relax among Romanies at one of their most traditional events.

At last the day came and the sisters were reunited for the first time since they were sixteen years old - it was twenty years since they had been together. The following day they went to see Sean and Rosalee at the main house.

For William it was their first meeting. He and Django greeted each other cordially before William led them into the lounge for drinks and a light tea. But Rosalee had other ideas.

"You must come to see Hans," said Rosalee, taking her aunt Mercy by the hand. *Where's Hans?* she thought. The stallion was in the stable behind the house as luck would have it.

Mercy entered the stable and moved quietly round Hans. He was calm, relaxed, but clearly attentive towards this new visitor. But as soon as he sensed the powers possessed by the Romani seer, he changed, responding to her every touch.

Hans flinched slightly as Mercy brushed his flanks with her fingers – first one side, then the other. She moved away, then blew gently through her own nose and into the nostrils of Hans. Rosalee, Sean, and now Django looked on, intrigued by Mercy's interaction with the horse.

"I can sense that he looks out for you as much as you two look after him," she said, stepping back to give Django the chance to get to know the stallion. Mercy could see how the part that Hans played in the lives of Sean and Rosalee was just as she had foreseen.

"His scars. The ones Chanter made with his cruel spurs. They're gone!" said Sean. Rosalee checked both flanks of Hans, confirming the same on the other side.

"No sign on either," she said. "What did you do, auntie?"

"It was just a cleansing," she replied. "He still held some memories of being poorly treated by his previous master. My blessing will cure any physical, as well as mental, scars."

Django said his final goodbye to Hans before they returned to the house where William and Florence already had drinks prepared. But as he left he remained mystified at the notion that the 'star' –

the sign of the rose in the centre of Hans' forehead – was glowing softly. *Or did he imagine it?*

Ernest was at the house too, having called on Florence. Django and Mercy planned to stay for the rest of the week. Their own boys, James and Jarvis, had remained behind in the West Country to look after the vardo as well as the two long-dogs, Jake and River.

William had already found Romani company especially pleasant and rewarding, having gained faith in the immigrant navvies that his own boys had conscripted from Ireland, to work on the viaduct. They were good workers, and honest. Django and Mercy appeared to be no exception. He made an open offer for James and Jarvis to apply for work on any of his future projects and contracts.

After his guided tour, Django was certainly impressed by the finished viaduct, which William had been proud to show off at the earliest opportunity. His work was not only very important as a commendable piece of engineering, it also restored enormous benefits to the local economy. It was much more significant than just repairing the rail link for travel.

Starting first from Derby and/or Nottingham, then through Leicester and on to Rugby, it was a main line to central London and beyond. On changing stations in the capital, a 'Boat Train' would then take French-bound passengers to the south coast where they would get off at Dover. Once through customs they would board the cross-channel ferry, re-embarking for a final train to central Paris.

William's rebuilding of the stricken bridge not only ensured that the wheels of Midlands' commerce began turning once more, but it made continental travel a possibility again. The viaduct design, lifted from similar engineering projects that show-cased the enterprise necessary for the ever-expanding rail system, was a thing of beauty to some eyes. It attracted sightseers from quite a wide area. Tickets for day-trippers to actually cross the viaduct often sold out.

On a technical note, blue bricks formed the base tiers of brickwork – bought in from Staffordshire, whereas William's own-designed and modified Hoffman kilns delivered the red bricks from Devonshire. The cast iron girders were brought in from factories in Doncaster and Scunthorpe, all transported by rail, of course.

That was one of the strange ironies – almost contradictions in purpose surrounding the rebuilding. It was the recent flooding from the soon-to-be-redundant waterways that had caused the destruction to the railway network. Was it a statement? Retaliation? It was almost as if the canal system was hitting back at the rail network that was threatening it.

The double irony was that the same Irish 'navvies' who had been recruited in their thousands to complete the canal system, just a decade or so earlier, also built the railways. Not only that, they used the same principles of cutting through the countryside regardless of obstacles – hence the slang name for a canal as 'the cut'.

But the main differences were the effects on surrounding landscapes and substantial commercial benefits.

The railways were fast, efficient, and more cost-effective – but they created more noise and increased disruption to their surroundings. In contrast, the canal system nurtured and *added* to the natural environment.

Those were Django's initial thoughts as he witnessed the rich pastures and beauty of the nearby farmlands, during the temporary suspension of the rail system. He bathed in the quiet and peace of a Leicestershire rural pace that had been like his beloved, adopted Devonshire, a mere twenty years or so previously.

For the time leading up to the reconstruction, at least, the call of the pheasant or corncrake, the flight of the merlin hunting just a yard or so above ground level, the well-worn paths of the badger – so far unchanged for centuries, and the baying of the milk-laden cows in late afternoon before milking – all these sights, sounds and smells had returned, unhindered by the relentless progress of industry. Those thoughts, those re-imaginings, invaded Django's consciousness as they neared the site where William's planning and engineering brilliance were on display.

Passing over the old canal bridge, William's words brought Django back to the present.

"It's built to last centuries, unlike the wooden structure that was washed away in the floods," declared William as soon as he and Django arrived at Crow Mill. It was true, but he would have been mortified had he known that, by a stroke of a Conservative politician's pen, it too would be rendered redundant and demolished in the 1960's! He would realise that nothing is scared, nothing is forever.

Mercy had no interest in engineering or railways. However, even though she led a simple life in the countryside, and away from sophisticated city life, she had always remained creative, with a reputation locally as a skilled seamstress. It was how she earned a living at market in and around the Devon and Cornwall towns where they lived. Whilst she was visiting she was keen to see the fashions about which she had heard so much from her sister.

Grasping a golden opportunity, they arranged a special trip to Leicester city centre – 'they' being Rosalee, Mercy and Maureen, Florence, and Frankie's wife, Annie. They took the tram, which Rosalee and Florence caught first from the Aylestone terminus before picking up the other three ladies on the way through to The Clock Tower.

The main reason for the whole expedition, however, was to treat Rosalee – or rather her new baby – to new clothes, even without knowing whether it might be a boy or a girl. Coupled with that, everyone was excited by the expansion of the new knitwear company, Corah's, and eager to seek out local shops where their latest fashions were on display.

And if that wasn't enough, coffee shops had recently opened up as a new social trend and as an alternative to pubs and other non-temperance hostels. They were perfect places for genteel ladies to relax in after a hard day's shopping.

Leicester was by that time considered the second richest city in Europe. Mercy was so overcome by such a level of sophistication and prosperity compared with rural Devon. Maureen, on the other hand, during the short time she was there, had adapted to a new style of living very well.

But by mid-afternoon Rosalee was feeling tired and ready to catch the next tram home. She was physically fatigued, being so far into her pregnancy, as well as finding the job of keeping up with the constant chatter of her aunts quite exhausting. The Clock Tower was only a short walk away, so she made her own way there to catch the next tram home.

"Aylestone Terminus!" called the tram driver, waking her up from her doze. She had slept nearly all the way and had been dreaming. She had dreamt that the baby had been born – it was a girl after all, just as Sean was hoping, *so she could grow up as pretty as she was*, he had said. They were on a picnic by the River Sence, just up from where The Ford crossed it on Mill Lane in Blaby.

It was just herself and Sean – and Hans, grazing nearby. The warm afternoon sun shone down on them from a cloudless blue sky. Suddenly it became dark. A jet black bird – it must have been a raven – blotted out the sun as it swooped down upon them. "Terminated!" it shrieked, talons stretched out in front of it, ready to strike – ready to steal her baby.

With that, Rosalee had woken up, suddenly realising where she was. The fear that came over her during the dream stayed.

Still in a partial daze she arose from her seat, walked down the aisle between the rows of seats, carefully clinging onto the metal safety rail as she stepped from the tram to the road. A hand reached out to help. She took it without thinking.

"Allow me," said the owner of the hand, but his face was dark and shaded by the afternoon sun as it crept over his shoulder from behind. All she could see was a dark shadow.

"Thank you," she said, before she could pull away. The touch was cold, clammy and gripping her so tightly she was unable to let go of its grasp. Then, as she turned, the sunlight caught the side of the stranger's face. It was a profile she knew, the one recalled from the first day of her honeymoon in Plymouth. It was the unmistakable face of Ben Chanter.

"You!" she shuddered. But the tram had now already pulled away, leaving her stranded and in the merciless hold of the dark figure. It was Chanter sure enough, Ben Chanter and brother of the highwayman Sean had helped put away in Dartmoor prison.

Of course, she thought, *it all makes sense now. He was a friend to the Count, and the one who vowed his revenge on Sean.* Count Bonnier and Ben Chanter both had a score to settle with Sean, but it was Rosalee who was going to pay.

She tried to scream. It was useless. She was still in a daze, half awake, half in the dream she was immersed in just minutes earlier. She tried to escape but Chanter was too quick for her. She breathed in a sharp, pungent smell as one hand covered her mouth and nose whilst the other encircled her now swollen waist, pulling her to him.

She couldn't move let alone resist. Her last recollection was of being forcibly lifted into an awaiting coach and pair. She lost conscious. The hand over her mouth held a cloth – a cloth laced in chloroform.

She had no idea how long the coach journey lasted as she drifted in and out of awareness of where she was. She had no strength to fight against the grip of her captor, her will was broken, her vision blurred.

After a while she felt herself being helped down the steps of the coach before returning to the vice-like hold of Chanter. She heard voices in the background, but could not tell what they were saying.

Then there was the sound of clattering horses hooves as the coach pulled away. But where were they?

She was looking for a sign, a clue as to their location and only when she heard the unmistakable shrill sound of the guard's whistle did she know they were at a railway station. But which one?

Her vision cleared for a moment and she saw the sign – literally. It read 'Wigston'. Soon this was followed by another sound – the rush of steam and steady pulsating rhythm of the wheels of the train, seeking to grip the slippery track. She lapsed into unconscious once more.

Some time later – she had no idea how long - she awoke with a jolt, finding herself sprawled across the seat of a railway carriage. She lurched forward as the train pulled away, gradually forcing her eyes open. It wasn't a dream after all.

On the seat opposite sat Chanter, peering nervously out of the compartment window as if expecting something, or someone. He was checking to see if they were being followed.

"What...? Where...? she murmured, still groggy from the drug he had administered.

"Well now, my pretty," he replied. "You're on your way on a new adventure. To Paris, and a new life – for both of you it looks like." Her condition had not escaped him.

She looked around her then sat up, rocking with the gentle movement of the train as it picked up speed. She was in a railway carriage, but they were alone. Just the two of them. There was no corridor. It was a self-contained compartment with doors on either side – the only ways out. Each would open onto a platform or, as they were now in the open countryside, onto the hard stone embankment some six feet below. It was a prison on wheels. *She* was the prisoner.

"There's no escape, so don't even try. There's more than a five foot drop onto the embankment and, at this speed, they wouldn't even recognise your face afterwards if you jump."

She looked out of the window and across open fields. They were *so* high up. Then she saw they were just about to cross the viaduct at Crow Mills.

"I'd rather die than come with you, or that bastard Frenchman," she said. The train had picked up speed as it headed towards the next station – Countesthorpe.

"I'll bet you thought you'd seen the last of the Chanters," he began, "once you'd put my brother behind bars. But I've been after you – or your worthless husband – ever since. Thanks to the Count I found out where you were, but you're soon going to wish I hadn't."

"You won't get away with this," she shot back. "When my husband catches up with you, you'll wish you *hadn't* found us."

If Rosalee had known how prophetic her words were she would have remained calm and waited until help arrived. But she was eager to get away, looking for the first possible chance to make her escape.

Earlier, the tram had dropped Rosalee off at the terminus and just a short walk from the Sercombe house in Aylestone. It was there, in the old village, that Chanter had been waiting for most of the day. He had hired a coach and pair, ready to snatch Rosalee when she returned from shopping in Leicester. He had arrived early that morning, seeing her get on the tram - but he was just a few minutes too late to put his plan to kidnap her into operation.

Since then he had been waiting – waiting hours - for her return, during which he had attracted the attention of one or two locals. It was unusual to see a stranger loitering in the village, a fact that didn't go unnoticed. Later, it was the butcher's boy, as he was clearing the display from the shop window that afternoon, who had witnessed Chanter carry out his dastardly deed. But he was too shocked, not believing his own eyes at first, and too late to intervene.

Once he had collected his thoughts and realised what was taking place and, recognising Rosalee, he jumped onto his butcher's bike and pedalled up to the Sercombe house to raise the alarm. Luckily, Sean and William were in their office at the front of the house.

Sean ran out to meet the frantic boy as he charged up the drive to the house, shouting. "Mr Sercombe, Mr Sercombe! It's your wife. She's been snatched."

Sean had intercepted the boy half way up the drive, anxious to find out what he was talking about. "*Who's* snatched her?" he screamed.

The boy, now out of breath, managed to explain how a tall, well-to-do man had taken her as she got off the tram, before whisking her into an awaiting coach.

"Where did they go?"

"He took off towards Wigston," said the boy. "I think I heard him mention the station to the coach driver."

"*When* was this?" asked Sean, his voice shaking.

"No more than five minutes ago. I rushed straight up to tell you," replied the boy. Sean muttered his thanks. He was now trying to think – to take it all in.

What should he do? In a flash he headed for the stables at the rear of the house – and Hans. There was only one thing he *could* do, but he had to act fast. He saddled up the stallion and tightened his girth. Minutes later he was in pursuit.

"There's a train leaving Wigston in ten minutes," he called out to the astonished William through the front office window. "If she *is* on that one I won't get to Wigston in time, so I'll ride direct to Countesthorpe to head them off." He left the butcher's boy to explain everything else to William.

Sean urged his horse forward, first along the Leicester Road towards Glen Hills and then Blaby. As soon as he reached the edge of the village he left the main road to cut across the park, riding towards Mill Lane along the bank of the River Sence.

There he crossed the lane, past the cemetery, making his way across open fields to Hospital Lane where he would take the Countesthorpe Road. Hans needed no encouragement and flew like the wind, clearing hedges and ditches without breaking his stride, somehow understanding the urgency, as if he *knew* Rosalee was in danger.

It was only when Sean and Hans had reached Hospital Lane that Rosalee first saw a shape in the distance. She *knew* it would be Sean. Careful not to give the game away to Chanter that help was coming, she stood up to face him with her back pressed against the door.

The train was slowing down, nearing Countesthorpe. The compartment where she was captive was now just a few yards away from the bridge that ran *over* Hospital Lane. She could see the shape clearly now. It *was* Sean - and Hans - galloping at full speed along the lane, straight for the bridge. She leaned heavily down on the handle behind her, relieved as it gave way under the force of her weight.

Suddenly Chanter realised what she was up to and reached forward to catch her as the door obediently swung open. He was too late. Still clinging onto the door, Rosalee was flung wide and clear from the train and the track. She was right over the bridge now and could see Sean's startled face as she lost her grip.

She was falling, heading onto the hard stone embankment. It was at least a six foot drop. She seemed to be flying through the air in slow motion. She screamed. Sean cried out in horror and disbelief. "Nooooo!"

But it was over in seconds. The train trundled relentlessly to its next stop at Countesthorpe station, little more than a mile away. Rosalee lay where she had fallen. Unconscious. Hurt. But still alive. Just.

It was Hans who took over now. Sean merely clung onto his mane with one hand, reins in the other. The brave stallion cleared first the roadside hedge into the field bordering the track, then jumped the fence between the field and the track itself. In no time at all he was trotting gingerly on the stone surface towards where Rosalee lay.

But were they just moments too late? Seeing what was happening, Chanter had jumped too and arrived there before them. He was kneeling over her. She wasn't moving.

"Get away from her!" yelled Sean. Hans snorted, hot breath from his nostrils crystallising into vapour as it hit the air.

Chanter came to his senses. He saw the horse and rider bearing down upon him. "You're too late, Sercombe," he yelled.

Sean and Hans edged closer, but paused as Chanter reached into his inside coat pocket. He drew out a revolver, cocked it, aiming point blank at Sean.

He had no time to react but Hans did. Without any signal from Sean, Hans lurched forward but not before Chanter could fire off two shots.

The first missed both horse and rider; the second found its target – or *a* target. The bullet travelled through the cerebral cortex towards the brain stem - of Hans.

He crashed heavily to the ground and died instantly but without suffering. Chanter cried out in pain as two flailing front hooves, striking out from the stallion in his final death throes, came into contact with his skull. He was propelled through the air and down the bank and away from Rosalee, landing in a twisted heap in a thick bed of nettles below.

His face was no more than a pulp. He was dead, a bitter sweet revenge for the brave Hanoverian on his former master. Chanter would lay there motionless as the flies gradually, on that late afternoon, feasted on his worthless form. His soul had already descended to hell.

But that was not the end of the tragedy. In the one last desperate move to end Chanter and save Sean, even though he was dying, Hans had reared so high he was almost vertical.

It was too much even for an experienced rider like Sean. It

unbalanced him. Reeling backwards he involuntarily let go of the reins, somersaulting over the back of the horse.

"Rosalee!" he shouted as he, too, was now falling through the air.

It was the last word he spoke, the final thought he had, as his head came crashing down on the cold steel railway line.

Sean died seconds later, lying side by the side next to his one and only love – Rosalee, mother of his unborn child.

Chapter Twenty Eight
A true miracle offers at least some comfort.

It was almost half an hour before bodies were discovered by would-be rescuers, arriving by the station's open carriage normally reserved for rail passengers.

Chanter and Rosalee had occupied one of the front carriages. Some passengers travelling in the compartments following behind had witnessed the bloody drama in disbelief. It was those shocked witnesses who had alerted the Midland Counties railway security guards at Countesthorpe station.

The station master jumped from the open carriage and was first on the scene. *What on earth has gone on here?* he was wondering as he cast his eyes from body to body before checking their pulses.

Another guard joined him. Coming upon Chanter he shook his head with no attempt at checking for vital signs. The guard carried on up the bank where he found Hans. A lifelong lover of fine horses, he knelt to feel for signs of life in the stallion.

He checked the radial artery on the inside of the knee on the Hanoverian. *Nothing.* He closed the horses eyes before getting to his feet to check the two remaining bodies.

Rosalee and Sean lay side by side but he failed to see either of them moving. It looked as though Sean's neck had been broken. There was no pulse. Sean's hand was still resting on Rosalee's as she lay next to him.

"He seemed to be reaching out for her," muttered the station master, "even in death."

Moments later he heard a plaintiff female voice, barely audible, followed by a slight movement of a hand, grasping the one that lay on hers. "Sean!" she gasped. The guard turned his gaze to where Rosalee lay. Then another cry, "My baby!"

He didn't have to check her pulse, beckoning to the   second guard who had just joined them. "Over here!" he called. "One of 'em's still alive."

At the sound of the guard's voice Rosalee tried to get up and with every strength left in her body raised her head to look for Sean. Even in death as he lay, motionless, his grip on hers remained firm. It might even had tightened.

"Sean?" she whispered.

"I'm sorry," soothed the Station Master.

"My baby. You have to save my baby." she cried, softly. She was too weak to become hysterical, but they could hear the panic in her voice. "Don't let me die yet," she managed to say, before she finally passed out.

"There's an infirmary about a mile down the road," said one of the guards. "We'll get her to The Cottage Homes." They carried her carefully down the bank and into their carriage.

They drove slowly for the mile journey to the infirmary. Even at the steady pace, the carriage and pair arrived at its destination within minutes. They were met at the entrance to the hospital by one of the nuns. Nuns formed a large part of the limited nursing staff and were experienced midwives. Rosalee was in the best care under the circumstances.

Their first priority was for the health of the mother. Rosalee had several superficial wounds caused by her fall from the train; she also suffered a more serious injury from the blow to her head. As a result she drifted in and out of consciousness. In her waking moments she did not appear to be in any pain.

"It's a miracle," said the head nurse.

It was fortunate that the baby had survived Rosalee's fall, but the unborn child was the nuns' second issue to deal with. She was a few weeks away from full term, when the birth was due to take place. All they could do until then was to monitor her round the clock.

Owing to the recent trauma that Rosalee had gone through, they were not too surprised to find her going into labour soon after midnight the following day. After little more than two hours, by dawn, they were all presented by a healthy girl – albeit not at full weight due to the premature birth.

The remarkable fact was that Rosalee was not conscious during her labour, nor at the actual birth. She never woke or even regained consciousness but died soon after the child was born. Maureen was by her daughter's bedside for the birth of her granddaughter and the passing of Rosalee, as was Mercy.

The nurse who delivered the baby was especially moved. "I have never experienced anything like it before," she said. "I have *heard* of rare cases where the mother gives birth whilst unconscious, or even in a coma, but I have never *seen* it.

"There is only one other type of miracle birth that I know of, and that one is at the centre of my faith."

Annie had been the third sister in the family delegated to be close at hand during Rosalee's final moments, and on the birth of the newest arrival to the Sercombe line. The nurses at The Cottage Homes advised them to have the newborn kept under observation for a few days given that she was premature, albeit slightly.

After a few days, and once a feeding regime had been established in the absence of a birth mother, Annie, Maureen and Mercy made arrangements to collect the wee mite from the hospital. It was then that a further mystery unravelled.

"How is the father?" asked the nurse.

"Why...? He's....didn't you know?" said Annie, pausing. "He was killed."

The nurse's face went a pale white. "But, how can that be? He was here... just before the girl went into labour. I saw him."

"Impossible," said Annie. "He died on the bridge over Hospital Lane, along with his horse."

"But they were both here, the father and the horse, that very night. She... your daughter-in-law... was talking to him as he sat by her bedside, just moments before her contractions started. He called me in as soon as she went into labour. I tended to her right away then I looked round - and he was gone. It was all rather strange."

"And your saw his horse, too? The stallion?"

"Yes... no... not exactly. I assumed he had ridden over here because, soon after he had left the ward – vanished as it were – I heard the sound of horses hooves. They seemed to come from round the back by the stables then fade away as he rode down the driveway. I assumed he was going back to Aylestone. To his family. To you."

The nurse's story sounded incredible but it was impossible to contradict the word of a nun. "There's one more thing," she added, "... this."

With that she handed over a silver pendant to Annie. It was the one she had given – that Frankie had given – to Sean on the day they were evicted from their cottage in Ireland.

"Where did you get this?" asked Annie, tearfully. Maureen drew closer to her to comfort her, still holding the child.

"From the mother. We found it grasped tightly in her hand as she was giving birth," said the nurse.

"The sign of the rose," said Maureen.

"The pendant I gave Sean, back in Ireland," joined Annie.

William, Frankie and Billy busied themselves making arrangements for the funeral and the burial of Sean and Rosalee. A local coroner's report had to be prepared, as well as a police investigation into the whole incident. Soon the full picture had been assembled following statements from key witnesses.

The local police interviewed William and the butcher's boy about the circumstances leading up to the tragedy, as they were the sole witnesses to the kidnapping.

Initially they had no idea who the dead 'stranger' was, not until the butcher's boy gave police the name of the carriage company. They interrogated then arrested the driver involved in the kidnapping, as an accessory. From him they discovered the name of Chanter as the one who had hired the coach.

The French Count Bonnier was named as a co-conspirator in the crime. He was seen as the main reason why Rosalee had been targeted by Chanter.

The Frenchman's name arose when the police extended their interviews to Frankie and Billy, who described the altercation that occurred months earlier at Blaby Hall. Enquiries were then extended across The Channel.

The story made the national as well as local newspapers, so in a short period of time news of the death of Sean – or rather Sercombe Lee-Ryan as the governor of the National Gallery knew him - reached his Patron, Sir Clive.

It led to the matter of legal title to the remaining collection of Sean's paintings, sponsored by Sir Clive. The portfolio value was not inconsiderable, a factor upon which Sir Clive was intent on capitalising. *He* claimed he owned it.

He took the matter to court. The foundation for his case was messy and dirty and one that angered the Sercombe family due to certain cruel inferences. One of these was the absence of living heirs, coupled with the challenge to Sean's fatherhood of the new baby.

By going to court, Sir Clive introduced a slight on Rosalee's honour and reputation centred around events and behaviour of Sean and the French Count at his dinner party.

"This is scandalous!" said a disgusted William. "How *dare* they question the reputation of the dead for financial gain? Just because he's got the money to fight this in the courts..."

But once more Romani lore, legend and heritage stepped in. Recent events were so traumatic for the family. Django and Mercy extended their stay in Leicester, purely in support of Mercy's sister,

Maureen. As it happened, their presence became a trigger for the turning point in the case, which led to it being settled without making it to court.

The sisters had taken temporary custody of Rosalee's child, pending Annie being given full custody. As they were bathing the child one day, Mercy noticed the birthmark on the little girl's shoulder. It was in the shape of a rose!

It was *so* real it could have been a tattoo, but it was a genuine and natural skin blemish. It was as tiny and as perfect as the silver pendant.

"Frankie has one of those birthmarks," said Annie when Mercy brought up the matter a few days later, when they were having tea together. "So did Sean."

"Should we ask William if he has one too?" asked Mercy. "It might be all we need to prove the child is Sean's."

They were right. It was a family birthmark – the sign of a rose that ran throughout generations of the male and female bloodlines of the Sercombe family.

"Billy will be disappointed," said Maureen. "He'll feel left out without one. Maybe we arrange for a tattoo for his next birthday!" They laughed, toasting their news with tea.

The next day they announced the good news to their solicitors, but it was bad news for Sir Clive. Against such compelling evidence he dropped his case. The collection of the artist, 'Sercombe Lee-Ryan', belonged to the daughter of Sean (of the same name) and Rosalee.

"The child needs a name. We can't keep referring to her as 'the girl'." said Annie. "She *is* my granddaughter after all."

"And mine," said Maureen. The three took the decision to consider all options, then vote, involving husbands and their father-in-law. They agreed on Rose. Rose Frances Sercombe.

And so the Sercombe family moved together into the 20th Century. A modern-day Romani took the bloodline forward, with the reputation for art combining with a gift for true entrepreneurial spirit and invention.

Even Florence enjoyed a life tinged excitement – involving the latest invention to dominate the early 1900's. She married Ernest, travelling together to America and Canada where he was at the forefront for the development of the new miracle – the internal combustion engine and the birth of the first mass-produced, powered vehicle – the Model T Ford motor car.

But on purely family matters, Frankie and Annie were soon granted guardianship of Rose as expected, and as per the wishes of the rest of the family. Even so, Billy, and especially, Maureen, enjoyed as much access to their daughter's son as they wanted.

As far as their husbands were concerned, the brothers had never been closer and now became even more so, to the delight of William Senior. With their support and expertise, he fulfilled a final dream by building rows of terraced houses in Aylestone for the benefit of the ever-growing number of workers.

Skilled and unskilled labour was flocking to the city to fill the factories to ensure Leicester continued in its role as one of the foremost cities in Europe. William retired wealthy, surrounded by his family.

At the end of the day, however, the extended family would never forget the two young people whose inspiration formed the base for their enduring strength through family values. Rosalee and Sean – theirs was an undying love, nurtured by a gift that had been born centuries earlier, surviving for centuries going forward.

The gift was a sign, and that was the sign of the rose.

Chapter Twenty Nine
The sign of the rose – the emblem of hope for generations.

But there was another doorway into the spiritual legacy that remained within the family to be passed down the generations. Once again, Mercy was instrumental in its revelation. It came about one evening when she was feeding Rose, even though she had not anticipated it at the time.

Maureen had brought Hans' bridle into the kitchen ready to clean it while her sister, Mercy, was feeding Rose. They had decided to present Hans' tack to William so he could display it in pride of place in his lounge. It was to be a tribute to the heroic stallion. Hans had saved William's grandson's life not only once, but very nearly twice – at the expense of his own.

They were sat chatting in the kitchen where Mercy was 'changing' Rose, when she asked Maureen to hold the baby while she fetched a clean nappy. Maureen had the bridle on her lap at the time. She had been working glycerine soap into the leather to soften it, but she was a little irritated being asked to do two things at once.

"Hurry up," said Maureen in the end, increasingly flustered, "or I'll end up dropping either the horse's bridle, or the baby."

She had paused from cleaning, allowing Mercy to hand Rose over to her so she could fetch a nappy.

Maureen was looking down at Rose as she lay sleeping in her arms, when she froze. "Look at this!" she whispered.

The urgency in her voice caused Mercy to look round immediately. *What on earth was going on?* They thought.

Maureen and Mercy's eyes were now transfixed on the centre of the horse's headband where Sean had embedded a valuable ruby stone.

"The stone has started to glow! As soon as I took Rose in my arms, I felt a charge running through her body, then mine, then the ruby began to pulsate."

"Don't move," urged Mercy. She knew exactly what was happening. She explained it to Mercy, without taking her eyes off what was taking place right in front of her.

"Hans' spirit is moving across into Rose. It will protect her throughout her life. The stone is the conduit. Take a look at her birthmark now, but be careful not to wake her."

The little mite was lying in Maureen's lap, face upwards, still sound asleep. She lifted her slowly, just enough so that the mark on Rose's shoulder became visible.

The birthmark was glowing. The sign of the rose on Rose's shoulder also shone as it continued to receive the power from Hans. It was the gift of guardianship passing over from the nether world, from where the stallion's soul was finally coming to rest. It was passing into Rose.

Gradually, and after what had seemed the longest while, the glow in the ruby receded. It returned to normal. The birthmark on Rose's shoulder also softened as it returned to its lighter shade of purple.

Mercy joined hands with her sister, Maureen. "She's in good hands now," she said. "The circle is finally complete.

~~ **THE END** ~~

About the series 'Love should never be this hard'

Each of the four books chronicles the fortunes of a fictional Romani family mixed with a more conventional culture.

Lives inter-twine and interact from the mid-to-late-1800's right up to the start of the 1970's. Where relevant, real historical context is introduced.

From early beginnings in Southern Ireland there is a migration to and from England, thereafter the background to the novels develops from Cornwall to Devon, and on to the Leicestershire countryside and the village of Blaby - where much of the chronicle is set.

On the way there are episodes taking place in Tavistock, short excursions in St Ives and Exmouth, before events finally unfold between Teignmouth and Plymouth - by which time 100 years have flown by.

The depiction of life in these locations has already struck a chord with, and approval from, readers familiar with certain locations, justifiably so, as John draws on personal experience in his descriptions.

Each has messages of hope rewarded by perseverance and faith.

About John Morey

John Morey was born in the Leicestershire village of Blaby, to the background of 1950's rock 'n' roll and 1960's Beatlemania, then flower power.

Although never part of hippie culture, he was influenced by its sentiments, freedom, and opportunity, now reflected in his writing.

John studied hard to forge a successful career in marketing and publishing, but it was not until he was in his '70s - after marketing 1,000's of books by other authors, in countless genres - he began to write, at the insistence of his wife and encouraged by close friends.

His emotional insights into relationships flavour many of the characters and the actions they take, although none of the works are autobiographical – merely drawn on experience.

Visit www.newnovel.co.uk for more of John's writing as well as valuable 'how to' articles to help aspiring writers discover the delights of self-publishing.

All books available in e-book and paperback on Amazon - search by title and author for details and to buy.

The Sign of the Rose (Book 1)

The novels have been called 'an easy read' where historical, location and factual elements entertain as well as inform.

They enrich and breathe life into the plot. Characters are believable, even though the story explores the mysteries of the unknown to stretch the imagination.

Leicestershire readers enjoyed experiencing the plot location in 'old Aylestone', Glen Parva and Blaby/Wigston, whereas those familiar with Devon will enjoy the journey across Dartmoor taken by Sean and Rosalee after leaving family behind in Southern Ireland.

But it is in Blaby where the Romani family – central to all four novels - set down roots, whilst integrating into mainstream society in an ever-changing world.

Within this first book in the series we are introduced to the mystical qualities intrinsic within characters and events, but they remain benign influences, not over-powering the reality and credibility surrounding the basic concepts of this fascinating tale.

If you are a romantic at heart, ready for mixing tragedy with good fortune, and appreciate love and emotion treated with sensitivity, then the series 'Love should never be this hard' – and this novel - is for you.

The Black Rose of Blaby (Book 2)

* Myth - was there really a black rose cultivated in Blaby?

* Legend - if the dancing maidens did exist - where is the site of the standing stones now?

* Reality - if what they say is true, did the Leicestershire village of Blaby really feed England with a rare commodity during WW2?

* Lost love - Mary Alice Baker Sercombe graces the cover of this novel. What was the truth behind her ancestors' tragic love affairs?

Myth, legend - reality? You never know the truth with John. That's what makes them intriguing reads.

Many locations actually exist - or used to, captured here for austerity. Characters enjoy a life of their own, often 'composites' of the several people who actually lived. These features add credibility to what are, after all, enjoyable works of fiction.

Beyond that, however, you will relish the escapism built into the plot and sub-plots, right to the final page where an unexpected twist or celebration of the tale holds you to the end.

The story majors on the post-war years up until the start of the 1960's but unearths much of the mysterious past surrounding the events emerging after the dramatic end to Book 1.

Rose: The Missing Years (Book 3)

Readers who know Blaby and surrounding Leicestershire villages particularly enjoyed the reminder of how the old village used to be. 'Rose: The Missing Years' covers the same period as 'Finding Rose', but goes behind the scenes to when she disappears from John's life to take up with Sean, and to have her daughter, Mathilda (Tilly).

Set predominantly in Leicestershire and specifically the village of Blaby, you will find references to its rich heritage and history, much of which is either forgotten or has never been recorded elsewhere.

Nevertheless, like 'Finding Rose', it remains a work of romantic fiction with a thread of mysticism throughout, embedded within imagined Romani culture. An entertaining romantic read, the book also serves as a fascinating social record of the rapidly disappearing country life within a definitive Midlands county.

As with all the novels in the series locations may be real but fictionalised, as are the characters introduced in cameo roles. In similar fashion, historic occurrences breathe reality into the fantasy - providing an element of grounding to the plot - but dates may be 'stretched'.

For maximum effect, read Books 3 and 4 in quick succession.

Finding Rose (Book 4)

The location of the story begins in Blaby before switching between Plymouth and Teignmouth - recounting events set some fifty years ago - with a brief episode in St Ives, Cornwall.

Romantic mysticism enters the lives of more people than we may care to admit. It does here, but without the trappings of horror or menace. Rose and John are, themselves, a benign force and, although their journey is not without sadness and heartache, their perseverance towards fulfilment remains undaunted.

Discover how two people embark on a journey without knowing how, where, or with whom it will end. Will they survive as one? or apart? And what did happen in Rose's life in the seven 'missing years'?

Answers were in the previous book but this fascinating read will take you a little further, leaving you with a feeling that 'some things do end happily after all'.

All books available on Amazon in e-book and paperback format. Search by title / author for more details and to order.

Printed in Great Britain
by Amazon

67936661R00132